THE GHOST MERCHANT

DEATH IS ONLY THE BEGINNING

By

Ben Andrews

Copyright © 2025

All rights reserved.

Edited by Eden Northover

Book cover design: Covers by John

ISBN :9781836548867

To all who have lost someone.
This story is for you.

Erin Layton

1992

Erin's heart raced, a grin stretching across her face as she skipped down the pavement—chasing the feeling she last experienced as a young girl. She never thought she'd feel happy again, but here she was, bounding along the road with her boyfriend Jacob, their hands breaking free. New York City was bustling with people and cars and birds tweeting in the treetops. Memories of the past few days flooded her mind, shopping with Jacob, eating high in the sky, watching over the city at the twinkling lights. She wanted to cherish them forever.

Erin stopped in the road to glance back at Jacob; his shaggy hair framed his almond eyes as he flashed her a broad smile, one she never tired of seeing. She stopped, her lips parted, trying to put the words she wanted to say in order. Was *'I love you'* something she was ready to say, something he was ready to hear?

A sharp pain stabbed through Erin's side, and a whirlwind of images engulfed her, captured in precise detail —family gathered around a newborn baby, the scent of flowers at her grandmother's funeral, the taste of success on her college graduation day, searching for her first apartment. Another wave of pain crashed through her, but this time, she wasn't sure if it was in her chest or legs. Erin didn't know what was happening. The blue sky spiralled, and then the world fell to darkness.

Erin's vision flickered in and out of focus as unfamiliar faces in masks gathered around her body. A stranger's voice yelled, "We're losing her!"

"I'm her boyfriend. Let me go with her!" Jacob cried.

Motionless inside the van, Erin sensed the swaying of her body as the vehicle hurtled across speed bumps and potholes. She closed her eyes, succumbing to the encroaching feeling of sleep that felt only a step away.

"We did everything we could, but we must call time. I'm sorry," a voice echoed.

Was she now floating? Erin felt like she could see everything at once. She drifted between reality and the ether, the sharp stings of pain interrupted by an icy breeze across her cheeks. Droplets of salty rain descended from the sky. She tasted the sadness on her lips, her entire being consumed by grief. Her father's scolding face flashed, as did the ripped-up picture of her family—torn apart for eternity. Darkness engulfed her as she slipped into a dream once again. Erin's breath faltered; the once simple act of breathing now required effort. In fact, she wasn't truly breathing at all.

But she was still here.

Erin peered around the void engulfing her, unable to see past the blinding golden light that was always a breath out of reach. Shadows consumed her body, creeping through her fingertips and festering along her arms. Suddenly, the sharp pain in her side intensified, and a crack sounded. Agony tore through her right leg. Erin screamed, yet no sound emerged. She could hear everything around her—sounds and senses she'd never once experienced. She rubbed her eyes and hoped to wake up in bed beside Jacob, the shrill beep of her alarm disturbing her peace. Anything to take her away from this void.

Time seemed to shift differently here. Had minutes or decades gone by? Closing her eyes, Erin pictured herself at the job she'd left a few years ago, the one she hated in the coffee shop, the one where she met Jacob, then she was a child again, in her grandmother's home. Sitting on the hard oak floors, listening to her grandmother in the attic, the chain necklace running through her fingers. Tears of laughter flowed freely from her, but further agony shot through her body as a reminder of those final moments. The stench of burnt rubber filled her nose, and a horn blared somewhere in the distance. A woman screamed. Broken glass crunched and red lights flashed. Jacob's face glanced down at her, his tears landing on her lips.

"She's gone."

Quill Darlington

The floorboards creaked beneath Quill's feet, stirring up dust particles that glowed in the sunlight. Downstairs, the shop bell rang for the second time that morning, while his cat Wilson slept soundly on the floor. Quill caught a brief glimpse of his reflection, though the dust on the mirror mostly concealed it. The passage of time etched into his wrinkles; lines carved around his eyes, a testament to the many years of his lifetime. He prodded his copper wire spectacles further up the bridge of his nose.

As Quill crouched to stroke Wilson, he noted the peeling wallpaper in the hallway — another job to add to his long list of tasks. While he had eternity to complete them, it often felt like they would never get done. Quill descended the staircase, the old wood croaking in protest beneath his weight. One more task, he thought.

The shop bell chimed again and again. Quill checked his pocket watch. Three more minutes before he was officially on the clock. He savoured the sight of the spirited October sun through the shop window, onlooking the village of Ringwood, now cast in yellow and orange hues. He had left the shop sign to *'open'* all night; though he hadn't slept, so technically, it was no mistake. Quill still had endless amounts of papers to read through and paint brushes to clean. *Rest was for those who deserved it*, he thought.

The shop was a haven of forgotten treasures. Dusty trinkets lined the shelves, their lack of value and worth warding off curious customers who dared to venture beyond the door. He often thought of adding to his night-time activity, cleaning the shop, offering a more welcoming environment. He had so many hours to fill, so many thoughts to distract, yet he never found the time, even with endless amounts of it.

The bell rang again, but death could wait, so he took his time before tending to his duties.

Outback, the bottles rattled on the shelves. Quill stopped by Alma's bottle. The content inside were calm, flowing like the red desert. Quill leaned his face towards it, running his hand along the cold glass. He remembered her kind eyes, her wild mind. The secrets he had told her. No other soul here had he opened up to, not one soul left on this earth he could speak to like he did to Alma. "I hope you are okay in there. I'm sure we will find a place for you soon."

Quill returned to the shop. Underneath the counter, wooden shelves lined the cupboard walls, home to Quill's books and paperwork. The Great Book trembled with anger and rang the copper bell on the counter top once more. Another poor soul arriving. There were always more this time of year. Even Death follows a pattern.

Wilson pushed his head through the slates on the stairs, meowing as he prowled towards the counter.

"I know, Wilson. I'll give this place a sweep later today," Quill said. He opened The Great Book and thumbed through the newly added pages at the back. Information etched onto the blank page. Wilson purred as he weaved in between Quill's legs. "I'll feed you in a second, my boy. Let me just check our latest arrival."

Eyebrows raised, Quill stretched and turned to the newly added pages. He pushed the glasses back up his nose, darting his eyes over the text, extracting only what he needed.

The bell above chimed. The Great Book slammed closed with a thump as a young girl walked through the door, her footsteps unsteady. Lifting his head, Quill greeted her with a smile, yet she stared back, expression blank. Her denim dungarees complemented her short brown hair. She clearly hadn't caught on to what had happened to her yet. Types like her were always the hardest to get in line. The ones who refused to see what was before them.

The Great Book never failed. Erin was exactly as he imagined.

He passed Wilson, who was now curled atop The Great Book and marched towards the young lady. Keeping his grin, Quill outstretched his arms to put her at ease.

Erin's wide eyes darted around the shop, and she pressed her trembling hands against the glass door. "Where am I?" she stammered.

Quill extended a hand towards Erin, who refused to

budge, as if searching for an escape route. "I'm here to help," he said. "Why don't you have a seat, Erin?"

Erin eyed him, her gaze flitting between Quill and the door. "Who are you? How do you know my name?"

Quill sighed and snapped his fingers, summoning Wilson to his side, who swayed to Erin, rubbing his head against her leg. "I know all of this seems strange, but we have lots to get through, and I'm here to answer any questions you may have."

Erin perched on the window seat and stroked Wilson's back. Quill hid a smile. Having Wilson here always helped settle even the most wild of spirits. He wondered how he coped for so long without him by his side. "What happened to me?" she asked, looking up at Quill, innocence still alive in her eyes.

He gathered The Great Book into his arms, which shrank into a single page. "I think, my friend, that you passed away. It says here: a car accident. Erin Layton. Age twenty-four, died on the 2nd of October 1992. Does that sound correct to you?" Quill asked.

Erin's mouth fell open. "I'm dead?"

Quill nodded. "I realise it's not pleasant to hear, particularly at your age, but unfortunately, there's nothing we can do about it now. I've found the sooner you get used to that, the better it is for everyone involved."

Erin glanced at the floor. "So, is this heaven, then?"

Quill chuckled. "If this was heaven, don't you think this place would house a lot less dust and dirt? This, my dear, is The Ghost Merchants. A shop open for eternity. A spot where we shall be together now, and for the many years to come."

Quill Darlington

Shoulders slumped, Quill took slow, measured steps to the back of the shop, sagging beneath the weight of his eternal duty.

"Follow me," He waved at Erin to join him, then pushed open the door. A low rumble reverberated through the room and clouds of dust spiralled in the faint light, casting eerie shadows on the old, weathered shelves. Erin hesitated, her fingers trembling around the doorknob. The darkened room was bursting with mysterious bottles.

"We store the spirits back here," explained Quill. "When you hear a rumble like that, it means one of them is restless, but it soon dies down."

More frequently in the modern world, young spirits found themselves here. There was nothing he could do; after all, his job was to tick boxes. He had no control over the decisions.

"Erin, I imagine you must have plenty of questions. Feel free to ask anything that comes to mind," Quill said.

"Can I go?" Erin whispered. Her gigantic eyes reminded Quill of a puppy begging for a bone.

Quill smiled, but shook his head. "I'm sorry, but that's not something I can allow. You have a job to do."

"A job? Even in death?" Erin glanced around, examining the countless jars positioned atop the wooden shelves. One rattled before her eyes. "What's happening?" she asked, her fingers tracing their edges. Quill glared at the bottle Erin had touched. A soul showed itself through its void. She'd picked well. A blue essence floated inside the glass bottle. Grains of sand trapped in an endless dance. "What's inside?"

Quill stepped closer to join her. Souls lived enclosed inside the bottles, and he rarely examined them. It felt like an invasion of privacy. To the casual observer, they all looked the same, but upon closer inspection, every soul was different. This bottle, with its dark colour and wild movement, held Arthur, whose void was somewhat gloomy —even more so than the other souls around him. Quill hoped things weren't too bleak for Arthur, who had been imprisoned for some years.

"Before you came here, do you remember where you were?" Quill asked.

Erin peered back into the bottle. The shaking stopped the second she placed her finger on the outside. "I was with Jacob. We were on holiday in New York for our anniversary, and then..." Erin's voice trailed off, the last pieces yet to form. Quill placed a hand gently on her shoulder. She turned to him, though it was as if she stared right through him. "Then I was... here, I think."

"What about in-between? Do you recall being in the void?"

Erin nodded. "Yes. I was floating or asleep. It's difficult to remember the details or find the right words, but I was in some sort of limbo. I heard people calling my name. There was a pain in my side, too, but I was distracted by memories from my family, my life. Then, I was here. It felt like an eternity, but thinking about it now, it was over in a few seconds."

"Well, that's what you're looking at here," Quill said, tapping the bottle. "This void is where we store your soul when it's not needed."

"What's the purpose of bottling up souls? Why do you store them here?"

"There are many uses, my dear. Some you could never imagine. Everyone who comes here has their reasons—their desires. My job is to sign the contracts and match the souls up as best I can."

"I remember you called this place... The Ghost Merchants. Is it really that literal? Do you sell ghosts?" Erin inquired flatly.

"It's a good name, isn't it? Humans often overlook what's right in front of them," Quill replied. "We have items for sale, ones from house clearances, from recently deceased. Some even donated. I do my best to make sure no sane person would come in here for any reason other than buying a soul."

Erin turned back to the bottle and pressed her face against it. "Is this where everyone goes? Can I visit my grandma? Is she here somewhere?"

Quill shook his head as he picked up an empty bottle. "I'm sorry, kid. Only a few end up here. The rest move on."

"Move on? Where? Why was I chosen to come here?" Erin asked, her eyes darting around the room.

"There are many reasons for a soul to end up here, but this is no punishment or retribution for your past mistakes... it's different for everyone," Quill said as he marked the container with a black pen. Erin followed him to the front of the shop and closed the door behind her. "Let me see... Birthplace, Southampton. Oh, just down the road from here. Age... twenty-four, not married, ah... here we are." Quill placed his glasses beside the bottle and rubbed his temples.

"What? What is it?" asked Erin.

Quill drummed his finger on the worktop three times in rhythm and Wilson jumped up, nearly knocking over the empty bottle.

"You see, when you sign a contract to purchase a ghost—or soul or spirit or whatever word you want to use—you can pay with your own soul to be exchanged here when you pass away," Quill explained. "Think of it like a recycling system, if you will. It appears Gertrude gave the soul of her seventh granddaughter as payment over her own. One hundred years later, and well, here you are."

Erin blinked.

"You mean a family member bartered my soul for eternity before I was even born, and that's allowed?"

Quill shrugged and lodged the end of the pen in his mouth. "She was warned, but during that period, seven generations looked like an inconceivable thing. Maybe she never thought the payment would be due. Nevertheless, here you are, Erin, and there isn't anything anyone can do about it."

Erin paced up the store, stomping across the creaking floorboards. "So, what am I supposed to do from here? Will you sell me to the next person who enters this shop? Am I a slave? What will people use me for?"

Quill glanced out the window at the empty alleyway

outside, where the shop was tucked away down a cobbled side street. Being a Ghost Merchant never got easier, and each afflicted individual filling his shop over the years pained him more than the last. This young girl bore this curse from birth, having been full of life only a few hours before. Now, all she had to look forward to was a lifetime stuck with some sad old man in a dusty shop. Maybe he could find someone sympathetic to her—someone willing to give up their own soul when the time came to let her go. Sadly, it had been years since someone sacrificed their freedom for another so willingly. He stared up at Erin, who awaited his answer.

"I'll do my best for you," he sighed, and it clearly wasn't the answer she wanted, nor the one he wished to deliver.

"Can you sell me to Jacob?" Erin suggested. "At least then, I could be with him forever."

Quill shook his head. "It doesn't work that way. I'm sorry."

Erin spun to the door and yanked it open, and Quill froze at the sight of such strength. Spirits rarely had the power for such force. He waited for her next move. She didn't look back as she stepped onto the concrete outside.

"Bye," Erin called, "I hope to never encounter you again." She smacked into an invisible wall and stumbled backwards. She whirled to face Quill, her face contorted. "What have you done?"

Quill raised his hands. "It wasn't me. We must hold you here until someone acquires you and binds you to them."

Erin let loose an exasperated sigh and flopped onto the window seat, disturbing Wilson, who raised his chin in defiance. "How is being dead more controlling than being alive? I should be free to do... well, whatever ghosts do.

Please, let me leave!"

Quill took a seat beside Wilson and stroked his fur; handfuls of his white coat shed into his palms. He made a mental note to give him a good brush later. "Erin, I understand it's difficult to accept, but I can pair you with an ideal companion. Someone who might swap your place for theirs."

"What if they refuse?" Erin asked. "If someone is callous enough to purchase a human, living or dead, why would they be willing to surrender their own soul for all time? I'm doomed to be stuck here forever, just like all the other souls locked in the back!"

Quill placed a gentle hand on Erin's shoulder as she stared into the bottle in his spare hand. "You've been through a lot," he said, his eyes glinting with empathy. "But there's no other way. It must be done."

"I won't go in there," Erin declared, searching the shop for an escape route. "You can't force me."

Quill uncorked a bottle and Erin's body faded, her arms and legs contorted, folding up like a piece of paper until finally she vanished in a flash, leaving only a faint echo of her presence. Silently, Quill watched while guilt settled in his chest like a lead weight. Erin's void was dark purple, like a brewing storm, and the jar shook as she fought against her fate. He re-corked the bottle and placed it on a shelf in the backroom.

"I'm sorry, Erin, but it's out of my hands. I'm as trapped here as you are," Quill said.

Quill Darlington

The cobwebs between the wooden beams quivered as another chill swept through the ageing store. It had been two weeks since Quill locked Erin away, two weeks of silence. Quill peered down at the untouched page as he waited for his customer to arrive, tapping Arthur's glass jar with a knowing smile and a spark in his eyes. Quill's matchmaking was spectacular. This woman was the precise client Arthur would work well with, or at least work well at solving her problems. He had some time before she was due; women like her were usually late, anyway. Quill pulled the cork from Arthur's jar. A white glow burst into vision, pieces of Arthur's soul gathered from the bottle, connecting like a puzzle.

Arthur stood before him. Those dark eyes of his always

brought forth an image of a winter lake, never knowing what was really lurking beneath. He wore the same pinstriped suit he had died in. To this day, he refused to change it.

"How are you?" Quill asked as he picked up a pen and marked the date on Arthur's bottle.

"What year is it?" Arthur asked, bending down to scratch Wilson's chin. Quill wondered who felt more relaxed out of the two.

"It's been eleven years, Arthur." Quill replied, withdrawing a sheet of paper from behind him and clearing his throat. "I've taken the pleasure in noting down what you have missed."

"You did? Golly! So you do like me, Mr Darlington!" Arthur said, walking towards the reception counter and resting his arms on the desk. "Come on then, what did I miss?"

"Remember that royal wedding you got so worked up about?" Quill asked, pushing Arthur's forearms off the desk. Arthur may be but a soul, but Quill still had standards to keep, and manners were so quickly forgotten when you die.

"Sure do. Lady Diana," Arthur replied.

"Well, she evolved into the people's princess, adored by everyone. Although not so much by her family. Rumours are rife with divorce and I know how much you love a good rumour. What else do we have here? Oh yes, that terrible game you enjoyed watching... where the yellow ball chased phantoms."

"You mean Pac-man?" Arthur asked with a gleam in his eye.

"Yes... well, that turned into a worldwide phenomenon."

"I knew it would," Arthur beamed. "Although, I think you'll find the ghosts did the chasing, Mr Darlington."

"Quite. A nuclear calamity happened in Chernobyl in the year 1986. Truly awful event." Quill pushed his glasses up the bridge of his nose as he let the shock settle in. "They ended the Cold War and tore down the Berlin wall in Eighty-Nine. Do you want me to continue?"

Arthur shook his head. Quill noticed Arthur's foot tap the floorboards. He clearly thought about why they had summoned him from the void. "No, not right now. I'll do some reading up on it all. Who have you linked me up with this time?"

"Lady Chapman-Webb. She will be here shortly to provide me with the full details, but when I heard her request, you came straight to my mind."

"Another short one, you think?" Arthur asked, mind seemingly elsewhere as he watched the gusty day outside. Quill always welcomed the bad weather. It kept the village quiet, and unwanted eyes away.

A silhouette appeared behind the shop door as the bell rang. A well-dressed blonde woman stepped inside, her heeled shoes clip-clopping with each unsteady step. She stopped shy of Quill, her fingers trembling as she pretended to examine the dusty souvenirs. Eyes glancing across some candles, a handful of small glass bottles and a hairbrush, avoiding Quill's gaze. Arthur stood beside the window in awe of another living person. She, of course, couldn't see Arthur, but Quill was sure she could at least sense something.

"Can I help you?" Quill asked, shuffling the paperwork.

She turned, her face pale, sunken and shallow. Her eyes swept the room, but never lingered. "I heard so much about this shop. I had to come see it for myself," she replied, picking up a silver necklace dangling in the cabinet. "What a charming piece." The fine chain trickled through her fingers.

"Yes, old costume jewellery is all," said Quill, "although I expect a woman with a discernment like yours already knows that. Interested in viewing our range out back? The shop offers much more than what the human gaze can discern. Come," Quill spun and outstretched his arm, leading the customer to the back room. She glanced at the front door again, ensuring she was alone before following his lead.

Every patron was the same.

Quill escorted her past the shelves of bottles as she delicately navigated the archway. The light from the soul's faintly illuminated the entrance to a small room at the back, where inside sat an unassuming chair and table. Candles lit the interior, hanging from the walls. "Have a seat." Quill pulled out the chair. Kaitlin picked at her nails as she took a seat.

"Thank you. This place certainly has a lot of... character, doesn't it?"

"Full to the brim, Lady Chapman-Webb."

Her face came alive, eyes widening and body tensing at the mention of her name. She wore a thick, cream cotton jumper, immaculate. A white pearl necklace clung to her neck, shimmering in a silver hue as they laid perfectly along the neckline of her top. "That obvious, was I?" She folded her left leg over her knee. "Please, just call me Kaitlin."

Quill ruffled through the paperwork. "Of course. So, why don't you tell me a bit more about why you are here today?"

Kaitlin smoothed her skirt and cleared her throat, finally locking eyes with Quill before averting her gaze to her folded hands nestled in her lap. "Is it true what you can offer here?"

"Whatever it was that brought you here, it did not lie to you."

Kaitlin ran a hand through her hair. "It felt like a dream. I didn't know if it was true or not. I looked up the store, found out it was real, although I'm not sure what I thought was actually true. A meeting like that. Coming in your dreams could make a woman go mad."

Quill nodded. "The offer comes when you need it, when you truly want it. I don't make the rules. I only follow them."

"As long as this is no scam." Kaitlin rolled her eyes, doubt set in her face.

"What you know is correct," said Quill. "But this is no joke; you must treat it with the utmost responsibility and care. Very few reach this point without being certain it is what they truly desire, seeing as you're here in my office, I know you are in the right place."

"What do I need to do? What are the rules?"

Quill placed the documents in the centre of the oak table. A rattle came from the other side of the door. Quill coughed, hoping to disguise the noise. Erin had been restless since he bottled her away. Usually, even the most determined spirit would have settled by now. "Why don't you start with why you want a spirit? What is your need?"

Kaitlin searched around the room, the walls obscured by dancing shadows cast by the flickering candles along the walls. "Is it here? In this room with us?"

Quill smiled. "Let's not get ahead of ourselves. Just tell me what you're looking for."

She placed her trembling hands on the table, her eyes pleading. Quill remained upright, his shoulders back and his fingers entwined. His eyes watched Kaitlin as they darted around the room. Arthur was in the shop, he knew this, and Kaitlin did too, deep down. "I need to find out who murdered my husband. The killer is someone close, I'm sure of it. But I need an extra set of eyes, someone who can witness what I can't."

Quill gave a brief smile. Murder was as old as time. Many scorned men had passed his doors wanting justice, answers to the unknown. He enjoyed tasks like this. Knowing there was some purpose to the sale, that justice may be served, in some way.

"I understand."

"Is that something you can provide?" Kaitlin asked, glancing at the walls again.

"I have a spirit that has resolved similar issues before." Quill darted a look towards the door. He should have kept Arthur in the void, but keeping him occupied with Wilson should be distraction enough.

"How long will it take?"

Quill chuckled. "This isn't like scheduling a contractor, Lady Chapman-Webb. You will have the spirit under your control until the task is done."

"I see. And how will I know if this... spirit is even real?"

"You will see the spirit once it is in your possession. You can also communicate with it. Wherever you go, you will remain linked."

"So, I can't let it leave my side?" Kaitlin raised a brow. "How can it find anyone if it's with me the whole time?"

"A spirit can wander around a building, a region, or a garden, whatever you desire, as long as you have been there yourself. It will always respond to your call when you need them back."

"Okay," said Kaitlin. "So, what do I need to do? You mentioned a contract...?"

Quill rested both the contract and a pen on the table, then slid it towards her, keeping his fingers firmly on the end of the document. "Once you sign this, there's no turning back. If you are dissatisfied and return the spirit, you will still be obliged to pay."

"Yes, I understand that." Kaitlin wiggled the contract from Quill's grasp and grabbed the pen with trembling hands.

"We specify your payment below, and show where you need to sign."

Kaitlin's eyes widened as she read the contract terms. "One year?" her voice trembled as uncertainty flickered in her gaze. "Are you certain?"

"Absolutely. One year of your life for his services should be enough," replied Quill.

Kaitlin sighed, leaning back into the chair. "What if I die before I get the answer I'm looking for?"

Quill shrugged. The living had such a strange concept of time and self importance. He was the same all those years ago. "We can't control everything, but within reason, you won't die before you get your answer."

"Within reason?"

"Just don't go doing anything reckless or dangerous, and you'll be fine."

"At my age, a year could be a lifetime."

Quill hid his smile. Kaitlin read through the contract. He knew the deal was done. He always knew when they read the fine print.

"As long as I get my answer, a year isn't that big of a sacrifice, I suppose."

Quill watched as Kaitlin put pen to paper and signed the contract. He couldn't help but wonder about the weight of her decision. Was she fully aware of the consequences? A year to some is nothing, but not the case for everyone. Quill tried to not think of if the burden fell onto his shoulders. He's doing what she wants. Who is he to make her question things further? His thoughts turned inward as he observed her signature taking shape on the parchment.

Quill took the agreement and tucked it into The Great Book. It grumbled as it consumed the contract, binding it into its pages for evermore. "Excellent. This contract will bound you with Arthur Leech. Once you pass, you can choose to release him or return him to me."

Kaitlin turned her head, glaring around the room, her eyes landing on the shadows on the walls.

"What kind of spirit is Arthur?" asked Kaitlin.

"He's a gentleman from the 1920s with a love for modern life. He's had many satisfied customers and I'm sure you will be pleased with his work," replied Quill.

"Will he be with me on my way home? I can't see him." Kaitlin rubbed her fingers across her forehead. "I feel so foolish taking your word on such a ridiculous concept."

"I'll brief him, and once you're home, he will appear," Quill said, placing his arm around Kaitlin and gently escorting her to the front door.

No matter how many years passed, people stayed the same. Always arrive full of doubt, never quite trusting the service. "Make sure you're alone tonight, and I'll deliver him to you afterwards. We hope you'll be very happy with our service, and we thank you for your generous donation."

As Kaitlin left the store, Arthur yawned, stretching out across the window seat while Wilson snuggled up close beside him. "She was quite posh," Arthur grinned as Kaitlin stormed past the window. "What have I got to look forward to this time?"

"A murder case. She thinks someone close to her killed her husband. Her partner was a news reporter, Derek Chapman-

Webb, been around for years. Been all over the newspapers, even I couldn't avoid that. Although I never read the death described as a murder. However, I'll let you get the full details from her."

"Will do, boss," Arthur said, saluting Quill.

"Arthur, before you go," Arthur lowered his hand. "Make sure you get this one done swiftly. She needs closure on this before it's too late," Quill said, rubbing his temples.

Arthur's face fell as he glanced at the contract. "One year?" he mumbled. "Is that all I'm worth now?"

Quill looked up at Arthur, observing Wilson sleeping on the sun-faded cushion. "Just make sure you're prompt. That year is practically all she has left."

Arthur Leech

Arthur's surroundings flickered into focus as he blinked away the bright light and flashes of crimson. The soft lamplight cast a gentle orange glow on the textured royal red wallpaper, the intricate patterns dancing and entwining. He breathed a faint smell of burning, a rare scent that would cross over to the plane of the dead. In the corner stood the woman who had bought him, staring aimlessly out the window with a cigarette poised between her fingertips.

As Arthur approached, Kaitlin's breath caught in her throat as she whirled to face him with wide eyes, her fingers trembling as they tightened around her cigarette.

Peering at the grandfather clock beside the fireplace, Arthur realised it was already two in the morning. It only felt like a few seconds ago he was speaking to Quill in the shop. Now he was miles away. Gently, he placed his palm towards her shoulder. Kaitlin recoiled, her gaze locked on him. Wrapping her arms tightly around her stomach, as if to shield herself from his presence, she asked, "Are you... Arthur?" Her voice quivered, and she stubbed out her cigarette. A cloud of smoke shadowed her as she stepped closer, gesturing at his chest before backing away like a frightened kitten.

"It's an honour to meet you, Mrs Chapman-Webb," said Arthur as he turned towards the fireplace. He paused at a framed photograph and focused on the balding man captured in this brief snippet of time. A piece of card leaned against the frame, bearing the words, *'Derek Chapman-Webb. Beloved Father and Husband. 1923-1992.'*

The date. 1923. Something stirred within Arthur, but he repressed it and faced Kaitlin once again. "I can't hurt you. I'm here because you wanted me to be," he continued. Kaitlin clutched a small glass bottle, the one Quill had given her as part of their contract. A reminder she could always send Arthur back to the void.

New owners often gripped the bottle during their first meeting, hoping to repel the evil they had regrettably summoned.

"I am under your command," Arthur said; he kept his distance and stood beside the fireplace. "Please, take as long as you need. When you're ready, you can tell me your request."

Kaitlin crept closer, the candlelight casting hard shadows across her pale face. Her wet eyes flickered to the photos on the mantle and back to Arthur. "I didn't think this was real, you know. I was desperate, and I suppose this was my last hope. Seeing you here now makes me wonder if I'm going insane. Am I?" she asked, "Going insane, that is?"

"People often have that reaction when they see me." Arthur said, following Kaitlin as she turned to face the window. "The contract you signed was real, Mrs Chapman-Webb. You gave part of your life for this. Don't waste it with countless questions."

"You can call me Kaitlin, you know. I hate being so formal," Kaitlin said, turning to gaze out at the gardens and fields outside. From what Arthur could see in the night, the grounds stretched for miles. He wished to breathe in the rich country air, to experience nature one more time.

"Even in a place like this?" Arthur asked, leaning through the open window for a better view.

"This opulent life wasn't mine. It was Derek's dream. He always wanted more—bigger and better. The only reason he kept working was to pay for this lifestyle, but I'm considering selling once I sort everything out," Kaitlin said. Leaning against the back of her chair, she lit up another cigarette. "He was a good man, my Derek. He looked conservative and had views I didn't always agree with, but he was a good man deep down. That's why I can't rest without knowing the truth. I hired all the private help I could find, yet they found nothing. You are my last resort, Arthur. I pray you are up to the job." Kaitlin lifted her chin, her lips tight.

"I'll do my best. Tell me more about him. What did he do for work?" Arthur asked.

"He worked as a broadcast anchor. You must have heard of him or watched him on the ten o'clock news?" Kaitlin said, raising her brows.

"I'm a ghost that's been dead since the twenties," Arthur chuckled.

"Of course. How foolish of me to assume the dead watch

television. Derek worked as an anchor for years. Loyal to the same channel throughout his entire career. I always told him he'd triple his salary in half the time if he were to move to a commercial channel, but he refused. The news was his bread and butter, but his genuine passion was in documentary making, investigative journalism. You know, speaking to people, asking tough questions."

Arthur could feel Kaitlin's passion for Derek with each breath. It was clear she loved him almost as much as Derek seemed to love his work.

"How did he die?" Arthur asked.

"Our housekeeper discovered him in the annex inside the wardrobe, naked, and with a belt around his neck. The authorities 'officially' marked it as accidental suffocation." Kaitlin wiped the chair with her hand and slumped deeper into it, gazing out the window once again. "Of course, the public doesn't know that. They were told he died from a sudden illness. But I don't believe the official report. That wasn't something he'd do."

"He could he have taken his own life? Maybe there were things you didn't know about him."

"You really are innocent, aren't you?" Kaitlin flashed her eyelashes at him. "The belt around a neck, it gives a certain pleasure. One many men get involved in, but not Derek. He loved life, loved his work, but didn't exactly love the bedroom."

"So, you believe someone made it look like an accident?" Arthur asked.

"Yes. He was very... plain, my Derek. When it came to decoration, his food palate, his *ways* in the bedroom. That isn't something he would have done."

"So, who would have a reason to kill him and set him up

like that?" asked Arthur.

"I don't know. He had lots of jealous young journalists who wanted his prime-time spot on the news. He reported about a lot of people—anyone could have held a grudge," Kaitlin said.

"Did he have any close acquaintances?"

"He wasn't one for close friends. We went to plenty of events and dinners, but that was all business, really. He has three sons from his first wife, and two daughters from his second." Kaitlin cleared her throat. "They're all still waiting for their share of the pie. Unfortunately, I need to go first before they can get anything."

"I see. Quite the busy man. You never had children together?"

Kaitlin laughed. "You really have been dead for a while, haven't you? No. By the time my turn came, we were both way past children, my dear."

Arthur tapped his fingers, his foot going along with the same rhythm. The suspects were mounting up. Ex-wives, kids all over. Countless workers and any super fan with a grudge. He thought about John Lennon, how a crazed fan killed him. Perhaps the same happened to Derek?

Arthur rubbed his face, tapping his finger along his jaw as he did. "I'm going to need access to some of his closest contacts: his kids, work friends, that sort of thing. Did he have a workspace I could look through?"

"I don't want any of his acquaintances knowing of you," said Kaitlin, raising her voice.

"They won't know about me. Only you can see or hear me, but I can eavesdrop and examine things. I can observe if anyone says anything."

"How will you get to his office? They've refused to grant

me access and none of his associates will talk to me now he's dead."

"His kids. Have you been to their homes before?"

Kaitlin tutted.

"Of course I have! I'm not some wicked step mum who they all hate, you know."

"Okay, well. If it's a place you have been to before, then you can send me there. I can listen in and do some digging," Arthur suggested.

Kaitlin furrowed her brow. Arthur watched as she moved her fingers along her palm.

"I'm not sure about this. Their lives are personal. They wouldn't have hurt their father."

Arthur tried not to let his anger show. They sent him here with a job to do, a job she sacrificed her life for, and now she's questioning every step.

"Just give me a chance. You gave up a year of your life to have me here," Arthur pleaded. "Let me gather the answers you need."

Kaitlin peered into Arthur's dark eyes; doubt etched into hers. "Why are you so keen to help me? What do you gain from this?"

"It beats being stuck in that bottle for years. I enjoy helping people."

Kaitlin grunted, and with a shrug, she turned away. "What place do you want to go to first?"

"I'll start with his kids, and then maybe a colleague of his at his office?"

"Fine." Kaitlin leaned towards her glass of gin on the side table. "What do I have to do?"

Arthur stiffened his back. Moving through space was harmless. It didn't hurt him, nothing could any more. But it didn't mean it was easy on his soul, either. God knows how far away he was about to be sent. It was usually over in a flash, but his stomach tightened thinking about it.

"Consider the place you visited, where you want me to go, and I'll go."

"And if I want you back?"

"The bottle," Arthur nodded to the void clasped between her fingers. "Make sure it's close."

Without replying, Kaitlin sparked another cigarette, and Arthur's world vanished.

Arthur entered a darkened room, the only source of light from the flickering television casting sporadic shadows across the walls. Luxurious chairs and tables, detailed in gold with sharp edges, filled the room, which was decorated with cold marble. A dark-haired man wept in the corner, sobbing into his arms. He reminded Arthur of an old friend, one whose good looks had often incited trouble. It dawned on Arthur that this must be one of Derek's sons, but he wasn't sure which one. There were three that Kaitlin had mentioned. Why did she pick this one to visit first?

Arthur peered around the room to try and piece together the man's identity. Abstract art adorned the walls, and the absence of family photographs did not go unnoticed by Arthur. A phone rang, interrupting the silence. The man hesitated before answering the call, while Arthur took a seat beside him.

"Hello?" muttered the man. Arthur leaned in close to hear both sides of the conversation, yet not close enough to impact the frequency. Spirits could affect technology, and while Arthur had asked Quill how that was possible, he had never given him an answer.

"Neil, I've been told you have requested the items from your father's office," spoke the voice on the other end. A stern and authoritative male, it seemed. "Let us be clear. You agreed to no interviews, press, or any of your father's unfinished work. I assume you will abide by those rules?"

Neil rubbed his eyes and rose, separating the slats of the blinds to peer outside. "Yes, I understand. But his office needs to be emptied. I thought that would be okay," he said.

"You've got a payout from the network, but you must stay quiet about it. We don't want the company being dragged into any of this. We have given your father a televised funeral and signed deals for three documentary series about his work. He's died a beloved man. Just leave it that way." The disgruntled man on the other end hung up.

Arthur narrowed his eyes. This phone call proves there was more to Derek's death. Neil seems beat up about the entire thing, a man way over his head. Arthur tapped his foot. There must be more answers to find at the broadcast company. Why are they so keen to keep this under wraps? It had to be more than keeping the company looking good in the public eye.

Loneliness enveloped Neil again, lost in his thoughts and grief. Arthur couldn't help but feel sorry for him, and the weight of his burden. His eyes were dark, sunken in with a clear lack of rest. His clothes hung from his shoulders, creases running along the seams. Arthur brushed down his own suit, still as crisp as the day he died.

He followed Neil into the bedroom and observed the emptiness of the space. The only personal touches being that of a few pictures dotting the walls and the soft cotton duvet draped across the bed. As Neil turned on the shower in the bathroom, steam quickly filled the room.

Just then, the front door opened. A blonde woman entered; she moved gracefully and seemed out of place in the sombre room, her flowing golden locks framing her face like a halo. Arthur wondered who she was, one sister, or someone closer?

Topless, Neil left the shower and walked past Arthur to the woman, who wrapped her arms around him, tenderly kissing him on the neck. Arthur turned away to allow them privacy, yet he caught snippets of their conversation.

"What's the matter, baby? I came down as soon as I finished my shift," she said; she lead him back to the sofa where he had been crying earlier. "Are they still threatening you?"

Neil took a sip of his coffee, half empty, no steam bellowing from the rim, and replied, "Cindy. I told you taking that money would be a mistake. I can't say or do a thing now."

Cindy caressed his back and leaned in close, brushing her nose against his neck. "You had no choice. With him gone, your allowance had stopped. This fancy place doesn't pay for itself, you know."

Neil pushed her hand away from his neck and stood. "I know that. But what if they're hiding something? Someone must know why Dad did this. I don't believe he would do something like that."

Her face flushed, and she stole a glance at the floor. "You never know what your parents are really like, babe. Maybe he was into that kind of stuff, and it went wrong."

Neil's anger flared, and he hurled his glass to the ground, where it shattered into countless pieces. "I don't want to talk about it Cindy. I haven't slept in days, and I need to clear my head."

"Why don't we accept your stepmother's invitation? We

could go to the house for a few days with the family. It might do you some good to be around his things." Cindy followed Neil into the bedroom, and Arthur watched as Neil entered his en-suite, stepping into the shower once again. The woman sat at the end of the bed, studying her nails.

"Shall I call her?" Arthur overheard her ask.

"Wait until morning. She's not sleeping, either. The same as me. But we can at least carry on and pretend we're coping," Neil shouted from the shower.

Arthur watched Cindy. She was beautiful, like a Hollywood movie star, with big blue eyes and hair that cascaded down her back. He could tell she was rich, with her opulent necklace and rings on each finger, but her style was timeless, a look that would stand out in any decade.

As the night went on, Neil and his blonde companion drifted off, clinging to each other in a restless slumber. While they looked content, Arthur, on the other hand, loathed nights like this. Nights when he was in a new location and no one knew he was there. The silence was tedious, as though time stood still. In the main room, a forgotten chessboard sat below the TV. Arthur blew the dust from it. He could never wrap his head around chess, no matter how much he tried. The men he used to serve drinks to at work would often discuss the game in detail—the strategies and moves Arthur couldn't even comprehend. No one had ever asked him to join in on a game, so he never got the chance to learn.

Arthur's mind wandered to his old friend, Billy—the handsome one possessing both the looks and intelligence Arthur lacked. During nights like these that stretched on forever, Arthur would often think of Billy. He'd wonder how Billy's life had turned out after Arthur left him. Not a single day went by that they weren't together, and Arthur couldn't help but feel a sense of guilt for leaving him behind. Maybe

Billy had found someone else to assist him whenever the local women flocked around him.

Quill last released Arthur from the void on the 50th anniversary of his own death—a chance for Arthur to share a few words. He had hoped to see Billy, in some form, or at least explain what he had been trying to tell him all those years ago, but Quill was adamant not to break the rules. At least Billy escaped the eternal fate Arthur suffers today. At least he had that to ease his conscience.

After decades of waiting for someone to release him, Arthur had given up hope. Perhaps Kaitlin might finally be the one to set him free. Every customer of Quill's signs the same deal in the end. The choice to set the soul you own free, but the burden of replacing that soul with yourself was one Arthur had seen no one accept. Given the choice, he isn't so sure he would either.

A buzzing from Neil's phone startled Arthur. Groggily, Neil felt for it on his bedside table, trying to silence it but failing to do so. In his drowsy state, his hand slipped, and the phone tumbled to the floor with a thump. Cindy stirred in her sleep, but she quickly settled down. Meanwhile, Arthur heard Kaitlin's voice through the phone's speaker.

"Hello?" Kaitlin said, her voice muffled.

Arthur leaned his ear towards the phone. "Kaitlin, it's me."

"Arthur? How are you doing this? What have you done to Neil? I knew I shouldn't have sent you there," Kaitlin exclaimed. Arthur peered up at Neil. He was asleep, but restless. His teeth were grinding, worry and pain painted across his face.

"He's fine. He's sleeping soundly with a beautiful woman in his arms," Arthur replied. "Can I come back to yours?"

Kaitlin let out a sigh. "I don't think there is much more I can do here."

Kaitlin hesitated for a moment before replying. "What am I supposed to do with you here?"

"At the moment, I'm getting a little tired of watching your stepson and his girlfriend sleep in each other's arms. I'd rather explore the grounds at yours if that's okay with you."

Kaitlin chuckled lightly. "I understand."

As Arthur materialised in the drawing room, Kaitlin remained in the same chair where he had left her.

"Thanks," he said, walking towards her. "You might want to arrange that family get together. Cindy was keen for Neil to come down here for a few nights."

"I bet she was," Kaitlin replied with a growl. "She always enjoys her stays here."

"She likes the high life, then?"

A smile crept onto Kaitlin's face. "She enjoys what this home brings, never had much before she met my Neil. She worked for Derek, some girl who sat behind a desk. Soon changed when a bit of money came her way, but who can blame her? If Derek was stupid enough to give it out, who wouldn't accept it?"

Arthur's eyes fell on the bottle of gin beside Kaitlin. "I see you've been keeping yourself busy."

Kaitlin turned to Arthur. Her eyes struggled to focus, but she seemed relaxed, less pain behind her eyes as the alcohol took over. "You want one?" She said with a wry smile.

"Nothing I'd want more. Do you know how long it's been since a drink passed my lips?"

"No, but I'm sure you will tell me."

"Too long, let's just say that. Why don't you have one for

me?"

"It would be my honour," she said, pouring another glass for herself.

"Wait. Come over here, to the bar." Arthur stepped behind the bar to his right.

"What are you doing?" Kaitlin asked, swaying as she made her way towards him, a smile creeping along her thin lips.

"Grab that gin, and pop open the champagne on the shelf."

Kaitlin raised her brows. "Champagne? My, my," she hesitated momentarily, then did as Arthur asked. "Now what?"

"Add four parts of Gin to the shaker, then a splash of lemon juice," Arthur's face beamed as he recalled the recipe, and as Arthur stood behind the bar, his suit tight around his shoulders, he felt alive again. "Now, slowly pour that into the glass and add champagne on top with ice."

Propped on his elbows, Arthur watched as Kaitlin did as he instructed. She finished the cocktail, and he closed his eyes as she took a sip. Memories of his long shifts behind the bar resurfaced. "Good, isn't it?"

Kaitlin licked her lips. "Marvellous, boy. You can stay. I have a question, though." Arthur nodded as he watched her swig the entire glass in one gulp. "Can you dance?"

Arthur laughed. "I used to know a few steps in my time."

"A man from the 1920s, you said." Her eyes lit up like flames. "Arthur, join me in a dance and introduce me to The Waltz, the same one from all those years ago." Kaitlin positioned herself in the centre of the room and outstretched her arms. Arthur inched closer; while he could not embrace or touch her in a physical sense, the energetic connection was enough to mimic the dance. Arthur draped his arm across her back and gestured for her other hand to join his. With tears in her eyes, she beamed at him, and they took a step forward, following his lead.

As they danced, the music transported Arthur back to the 1920s clubs, while Billy watched from afar. These were moments Arthur feared he had lost forever, from his brief existence that ended far too soon. Kaitlin looked over his shoulder at the mantle where her husband's photos were displayed; they danced for hours until the birds sang and the sun rose.

Quill Darlington

The rhythmic ticking of Quill's watch indicated that time was, indeed, passing. Yet the bus he patiently waited for appeared to be running late. Leaning against the brick wall of the bus stop, Quill let out a frustrated sigh. Vibrant graffiti now covered the once pristine paintwork—an artistic addition since his last visit. He retrieved the letter from his oldest friend, Isaac, and read it again.

> *If you can, please visit Jason's shop. I've tried to warn him, but he won't listen. Maybe seeing him in person will make him see reason. Our meeting isn't due for a while, and I want to ensure we're all still here for it. Well, the ones that are left, at least.*
>
> *Regards, Isaac.*

* * *

Slipping the note back into his pocket, Quill boarded the bus as it finally arrived. The journey would only take two stops, and the bus was nearly empty if not for the solitary woman surrounded by shopping bags, arranged like a makeshift fort. Quill chose a seat across from her and twisted to face the window. As the bus rumbled along, the pale stone walls whizzed past in a blur, surrounded by lush green fields stretching alongside the abandoned railway tracks. A group of sheep grazed, basking in the sun's warm rays, while Quill absentmindedly traced his hand along the metal handrail, poising his thumb over the stop button. Silently, he hoped Jason was faring better than their last encounter. After all these years, the weight of their shared responsibility still burdened him.

The village gradually came into view, its quaint charm reminiscent of Ringwood, Quill's hometown. This was his second visit here; the group had long ago decided to keep their meet-ups to a minimum—only meeting once every ten years at the same location. Quill adjusted his shirt. If Isaac had asked for this favour, Quill knew whatever awaited inside Jason's shop would be no straightforward task.

Outside the shop window—'Jason's wares'—was a vibrant display of handmade items: pillows, lamps, and paintings. Shaking his head, Quill pushed open the door, where inside, reclaimed wood covered the walls, adorned with hanging lush green plants intertwining with black metal beams. If Quill could smell, he imagined the air would be sweet. A young boy manned the desk. A warm smile crept across Quill's lips as the boy glanced up from his paperwork. His hair was a dishevelled mess, as if struck by a bolt of lightning.

"Hello, sir," said the boy, clearing his throat with a cough.

The Ghost Merchant

"Welcome to Jason's Wares, where you'll find all the wares you need. How can I assist you today?"

"Very good," said Quill, raising an eyebrow. "I'm here to see the boss. Is Jason around? I can go out back to meet him." Quill tapped his nose, winking.

The boy hastily stood and extended his hand. "Wait! I can't let anyone go back there. Please, sir. Stay on *this* side of the desk," said the boy, using his finger to draw an invisible line near Quill's feet.

"What's your name, boy? I'm Quill," Quill said, accepting the boy's hand and shaking it twice.

"Quill?" The boy's eyes widened. "Mr Darlington?" The boy darted past the counter toward the front door, flicking the sign to 'Closed' before rushing back to Quill's side. "Jason has mentioned you before. Oh, I'm so glad you've arrived."

The boy retrieved The Great Book from under the counter and slammed it onto the table, the air erupting with a cloud of dust. Quill waved it away until The Great Book came into view; it was enormous and countless pages stuck out from its edges. Quill surveyed the shop once more before watching the boy with fresh eyes—his untidy hair, the shelves of empty stock, the dust coating the plant leaves. Jason had always kept the shop neat and tidy, just like he had once kept the book.

"It seems things have gotten a little out of control here. Why don't you tell me what has happened? My friend Isaac sent me to speak to Jason and offer some help. Judging by the state of The Great Book, it seems things are far worse than either of us could have imagined."

The boy sighed. "I've been clueless about what to do all this time. He said I was ready and that I knew enough, but I didn't. Everything has gone wrong since he left."

Quill did his best not to react to the boy's words. Moving past the desk, he proceeded to the backroom, where bottles lined the shelves, trembling violently in the dimly lit corridor. "Tell me what happened here. Where has *Jason* gone?" Jason wouldn't abandon his duty. If he had moved on, he would have known. Isaac would have known.

"It happened a few days ago—or maybe a few weeks. I've lost track of time; it all blends together," replied the boy.

"Take a breath," Quill assured him.

"Jason told me my training was complete. I've been here for a few years. I arrived as a soul, and then he took me on as his apprentice. He said I could manage this place without him."

"He moved on? To whatever comes next?" Quill inquired.

The boy hung his head. "No, I don't think so. I don't believe he left willingly. I've been trying to figure out what happened, trying to remember everything he taught me, but it's all gone wrong."

Quill nodded, then clicked his fingers to summon The Great Book into his arms. He placed it on the empty table behind him. "Tell me about the last few days before Jason vanished," requested Quill, flipping through the pages in search of Jason's final meeting.

"Well, it was a busy day, and Jason had a late customer he didn't want to see, but I allowed him in. He was an old man, smoking a cigar. He didn't say much. Was quite nasty, really."

He flicked to the last entry in the book. "Dustin? Dustin Davis?" asked Quill, tracing his finger along the book. The boy nodded. "What happened?"

"He wanted to purchase a spirit."

Quill rolled his eyes. "Yes, I *gathered* that. But why did Jason leave a few days after that meeting?" Quill skimmed through the entry. Dustin had bought a soul. A thirteen-year-old girl.

"They argued. Jason didn't want to sell the soul to him. I think the man had already purchased some souls from other shops. Do you know him?"

"No," Quill replied, closing The Great Book with a loud thud. Jason knew the rules well—he couldn't refuse a sale when someone made an offer. "So, Jason refused, but then later changed his mind?"

"No. That was me who sold the girl. I didn't want Jason to get in trouble. He was breaking the rules, so I handed him the soul the man came for." The boy sat on a wooden stool. " I shouldn't have gone over his head, but he always warned me about The Boss. I wasn't ready to lose him, though I suppose it was inevitable."

"Did Jason leave anything behind? Did he prepare anything before he left?" Breaking the rules had been a struggle for both Quill and Jason, both in life and death, yet they knew better than to test The Boss.

The boy guided Quill up the narrow staircase, past the shelves of trembling bottles, and into Jason's office. "I saw your name there, along with a list of letters. There are a few other names there, too. I haven't opened them."

Quill settled into the comfortable leather chair, holding the wax-sealed letter. In one swift motion, Quill opened it.

'Quill, my longtime friend. I hope the shop is doing well. I've trained Oli as much as I could. He may not be the brightest—much like me—but he has a good heart. Take care of him; keep an eye if you can.' Quill glanced at Oli, who was fussing with his hair. *'I'm sorry I won't be at the gathering. You never know when it'll be the last time you see your mates. I've been a fool, a complete idiot, but I don't regret*

it. That man who came in, Dustin Davis, is a nasty bugger. I've sold many souls to him. Breaking the rules felt like my only option this time. I hope the darkness isn't too harsh. Perhaps it won't be worse than our last few months alive. The Boss is taking me tonight. They gave me a few hours to sort things out. It's not the ending I envisioned for myself, but I gave it my best shot. The Boss wanted payment for the rule break. He dug into a few things—small things I had missed over the years. Young Oli here should have been sold years ago, but he was like a son to me, and I couldn't do it. Make sure you do good in this life, mate. Make better choices than we did in our past. Perhaps there's still time to make a difference. But if you do anything, and I mean anything, be prepared for the consequences. I hope you make it to the other side and find forgiveness. I have three other letters to write, and I'm already struggling. Never forget me. Keep my name alive.
Jason.'

"Mr Darlington, is everything alright?" Oli asked.

Quill smiled. "Everything's fine, lad. You'll be okay here. Work hard, follow the rules, and make Jason proud. Do you understand?"

Oli furrowed his brow. "I think so, but there's so much I don't understand, sir. So much for me to learn."

Quill chuckled. "You have plenty of time. In the back of The Great Book, there's a list of all the Ghost Merchant shops in the world. If you ever need anything, write to me."

When Quill returned home, he arranged the easel and prepared his paints. He closed his eyes, summoning memories of Jason—his shaved head, his strong and stern countenance, and those friendly blue eyes. Quill recalled the kindness beneath Jason's tough exterior, the softness in his voice when he was at ease. For hours, Quill painted, pouring his heart and soul into creating the perfect portrait of his dear friend—the man who finally took a stand and did what he believed was right. A pang of sorrow tugged at Quill's heart as he contemplated Jason's final moments. Having his soul stolen before being taken to eternal darkness, with no hope of moving on. It was a fate Quill wouldn't wish upon his greatest enemy, and it served as a stark reminder of the dangers of bending the rules.

Quill reflected on his mistakes. Then, with the last stroke of his brush, he stepped back, gazing into the eyes of his friend one last time. Placing the completed portrait on the wall beside Mike's—the first of their group to depart—Quill smiled, his heart heavy with memories of the moments they had shared, the good, the bad, and the downright terrible.

Quill Darlington

Quill's fingers danced over the shelves, a whirlwind of dust swirling in its place as he meticulously cleaned each bottle. Even with every bottle having the same design, the voids inside told the story. Each colour, he could see, was like a window into their deepest desires. He kept a watchful eye on the desk, where he hoped Wilson hadn't drifted off to sleep. But then again, who could blame him? After all, he was over a hundred years old; he'd had likely seen more than his fair share of excitement.

Some souls placed in front of him were new, like Erin, whose bottle was full of colour, purple and crimson swirling around, mixing into one. Her ambition and anger swelling through. She was adjusting to her new afterlife; however, her fiery temper showed, and she was displeased with her life's outcome. Two shelves across at the back of the collection, Alma's bottle dimmed more each day. Quill leaned in close, listening to the faint humming from within. Alma was one of the oldest ghosts in the building, and Quill has never matched her up correctly. He sighed as he wiped the dust off her bottle. He'd let her down so many times. Alma was a gentle spirit—slightly irritating, mind you—but harmless, nonetheless. Even in life, her memory had been terrible, but back then, there was no name for her condition, not like today. If only she had received the help she needed, her life might have been better, longer, and more fulfilling.

The bell rang from inside the shop, and Quill turned to find Allegra standing by the desk; she owned the Wicca shop past the pub. Her hair was often wild, a muted red streaked with flashes of white; eccentric wardrobe mirrored the untamed chaos atop her head—a riot of colours. Her leather boots creaked against the floorboards as she walked to Wilson, smiling—a smile that softened even the hardest of hearts. Quill had known Allegra for a long time, longer than most people, yet despite their friendship, he remained cautious around her, maintaining a polite distance. Warily, he clocked her every move.

You couldn't always trust a witch.

"Good day, Allegra. Need me to fix your monocle again?" Quill propped himself up on the desk, sunlight flickering across his cheeks.

"I thought I'd come see my most experienced friend." Allegra's robes billowed as she scanned the shelves, stroking the frame with her finger. "Do you know what date is coming up?"

Glancing over his shoulder, Quill checked the calendar. 1990. Two years old.

"Your birthday?" he guessed. "Surely that hasn't come around again?"

Allegra sat in the window seat with Wilson eagerly curling onto her lap. "Your favourite holiday."

Quill sighed. He hated that date, always had. The generations of families showing their faces pushed him for small talk, stories of his year. Customers daring to come into his store. "No, not Halloween. I'll be closing this year."

Allegra cackled. "You can't! We need all the shops open, including this one! Now I've already spoken to the landlord of The Tavern, and the two ladies who run the stuffed toy shop. We are all in agreement, and I won't take no for an answer."

"But I have nothing to sell, just that junk up front, which is purely for show!"

Allegra gave Quill a hard look. "My new apprentice Renee arrived a few weeks ago. She can help bring my stuff over here. It will double my sales and I'll take 80%. It seems a fair agreement for bringing you so much trouble."

Quill unbuttoned the top of his shirt. "But how will I cope? I have... *important* work to be getting on with."

The raft of paperwork swelled through Quill's mind. More organising could always be done, and of course he had his list of never ending improvements to apply to the shop, too. There were also letters he needed to write. He wanted to update Isaac about Jason, give him the terrible news.

"That young thing you had come in a while back. Can't you use her?"

Quill strolled towards Allegra and nudged her hand away from the shelves of items displayed in the window. "How did you know about Erin?"

"That's her name, is it? Handy to know. Why don't you

stop being such a stubborn so-and-so and take my advice? You have a wealth of opportunity back there in those bottles. Use the help while you have it."

It always frustrated Quill, how Allegra dished out advice on things she didn't know about, and how she somehow was always spot on despite the fact.

"I've told you. It's against the rules."

"So? Rules can be bent, Quill. Every Ghost Merchant can have an apprentice."

"No. I won't do it. I won't put others at risk if they make mistakes. If The Boss finds out, they will punish them. Not me." Quill picked up the spare papers on the table and shuffled them. Allegra watched on, her eyes full of pity.

"One day, Quill. You are going to need to let go. You can't run this place at the rate you want to forever. Even the oldest souls grow tired." Quill kept his head down, chewing on the end of his ballpoint pen. "You want to know how I knew about her, then?"

"If it means you'll leave, then yes."

A smile crept along her face.

"I could feel her presence. I always do when you have a new arrival. My stomach tells me." Allegra pulled up a layer of her clothes and pinched her belly. Quill flinched, raising an eyebrow. "But this one... Erin. She was stronger than any other I'd felt before. Keep an eye on her. Get to know her. Use her to help in the shop. There's something different about her, and the sooner you know what that is, the better for all of us."

Quill set down his pen, intrigued. For the first time in countless years, he felt a hint of excitement, a movement of fear in his stomach. "What do you mean, different?"

Allegra stood and adjusted her robes. "I'm not sure. But I

have a feeling she's not like the others. And with Halloween coming up, we need all the help we can get, do we not?" She winked at Quill and turned to leave the store.

Quill sat at his desk. He had never given much thought to Allegra's intuition before, but there was something about the way she spoke of Erin that made him curious.

Allegra rummaged through her pocket and finally pulled out a can and popped it open. She set it down beside Wilson, who eagerly lapped its contents, while Allegra leaned against the door frame and faced Quill. "Remember what I said," Allegra smirked. "Erin could make a fine shop assistant with a bit of training. Ease your burden, Quill, while you can."

Quill grunted, forming his lips into a thin line. His mind was elsewhere, focusing on how he would handle the upcoming Halloween rush. Allegra was right, of course— Quill couldn't manage the store on his own forever, yet the idea of entrusting another soul with the secrets of his shop, and his past, weighed heavily.

"I'll think about it," he said finally; he met Allegra's gaze with a level stare. "But I make no promises."

Allegra flashed a sly smile; her eyes sparkled. "Oh, I know you'll do the right thing, Quill. You always do." And with that, she disappeared out the door.

Sighing, Quill returned his attention to the desk. He had a lot to do before Halloween and not much time to do it.

Quill rushed to the entrance, flipped the shop's sign to close, and secured the door. He glanced at Wilson, who happily licked the content of the can Allegra had left behind. Quill surveyed his cluttered shop, which he always left in purposeful disarray to deter casual visitors. It usually worked, but with Halloween approaching, he would need to sell wares to curious customers.

Quill disliked dealing with the living, but he couldn't deny the necessity of a helping hand. The unusual strength Erin showed on arrival had caught him off guard; the power emanating from her was impossible to ignore. She almost walked out of the shop, an act no other soul had achieved it. *Maybe Allegra is right,* he pondered, moving to collect Erin's bottle from the back of the shelf.

Quill sensed her presence the second he released her. Erin's emotional turmoil lingered in the air, amplified by her unwillingness to accept her own death. Quill approached her with his hands raised defensively. Her will was strong, her eyes like stone, clinging onto her past. "Erin. I wanted to talk to you again."

Erin stepped away, backing into the desk. "When will you let me go back home?" she asked. "I don't know what I've done to deserve this, but I want to go back home, back to Jacob."

Quill took in the look on her face. For a moment, Erin transported him to the lowest point of his life hundreds of years before. A look of absolute terror—a constant reminder of his mistakes. "I understand, Erin. I know I approached it wrong. Can we start over? There is no going back to your past life now. Please, let me help you move on."

Erin's eyes darted around the room. "If I'm dead, then why can I touch this desk? It means I've improved from before. It proves I'm still alive."

Quill exhaled, and when he snapped his fingers, Erin lost her balance and fell through the desk. "It's all a trick. I gave you that power and I can take it away. I thought you'd like to be solid again, to touch and feel while I explain matters to you."

Erin's eyes narrowed on Quill, and she ran straight through him. She skidded to a stop, turning to face him once more. She glanced at her hands and giggled as they moved through Quill's body. "I'm a ghost. So, this isn't a dream. I'm really dead."

Quill clicked his fingers again before placing a gentle hand on her shoulder. "There is still much more to do. If you want to look at this as a punishment, you can. Plenty have in the past. But maybe I can offer you something more—a purpose while we try to find you a match."

"A match?" Erin asked.

"If I find a customer who proves to match with you," continued Quill, "then I have no choice but to sell you. However, until then, I'm offering you something I've never offered another soul before."

"Oh, making deals with the devil now, am I? What are you offering, exactly?"

Quill moved behind the counter, returning The Great Book under the desk and into a drawer. "The devil doesn't need to know everything. How would you like to be my... apprentice?"

"You mean help you sell souls to the highest bidder?"

Quill slid his glasses back up his nose. "No, not quite. I mean, working here, in the shop, helping the public on busy days."

"A shop assistant? That's the best afterlife can offer?" Erin placed her arms on the desk. "You might as well kill me all over again. Go on. I'll close my eyes. Get it over with."

Laughing, Quill pushed her arms off the desk. "We can start right away, and if you show you can be trusted, I'll let you have more responsibility."

Erin tapped her chin. "Okay, but on one condition. If I

agree to this, then I want something from you."

"Name it," said Quill, suddenly curious.

"I want to attend my funeral. I won't believe I'm gone unless I do."

"Are you sure? Even the most confident of people would find the reality of their own funeral a hard burden to witness."

"If you want me to help at Halloween, then that's my offer."

"Who said anything about Halloween?"

"I can hear, you know. When I'm in that bottle, I hear bits and pieces. I'm aware of whats going on around me."

Quill froze. Hearing fragments of the world from inside the void was unheard of. According to the rules, any soul in the void should be in a state of sleep. How could Erin hear across different planes? While it went against the rule book to agree to her demands, Allegra was right. Erin was one to watch.

"Very well," Quill said. "I'll agree to your condition. However, you must clean this shop from top to bottom first. If you do a good job, we'll attend your funeral together."

Quill Darlington

It had been centuries since Quill last propped his feet up on the stool, with Wilson snuggled in his lap. Gazing out at the cobbled street, a vibrant carpet of orange autumn leaves rustled and swirled in the breeze. Erin had worked hard, despite struggling with the broom at first. She complained that hoovers did a better job. But, you know, some of the old ways work best, Quill thought.

Erin continued to sweep, the bristles scratching against the floorboards. "You really want to go, don't you?" he asked. Quill placed a hand on top of the paperwork as she moved a hand towards it to rummage through. There were some things he didn't want her to see, not yet.

"Of course. I won't change my mind. Never." She bent down to pet Wilson. "What else do you need me to do? Any more ghosts you need to trap for eternity?"

Quill cracked open The Great Book. A selection of names appeared, though some other Ghost Merchants around the world had crossed a few out. Quill skimmed through the list to check if it had assigned him any. "There are a few on here, but you're far too new to be checking on new souls." A name appeared. Madeline. She was to be expected in several days. Eight years old. Quill's heart dropped. Throughout the years, Quill had built up a wall against the emotions of the job, but it never got easier when kids arrived.

"Quill? What shall I do?" Erin pressed.

"Just sort out the rubbish," Quill snapped. "I'll go check on the souls out back." Erin marched off, and sighing, Quill made his way to the back room.

Striding in the dark, the jars of souls clinked as he passed by. The spirits within awaited their next assignment, and he couldn't help but feel the responsibility. He stopped at Alma's jar, checking to make sure everything was alright. As he wiped the dust off her glass, he whispered, "I'm sorry I've left you for so long, Alma. I'm still trying to find you a match, but it's not an easy task." He returned her bottle back on the shelf, carefully arranging it with the others. Alma was one of the few spirits he felt comfortable confiding in. She had a forgetful memory, so he knew he could trust her not to judge him, not to fully remember his secrets.

Quill glanced up at the clock above his office door and realised it was time to prepare Erin for her journey. She had proven herself these past few days, and if she truly wanted to attend her own funeral, he needed to get her ready to go.

Underneath a turbulent, overcast sky, the lush greenery of Hollybrook Cemetery seemed to defy the gloom. Oak trees filled the landscape and grass stretched around a tiny church. As Quill led Erin towards the church, he questioned his decision. Never had a ghost under his watch witnessed their funeral before, but Erin was determined to prove it was all a huge lie, as if she would soon awaken in bed, back in her old life. He hoped being here would let her mind settle, and her heart wouldn't break by what she witnessed.

"It's not too late to turn back, you know," Quill said, stopping before the church. Murmurs rumbled from inside, and music played in the background as the guests found their seats. "Erin?" He tapped Erin on the shoulder, who stared, transfixed, at the wooden church doors.

"I want to go. I want to see it. To see myself." She faced Quill with a smile. "Will you come with me?"

Quill had prepared to stay outside to allow Erin her space. After all, she wasn't a child, yet her plea drew him inside along with her. Immediately, he froze. Quill had expected the death of a young girl to draw a massive crowd, but only a few people sat on the hard wooden pews in mourning. Erin's boyfriend, Jacob, sat at the front, tears streaming down his face.

"I wish I could speak to them, to let them know I'm okay, not in any pain," said Erin. She released Quill's fingers and walked towards her coffin. She stood beside Jacob, her boyfriend, who had a dark suit on, accompanied by a multi-coloured pocket square in his velvet jacket. Each person had a bright item accompanying their dark attire. Funerals had changed much across Quill's lifetime. In the earlier days, everything was so structured. So traditional.

An elderly man seated in the back alone wiped away a tear with a bright handkerchief. Hard lines along his pale face, eyes that told a sad story. Perhaps her father, Quill thought.

The coffin moved as the music trailed away, and a red curtain swept across it. All attention focused on the vicar, who gestured to the exit on the left side of the church. Erin glanced back at Quill. "Might as well see me off to the very end. Come on." Linking arms, they walked beside her guests and emerged from the church, stepping into the vibrant courtyard of the cemetery. Vines weaved throughout the surrounding stone columns, and the gazebo offered an expansive view of the sprawling cemetery beyond. Bright bushes and flowers lined the stone paths, their colours a sharp contrast to the solemnity of the funeral.

"You're taking this much better than I expected," said Quill, breaking the silence.

Erin smiled. "You know, I was never in denial, not really. I just needed to see this for myself. To know Jacob was okay, and to see who really cared about me in the end."

"Did it give you what you wanted?" Quill asked softly.

"Yes, and no." Erin hugged her frame. "I miss him more now. I know he's only a stretch away. I want to just reach out and hold him. But that life isn't mine anymore, is it?"

Quill shook his head, averting his gaze to the ground. "Who's that man over there?" he asked, gesturing to the elderly man he'd seen earlier in the church.

"My father. He brought me up mostly—not well, but it was better than nothing, I suppose. My mother left when I was young, and, well… Dad did what he could."

"All any parent can do is try their best. Is that Jacob's mother over there, with her arm around his shoulder?" asked Quill, nodding towards a woman in the distance.

Erin's shoulders slumped, her eyes darting to the ground.

"Yeah, Maria. She was like a mother to me."

"Had you been dating for a long time?"

Erin chuckled. "No, not really. I make it sound like we're lifelong lovers, don't I? We were together for around two years. We've known each other for three and a half, though."

"Well, for what it's worth," said Quill, with a sad smile. "He seemed to really love you. I've seen a lot of loss in my time, Erin—some deeper than others. But the look in that boy's eyes tells me everything I need to know about how he felt for you."

"Can you find a way to let Jacob know I'm here? Even the smallest sign?"

Quill stood and rested a hand on her shoulder. "I'm sorry. I can't do that. It wouldn't be right."

"But he's hurting. *Please*," Erin edged towards Jacob. He wore a crisp suit, but looking at the details, Quill saw a broken man. He had undone his top button, his tie was slightly off-centre, his shoes were scuffed, and shirt was not fully tucked in. "Tell me how, and I will take the punishment. I don't care."

"Erin, listen to me. There is nothing you can do. Let him be and move on," said Quill. He attempted to pull her back from the crowd, but Erin somehow separated from him, swinging her arm and knocking a flowerpot off the wall. The guests shrieked, but Erin remained motionless. Quill gaped. How had she crossed the divide? He had only permitted Erin's ability to move freely outside of the shop—nothing more. Even he would find it difficult to move objects in the physical world while hidden. "What did you do?" he shouted. Erin stepped away from Quill, closer to Jacob. "Get back here now! Get away from him."

"Why? He can feel me near him, can't he? Look at him! He's looking for me." Erin gestured to Jacob, who scanned the crowd. "Let me have this, Quill. *Please*. Just one more conversation. I know I can change things." Ignoring the chance for Quill to answer, Erin moved towards Jacob and reached for his hand. As she grasped it, Quill clicked his fingers.

Erin whirled, staring open-mouthed now, back inside the ghost merchant shop. "Why did you do that?" she screamed, storming towards Quill. "You are the one who gave me hope! You said I couldn't hold him again, but I did it. I felt his hand brush against mine. Why did you take that away from me?"

"There is a reason the spirit world and the living do not mix. What just happened is a prime example of that. You and Jacob live two different lives now. I risked everything to give you that moment and you pushed it too far. I had to take us back before you exposed everything."

"I won't stop loving him."

"I'm not asking you to." Quill drew a breath. "But if you love him, Erin, then you must let him go."

Erin's determination burned in her eyes. "I need to reach him while his memories of me are fresh, while he still remembers me. You must have loved before, Quill. *Please*. Let me try."

Quill moved from Erin and perched on the desk, wrestling with the weight of his emotions. He'd never experienced a spirit like Erin's before, someone so eager to continue her old life. That wasn't an option anymore. Wiping away a tear, Quill watched her as she paced. "I'm sorry, truly," he said, picking up the bottle.

"Don't! *Please* don't send me back there," she said.

Quill hesitated, gripping the bottle. He looked at her, her large pleading eyes, those innocent haunting looks that had followed him into the afterlife. He wanted to be better, to not repeat the same mistakes. Quill slammed the bottle down and sighed. "Get out of my sight. I don't want to see you. You stay in one room, I'll go to another." He shouted, anger swelling. He was afraid of the power she had, of the repercussions from allowing this to happen.

Erin stepped back, her body closed in. "I didn't mean to upset you." She turned, went towards the stairs.

Quill flashed a quick glance at her, looked back to his desk. "You won't be able to leave this shop. Got it?" Erin nodded. "And from now on, all rules are followed, by the book. The Boss doesn't take kindly to rule breaks, that I know all too well. Now go, keep yourself busy. Read The Great Book, remind yourself of the rules. Of the importance of what you are doing here." Quill fell into the window seat, the silence of the shop swelled around him. The silence that had followed his life for centuries.

Arthur Leech

Laughter wafted into the courtyard from outside the dining hall where the family congregated. They were each dressed in light linen clothes, holding a glass of wine, as if on holiday in the French countryside. All of Kaitlin's stepchildren were present, and it was like Derek had never existed. Kaitlin played the perfect hostess; with a fixed grin, she offered drinks and observed her family's playful chatter. It was heartening to witness her smile and the vanishing of pain in her eyes; the same could not be said for night-time, where the pain resurfaced every evening and etched lines into her features. At night, she acknowledged Arthur, though she took every attempt to keep the topic of Derek from his lips.

Even if Kaitlin remained defiant, Arthur's dedication remained. He was on a mission, determined to unearth the answers Kaitlin now seemed to dismiss. In the games room, some of her stepchildren lounged in plush leather seats, enveloped in an opulent lifestyle that had become second nature to them. Neil, with a glass of swirling brandy in hand, appeared inebriated. Arthur spent the day observing the dynamics between them, noting how Neil projected confidence to his siblings—a stark contrast to the vulnerable man who privately wept about his father in the dark.

The dialogue between them proved monotonous, prompting Arthur to seek refuge from the stifling atmosphere. He took advantage of the absence of Neil's girlfriend, Cindy, who had wandered off, leaving the family to their discussions. Arthur tailed her, convinced that anything would be more captivating than what would conspire in this room.

He walked alongside Cindy through the sprawling hallways of Kaitlin's residence. The royal green wallpaper triggered memories of velvet dresses from Arthur's past. Cindy's footsteps echoed on the parquet flooring, and her demeanour suggested an attempt to conceal herself. As they passed Kaitlin's bedroom, Arthur caught a glimpse of her in a despondent state as soon as the door closed and she was left alone.

Cindy's journey continued well beyond her private quarters, and Arthur grew increasingly curious. Outside Derek's home office, Cindy hesitated a hand over the door handle before entering, and Arthur couldn't help but wonder why she was here.

Inside the office, adorned with dark oak panels, awards, and a cabinet displaying a lifetime of achievements, Cindy traced her fingers along Derek's desk. A photo of him garnered her attention, and she sighed, her lips forming a pout. Arthur circled the desk, leaning in toward Cindy. She glanced over her shoulder, perhaps sensing a presence. Holding his breath, Arthur feared he had made himself known.

"You were such a wonderful man," Cindy murmured to herself, settling into the plush leather chair, the wheels squeaking slightly as she moved. "I wish you were still here to help. Your advice was always so invaluable."

Arthur stroked his chin in contemplation. Why did Cindy harbour such powerful feelings for Derek? Memories of how Derek was found resurfaced, and Arthur wondered if Cindy's emotions exceeded what was normal for a friendship. Perhaps he had cut her off financially after an affair, and his death was her way of seeking retribution. These questions swirled in Arthur's mind, but he lacked any evidence—only a hunch that wouldn't hold up. Cindy gently caressed Derek's photo, old memorabilia, and awards he'd left behind and exited the office.

Arthur approached Kaitlin in her room, who sat by the window. He wanted to speak about her husband, about Cindy, to continue his search for answers.

"Busy day?" he asked, noticing her stifled yawn. "It's nice to see your son is doing better. Surrounding yourself with a few familiar faces really can do wonders."

Kaitlin glanced at Arthur, then gazed out of the window, moonlight illuminating the ground below. "Am I one of the best you've had, Arthur?" she slurred.

Arthur gasped, shifting in his place. The family who'd kept her so busy during the day now slept, and that meant Kaitlin's mind was free to wonder into the long night. "I'm going to need you to be more specific, Ms Chapman-Webb."

"You know, your previous owners..." Kaitlin replied,

waving her hand through Arthur's figure. "Tell me about them. Tell me I'm the best you've had."

Arthur couldn't recall a single moment when Kaitlin wasn't holding a drink. "I've had eight previous owners since I arrived at Quill's shop," he said, trying to steady his voice.

"Tell me about your first one," Kaitlin demanded. She swayed, and her glass of wine sloshed towards him.

Arthur observed her, puzzled by her fixation on the topic. "My first owner was Barbara Atkins. I stayed with her for about three years."

Kaitlin raised an eyebrow and laughed. "Tell me about another, one that wasn't a *woman*."

Arthur glanced away, peering across the landscape. "I've only had one male owner," he said.

Kaitlin urged him on. "Tell me about him."

"His name was Luke," Arthur began. "He was a fine young man, with good looks like his father. He had dark hair, black as the night sky, and a smile that kept you awake."

Kaitlin leaned in, interested. "Go on."

Arthur hadn't thought about Luke in a long time. "He was a foolish boy who went out of his way to please his dying father," Arthur told Kaitlin, who had stopped drinking. She gave a knowing nod. "When I died, I never thought I'd see my friend Billy again. But then Luke came to see Quill; he specifically asked for me. He traded in some good years of his life to get me to his home. His pa was sick, unconscious most of the time. He didn't have long left."

Arthur turned to the window, looked towards the open fields, the winding stone paths illuminated, endless freedom. "Luke told me how his father spent hours telling stories of his friend who died, and how he never had a chance to say goodbye. He had a whole life without me by his side." Arthur paused, noticing that Kaitlin had nodded off, the wine glass somehow perched between her legs.

It was nice to remember Billy.

By the time Luke signed the agreement with Quill, it was too late. Arthur arrived in time to witness Billy's departure from this world, never having the chance to explain his behaviour the night he died. At least Luke was around, though, Arthur thought. Yet Luke blamed him for not being there for his dad's final moments, and he returned Arthur to the void immediately. Luke had sacrificed years of his life to make his father's dying wish come true. To see an old companion once again, but was all futile.

Arthur's gaze fell to his hands. His body trembled. "All I wish for is to be able to close my eyes and not wake up in the morning, but I'll never be granted that wish unless I'm set free."

Kaitlin shifted, and the wineglass tumbled, staining the carpet. "Arthur?" she murmured, rubbing her eyes, and glancing at the spilt drink. She ran her hands through her hair. "God, this is all such a mess. What was I thinking having you here?"

"I'm here to solve a murder, remember?" Kaitlin looked away at the mention of her husband. "I still need to go to his office, the place he worked at," Arthur continued.

"You still want to do that? Why not just enjoy yourself here on the estate? I thought you enjoyed walking around nature."

Arthur looked into Kaitlin's glassy eyes. Her priorities changed so quickly. Moments of obsession over Derek's murder, clouded by a few good memories spent with her family. It was like she was trying to find an excuse not to uncover the answers.

"I do, and I'm most grateful, but I like to keep myself busy, too," Arthur said.

"Fine. Go... if you must," Kaitlin replied. "Although I cannot understand what you'll find there."

Quill Darlington

Raindrops pounded against the window like an angry drum, their relentless assault sending shivers down Quill's spine. Quill could feel the chill of the storm creeping into every corner of his small store. Quill strategically scattered buckets across the room to collect the rainwater seeping through the ageing roof. The air, heavy with the scent of dampness, clung to everything in the shop. As he watched the raindrops race each other down the gutters outside, he couldn't help but feel a twinge of disappointment. His next customer, Rupert, was late again.

Quill drummed his fingers on the wooden counter, bracing himself for Rupert's inevitable delay. He'd told Erin to stay silent. He still couldn't look at her, wanted to get through how angry and disappointed he was with what she'd done, but at the same time, he wanted to act as a teacher, to show her how things worked in the shop.

Quill had spent the morning preparing for Rupert's visit, studying his past purchases, and trying to guess what kind of spirit he might need this time.

When Rupert finally arrived, Quill masked his impatience with a forced smile. "Ah, Rupert. It's been so long. I almost got my hopes up that we'd cracked your problem. When I saw your booking, my heart broke a little."

Rupert seemed unfazed by Quill's teasing. In the later years of life, humans are often unbothered by most things. They have learnt to let things go, something Quill still needed to learn for himself. Rupert simply tipped his cap, his white strip of hair poking out from around his head, then made his way to the back room, tapping a steady rhythm with his walking stick on the floorboards.

"Has he been in before? Do people buy more than one soul?" Erin asked. Quill put a finger to his lips and scowled at her.

Quill trailed behind Rupert, his thoughts racing. He mentally sifted through the inventory, searching for Rupert's ideal companion. Rupert had cycled through so many over the years. Quill's steps faltered as he turned to Erin. "You keep quiet from now on, you hear? And yes, to answer your question. He has bought a soul before, but he comes in for an exchange now and then if he isn't happy."

"Is that an official rule break or just something we don't mention?" Erin said. "Because I'm sure I don't remember reading about that in The Great Book."

Quill rolled his eyes. "Do as I say, not always as I do." He replied. He knew it was a weak answer, but time was limited.

As he replied, Rupert's walking stick thumped against the floor—a clear sign he was ready to begin. Quill steeled himself for the delicate conversation that was about to begin. It was time to find the perfect spirit for Rupert, no matter how long it took.

Quill crossed the threshold into the shadowed room, where candles flickered in an enchanting dance, casting intricate golden patterns on the walls. Rupert was already seated in the wobbly wooden chair, and the bottle of his current ghost rested on the table. "Have you seen Wilson? I brought him some catnip," asked Rupert, searching the room with his eyes.

"He's still here, sleeping upstairs. I'll let him know you brought him a present," Quill replied, lining up some papers on the table. "So, Rupert. How have things been?"

Rupert picked up the glass bottle and tapped it on the table. "This one isn't working. Not at all like my Mary."

It had been a decade since Rupert's wife passed away, and eight years ago, he approached Quill in search of a companion. Quill had suggested a dog, but Rupert had already tried that. After a few meetings, Quill realised Rupert was looking for someone to replace his late wife. Originally, Quill had matched him with Veronica, a housewife from the sixties. Unfortunately, Rupert had returned her within a year. He claimed they had nothing in common. Quill had tried several other matches, but none had worked out. Finally, he suggested Lou, a receptionist who had lived a very loyal and dedicated life.

"So, Lou wasn't working out for you? I see she's spent around eighty percent of the time in the void. Is that typical for you, Rupert?"

"I couldn't stand her. She was mean and angry, like a

headteacher. I want someone... kind, soft, caring, someone like..."

"Like Mary," said Quill.

Rupert's expression faltered at the mention of his wife's name. Quill always noticed Rupert's heart ache when her name was spoken out loud. He knew he shouldn't feel this connected to a customer, or allow him to exchange so often, but Quill couldn't help but to try. The man was alone. His whole life was just him and his wife, and now he was here, with no one.

"Exactly," said Rupert.

"Oh, Rupert. This isn't what I like to see. You came to me wanting to find a new companion, but how will anyone ever replace your wife?" Quill asked, concerned.

"You must have had someone—someone new since I last came here," pleaded Rupert. Clasping his fingers together. Quill was sure if Rupert had the strength, he'd be on his knees begging now.

"You know, they say the love of your life is one of a kind. I don't think many get a second."

Rupert stared into his lap, a tear forming in his eyes. "Can't you try? Give me one more chance?"

Quill prodded his glasses further up his nose. "Okay, another shot. I can do that for you. I never want to see an unsatisfied customer, and I think I might have just the one. Please, may you wait in the shop while I prepare her?" asked Quill, showing Rupert to the exit. He turned to Erin, who'd stood by the door and watched. He glanced at the gift Rupert left for Wilson. "Take this up to Wilson and stay with him, will you?" Quill clicked his fingers, and Erin picked up the gift. "Remember, walk past Rupert. Don't say a word. He can't hear or see you anyway, but I don't want to chance it."

The Ghost Merchant

In the hallway, Quill's fingers caressed the wooden shelves, his touch a tender reflection of his reluctance. He lingered over the grainy textures and polished surfaces. Quill needed to let Alma go, but his heart felt heavy with the weight of what he was about to do. Reaching to the back of the mid-shelf, Quill stretched as much as he could before pulling Alma's bottle to the front. As he gazed upon her void, guilt niggled at him for having kept her for so long. But perhaps, just perhaps, her unpredictable nature was exactly what Rupert needed.

Alma's void had faded over the years, her time was running out, the colour was muted, the essence moving around the bottle in a slow swirl, energy drawing to an end. This might be her last opportunity. Souls can only endure in the void for so long until they vanish forever. With careful deliberation, Quill uncorked the bottle and released Alma, who slowly emerged, like a phantom stepping into the mortal world. She had styled her auburn-grey hair to perfection in an elegant updo. Her long dress cascaded to the floor, and her puffed sleeves ended at her elbows. Alma glanced around, dazed, then dropped into the seat.

"Oh my. Quill! How long has it been?" she asked, placing a hand on her forehead.

Quill laughed and gently pulled her hand back to her lap. "I know you can't feel faint, Alma. It's been a fair few years."

"What year is it?"

"1992."

"Oh, I see. Sixty years since I was last out of that thing. Do I get a prize? Is that why you have called upon me?" Alma's smile widened with anticipation. That kind smile, attached to her welcoming face, large cheeks and soft pale skin. She held herself like a child sometimes, clasping her hands behind her back, poking a foot out to the side.

"A prize of sorts. I have found a new owner for you to live with."

Alma's eyebrows crinkled. "You've sold me on? After all this time. Why?"

"I thought you needed to share your wisdom with another man, Alma. I can't keep you for myself forever now, can I?"

Alma giggled, then jumped to her feet. "I don't know what to say." Twirling gracefully, her dress flared in a perfect circle as she leaned towards Quill. "I don't know how anyone would compare to you."

Quill took her hand, slowing her to a stop. "He is a kind man. Rupert. He's looking for a companion. Someone to spend the rest of his days with."

"So, it won't be long then until I'm back here," Alma whispered.

"Not necessarily." Quill guided Alma back to the chair. "You see, spirits can last for so many years in our world, Alma. But there is an end date for us all."

"Not you," she protested.

"You are fading away. Reaching the end of your journey. Rupert could be your chance to get out, to be set free. From the beginning, he said he will replace the soul he ends up with."

Quill knew the chances of Rupert sending Alma back here, returning her for another and taking away her opportunity to move on, but he had to try to take a risk at some point in his life. This one could be worth it, if it meant she could move on in time, before she vanished completely.

Alma averted her gaze. "I don't know. It feels wrong being with another man. My Jean would have a fit if he found out. And my children. I can't let them be ridiculed by a hussy for a mother." Alma stood again and leaned against the walls, scrambling to find a way out. "I can't bring any more shame upon them. I don't want to do it, Quill. You can't make me!"

Quill held onto her shoulders and met her eyes. "Alma, look at me. Breathe. I can't have you acting like this. Your family is gone, remember?"

Life sparked into Alma's eyes. "Yes, I remember. Where were we? Am I to do some cleaning? Or did you want to talk more about the poor children?"

Quill reluctantly released Alma's shoulders, then turned away from her. "You've been sold to Rupert, Alma." His voice choked with emotion. "He will take care of you. Please, try to get to know him; be there for him with your wonderful sense of humour and fantastic listening skills, and I'm sure you will be free to be with your family again." With a flick of his wrist, Quill gently placed Alma back inside the bottle, his eyes swimming with tears.

Quill returned to the shop, where Rupert doted on Wilson with some catnip. Erin clearly didn't follow his instructions.

Quill approached him and handed over the bottle containing Alma. "She's all yours. Her name is Alma Edwards. Born 1757 and died 1820. She was a devoted housewife; she loved her family dearly," explained Quill, his voice wavering. "But I must warn you. She has some... memory problems. She forgets a few things sometimes, but it doesn't last long. Just calm her down and she soon settles."

"Thank you, Quill. I hope to not come back here again if I can help it," said Rupert, his voice solemn as he carefully placed the bottle in his bag.

"Just remember, she isn't your wife," Quill pressed. "If you can get past that, then I see no problem with you having a happy life together. Just take care of her. She's special, one of a kind. Someone I wouldn't give away without careful thought." Quill handed Rupert his umbrella, the tears now streaming freely down his face.

As Rupert made his way out of the shop, Quill stood, lost in thought. Out of all the ghosts he kept, he only ever confided in Alma. She was one of the select few who were allowed to get to know him; he had revealed his most inner secrets to her, knowing she would keep them to herself. Quill was optimistic Rupert would bring her joy, but the thought of saying goodbye to one of his oldest friends was almost unbearable. Still, Rupert would be the one to give her the greatest chance of freedom, and to depart from this life.

For that, Quill was grateful.

Arthur Leech

The news office was chaotic, to say the least. Arthur stood, absorbing the frenzy of activity around him. The chatter between co-workers was a constant hum, interrupted by the phone's ringing. Numerous televisions plastered the walls, each with a different program blaring. Arthur had fond memories of TV. He remembered a past owner, who's spend their days and nights in front of one in the 60s. Seeing the moving images in a home, coming from such a small box, always fascinated him. One advantage of living forever was witnessing new technology.

Arthur stepped aside from the crowded walkway, tucking beside the water cooler as people rushed by. Two men stood next to him, filling their cups. They discussed a show called *'Gladiators'*, and Arthur made a mental note to ask Quill about it later. For now, he had to focus. He needed to locate Derek's office and search for any clues that could shed light on his death. The call to Derek's son, Neil, originated here. There had to be an explanation for why it was off-limits.

In the communal area, no trace of Derek remained—not even a photograph to commemorate him. It was as if, beyond the cameras and public displays of grief, they had erased Derek's presence entirely.

Arthur paced the same walkways for what felt like days until finally locating Derek's old office, only to find he couldn't enter. A gold nameplate still adorned the door. While Kaitlin had been to the office building before, they must not have allowed her into Derek's private space. This meant Arthur couldn't enter, either.

A small crowd gathered around the main reception, where a man with balding hair stood, smiling, with a cigar dangling from his mouth. Arthur waited outside Derek's office door, hoping to glimpse something inside—anything. But he gave up, worried Kaitlin would call him at any moment. Two men arrived, entered the office and after a few minutes came out carrying boxes. This was Arthur's chance to peek inside, yet his anticipation was short-lived when they closed the door.

"Out of all the people to get his old office..." groaned the man in glasses.

"Don't think about it. Let's just get him moved in. Besides, his show won't last. He'll be back doing charity events and photo ops before Christmas," said the other man.

But the man in glasses wouldn't let it go. "Still, I don't think it's right."

"None of us do, but the guy's untouchable. Look at what happened to Derek. He wasn't the first to lose out to him, and he won't be the last."

Arthur glanced at the man who'd arrived beside the reception. He was all smiles, puffing smoke into the faces of the surrounding staff. Arthur wondered what he had done to Derek, if a man of that fame would risk his life and career for murder? The people watching on were clearly scared to speak, refused to look him in the eyes. He was already walking around the office like he owned the place.

"All it'll take is one person to talk for it to be over." The man in glasses said.

"I won't be putting my neck on the line—not while he's alive, anyway. Just hold off a few more years. Get the details now, then plan your big story for the future."

"What about Derek? You think his expose will ever get released?" asked the man, tapping the box.

Expose? Arthur gripped onto that word. What was Derek working on? And why has it been hidden?

"Nah, what use would it be now to show him as the hero? Destroy it and take the glory for yourself when the time comes," the other man gestured towards the bald man at reception. "I mean, look at him. He ain't exactly a picture of health."

The two men headed off, about to destroy whatever was written in that report of Derek's.

Arthur followed the new man closely, who was taking everyone's attention in the office. "Dustin, you'll move into Derek's old room. Just as requested, it's just been cleared out," a man in a suit shouted.

Dustin exhaled, puffing smoke towards a young female colleague. "Fabulous news, fabulous news." He clicked his fingers towards a younger man with slicked back dark hair; in fact, it wasn't too dissimilar to how Arthur had once styled himself. "You! Follow me. Don't be shy now, come on. Chop chop!" Dustin whistled, striding towards Derek's old space that was now Dustin's new office.

Arthur followed Dustin and the young man until they stopped by the door. "Thank you for giving me so much of your time, Dustin," said the young man.

"It's *Sir* Davis to you, son. Don't forget that. It's important. I worked very hard for that title."

"Yes, of course, sir."

Dustin pushed the door open. "We'll talk business in here. Go on, don't be scared."

When the door shut, Arthur leaned against it and closed his eyes, listening to the conversation continue from inside.

"Remember what I said? *Big* money we're talking here. All you need to do is join me on a trip to a shop, sign a bit of paper, and that'll be you sorted for life. Got it?"

The man didn't answer right away. Arthur could hear the tapping of his feet as he paced the office floor. "It's not dangerous?" he asked.

"Don't be so wet, boy. Men like us, we don't *do* scared. Now, sign this, and we'll get things going."

"What is it?" Arthur could hear the rustle of paperwork.

"It's a contract. It makes sure you can't go talking to anyone about this—about me." Dustin chuckled, his gruff voice echoing. "You know whose office this was?"

"No."

"Exactly, and you don't need to know anymore cause he ain't here. It's my name here now, and don't you forget it. I can make names disappear. I made his, and I can yours, too." Dustin snapped his fingers. "Just like that—poof, and you're gone. No one will ask why. Now, get signing."

"I'm not sure. I don't think I want to do this." Arthur could hear the young man more clearly now as he raised his voice. "I think I'll go."

"If you walk away, don't expect to have a job here tomorrow!" Dustin shouted.

The door opened and the dark-haired man stood in the doorway. Behind him, Dustin's face was red, his thin hair wild.

"Step away from me, and you will regret it." Dustin shouted. Arthur looked at the young man, whose hands trembled on the door handle. With a shake of his head, the man left, storming past the reception desk and straight out of the building.

Dustin marched towards the door, a hair's breadth from Arthur's face. "Make sure that kid doesn't show his face around here again, you hear me? No production or show I've ever worked on!" Dustin slammed the door. Arthur could hear him grunting and muttering to himself inside.

It all became clear then. The expose Derek had arranged must have been about Dustin's actions behind the scenes. The power Dustin wielded—the money—allowed him to arrange anything, even the death of a beloved news anchor. The threats Neil received over the phone from his office colleagues—warnings to stay silent and not ask questions—came back to Arthur. It all came back to Dustin Davis.

Arthur glanced toward the reception. Everyone was whispering, their faces etched with concern ever since Dustin had arrived, their concern only growing with his most recent fit of rage. It was obvious what had happened. Arthur was ready; he'd gathered what he needed. Now he had to relay it back to Kaitlin.

Alma Edwards

With widened eyes, Alma beheld the quaint little house before her. A mixture of wonder and puzzlement swirling within. She couldn't remember how she arrived here, yet the man beside her smiled warmly. A slight tremble wavered his grip on the walking cane, and his warm smile triggered a glimmer of hope in Alma. Perhaps he held the answers to the past she had forgotten.

The stone path leading to the house was worn by time, by weeds pushing through the cracks. Alma followed the man down the path, taking in the vibrant colours of the flowers planted in the flowerbeds. Ivy covered the brick garden wall, and a small greenhouse with broken windows stood on its lonesome nearby. She couldn't shake the feeling she'd seen those flowers before, though she recalled no memories.

"This is your new home," said the man, leaning towards Alma. "My name's Rupert." Alma glanced up at him, gaining a sense of comfort in his presence. He offered Alma his hand and guided her inside.

As they walked down the hallway, Alma soon became disorientated. The small kitchen at the end of the hallway looked unfamiliar, as did the sitting room on the left, and the bedroom on the other side. Each room appeared foreign to Alma, as if she had stumbled into an entirely different world. The kitchen, the sitting room, the bedroom—they all whispered secrets she couldn't quite grasp.

"It's no castle, I admit," said Rupert, "but it's home. Treat it as your own." Rupert shut the front door behind them, and Alma nodded, grateful for his kindness despite her confusion.

Rupert propped his walking stick against the wall, then rubbed his hands together. He watched her, his eyes refusing to blink, the start of a smile on his lips.

How did she get here? Alma wondered.

Alma's footsteps faltered as she entered the kitchen, her thoughts a hazy jumble slipping through her fingers like smoke. She gazed at the tiled floor, the oven, and sink, trying to piece together where she was and why she was there. "What is it you want me to do here? Did my husband recommend me?" she asked. Her voice quivered with uncertainty. "Shall I cook something? Give the place a clean?"

Rupert scratched his head. "No, no. You can't do any of that, even if I wanted you to. My Mary never could cook, anyway, so it always fell to me to do," he replied gently.

Alma didn't respond. Instead, she wandered towards the living room. "Shall I stay in there while I wait?" she asked. A cosy armchair bathed in the sun's glow, propped in the corner of the room. Without waiting for a reply, Alma sank into the plush cushions, relishing the sun on her cheeks.

Rupert's brow furrowed. "Alma, do you know why you're here? Quill usually prepares the guest."

"Yes, of course. I'm here to serve you. Do you want me to prepare dinner?"

Rupert's eyes widened. "No, no, my dear. You're here because you're *special*," he said, trying to gently explain the situation.

Alma's confusion deepened. "Special? How am I special?" she asked, her mind grasping for a memory that wouldn't come.

Rupert reached out to her. "You're special because you're... well, a ghost. You're here to help me," he explained, allowing his words to sink in.

Alma's shoulders lowered, her jaw loosening. "A ghost? Me?" Her voice trembled with disbelief. "Of course, I am. I remember now."

Rupert nodded, his smile warm and reassuring. "Yes. You're a ghost. But that doesn't mean you can't be of help. In fact, you're perfect for the job," he said.

Alma's confusion gave way to a sense of purpose as she finally understood why she was here. "I see. So, what can I do to help?" she asked, more confidently this time.

Rupert's face lit up. "Well, there are many things you can do. But, for now, why don't you take a seat and relax? I have a selection of books my wife loved. Maybe you'd like to read through them?" he suggested, gesturing towards the bookshelf.

Alma's eyes followed his gaze. "I'd love to, but I don't think I'm able to touch those things."

Rupert chuckled. "Nonsense. All the spirits I've purchased have been able to turn a single page. You can do it too, I'm sure. Go on, give it a go," he urged, pulling a book from the shelf and placing it beside her.

With uncertainty, Alma extended her hand toward the book, her fingers trembling as they hesitated above the book's worn cover. She waved her hand through the pages, unsure of what to do next. "What do I do?" she asked.

"Do what you would do if you were alive. Focus on the book, then turn the page."

Alma placed her translucent fingers on the page again, desperately trying to make the pages turn. It was no use. She couldn't seem to master the art of physical interaction, which frustrated her to no end as she turned to Rupert's warm face; his kind eyes comforted her.

"I don't think I'm very good at this," Alma admitted with a giggle.

"Try again. *Really* concentrate," Rupert encouraged. "You can do it. I know you can."

With intense concentration, Alma willed her fingers to contact the book's pages, yet they remained stubbornly immobile. "I can't do it. My hand goes through the page." She glanced around the room. "Maybe my Jean will be able to help me. He always helps me with this type of stuff."

"Jean? Who's that?" asked Rupert, furrowing his brow. "I can help you with anything you need."

Alma stood then, shaking her head. She peered out of the window. "No, no. My Jean, he always helps me. Do you know where he is?"

"Is he your husband?"

Alma whirled to face Rupert, her eyes wide with fear. "Yes, yes. Where is he? I haven't seen him in such a long time."

Rupert's outstretched hand passed through Alma's

translucent form, a gentle reminder of the insurmountable gap between their realities. "I don't think he's around anymore," said Rupert, gesturing to a rosebush in the garden. "That red rose bush over there. It was the last thing my Mary planted before she got sick. Every time I wonder where she is or what she's doing, I look out there."

"It's beautiful, Rupert. My Jean loved his garden. He couldn't get enough of primrose. Do you have any of them?" Alma smiled.

"We can plant some, so then every time you forget, or worry about where he is, all you need to do is you look outside. You will know he's not far. How does that sound?"

"Oh, that would be wonderful! Truly perfect."

A few pages of the book drifted open as Alma whirled around the room in a dream-like state. She stilled under Rupert's gaze. "Oh. I'm sorry." Alma leaned towards the book and turned the pages back again.

"You did it! See, I knew you could!" said Rupert, kneeling to pick up the book. "Do you think Jean will mind you keeping me company for a while?"

Alma shook her head and glanced towards the rose bush. "Do you think Mary will mind?" she asked, unsure.

"No. I think she would have liked you. She would have approved if she were still around." Rupert murmured, his voice thick. "Let me get started on dinner. Why don't you have a wander around and maybe we can try out the television?" Rupert leaned into Alma's ear. "It's much more fun than a book." He tapped her nose, then shuffled into the kitchen.

Alma watched him go, grateful for his kindness, and as she drifted through the house, she couldn't help but wonder what had happened to her, and why her memory felt hazy and incomplete.

Alma hovered in Rupert's wake, watching his hands painstakingly peel each potato with unwavering focus. It pained her to know she couldn't physically help him, but she was determined to make up for it in any way she could. Had Jean left her in Rupert's care for a reason? If so, she couldn't disappoint him.

As she watched Rupert work, Alma's mind drifted to the back garden. Passing through the walls, she felt the breeze brush past her. The back garden was breathtaking: a riot of colours and textures making her heart sing. It was a far cry from the place she'd been held when she died.

A deep sense of peace settled over her then. For the first time in what felt like an eternity, Alma truly felt alive, as if the beauty of the garden breathed new life into her spirit.

Alma smiled at the sight of Rupert cooking in the kitchen. He seemed a kind and gentle man. She wondered about Jean and their two sons. Her heart overpowered with yearning. The very essence of her being craved their presence, and she missed them more than words could ever express. But if she worked hard and did everything, she could to help Rupert, maybe someday she could be reunited with them again.

Arthur Leech

After countless nights in the dreary TV studio. He'd seen his fair share of Dustin, watched how the world of TV worked behind the scenes. Witnessed Dustin's destructive side in the office, how he'd bully and threaten any who were below him. Arthur yearned for Kaitlin's company, to finally tell her the truth, and eventually he returned to her countryside home. However, Kaitlin was evading him, filling her home with friends and family members at every waking moment.

Her house bustled with cheerful faces, a stark contrast to the television studios' gloomy atmosphere. Kaitlin was even getting along with Neil's girlfriend, Cindy, as they shared jokes over glasses of wine. The whole family seemed closer than ever before.

The only time Arthur had a chance to speak to Kaitlin was

in the evening when she retired to her bedroom after a long day. Despite Arthur's attempts to engage with her, she ignored him. Though Arthur was accustomed to being invisible, her ignorance hurt him deeply.

On this night, however, Kaitlin was sober. Perhaps she was hoping for a restful night of sleep without the wine in her system. She removed her jewellery, and Arthur joined her, hoping for a chance to finally speak.

"Will you talk to me now?" Arthur watched her through the mirror as she removed her earrings.

Kaitlin pouted, then wiped her face. "I apologise, darling. I've grown so accustomed to having you around; you're like my comfort blanket of sorts. I know you were here, but it's become so easy to forget at the same time. I didn't mean to ignore you."

"I informed you I had information about your husband and about what happened to him."

Kaitlin stood, resting her hand on Arthur's cheek. "Please, don't say another word. I don't want to hear it. Not anymore." Crossing to the bookshelf, Kaitlin took a small silver-framed photo of her husband. "Since my beloved Derek died, I was convinced this family would fall apart, that I'd be thrown aside like a useless stepmother." Kaitlin's voice was thick as she spoke to Arthur. "I convinced myself they had something to do with his death. One of his children, or one of his siblings, even one of the girlfriends. But I was mistaken, or at least, I hope I was. That's why I don't want you to tell me anything. Not yet. Not now. We're all getting on so well."

"Mrs Chapman-Webb, you've given up so much to uncover the truth. Are you saying that hiring me was all for nothing?"

Kaitlin moved away from Arthur and picked up a hairbrush. "I don't know. I don't want all of this to be ruined. Can't I just live in blissful ignorance?"

Arthur rubbed his temples. "It'll only take me a moment to tell you what happened."

Pressing her hands over her ears, Kaitlin began singing. "La, la, la. I can't hear you, Mr Leech."

Sighing, Arthur's patience waned as he stepped closer to Kaitlin. "You gave up the last years of your life for this moment, Kaitlin. I can't leave a job unfinished."

Kaitlin attempted to stroke Arthur's cheek, but passed right through him. "You're a truly beautiful man, Arthur. How fortunate are you to remain forever young like that? A tiny fragment of your prime self."

"I don't see it that way. I should have left here years ago. I don't belong in this world any longer. This job—this life—was forced upon me as punishment, and now, you treat my ownership like a joke, like something you can discard when you're scared to hear the truth."

"Arthur, please. I'm just some foolish old bag. Let me be happy. I'll do anything you ask—anything you want."

"You have nothing I need!" Arthur yelled, spinning to face the window again to gaze past the gates and to the hills beyond.

"There is one thing," Kaitlin said, joining him at the window. "The clause of the contract. I gave up a year of my life to own you, and when it comes to my end, I can choose to release you. Am I correct?"

"When you pass away, I'll return to the shop. I always do."

"Unless I decide to replace you, to set your beautiful soul free. In return, it will be me spending my afterlife on the shelf of a…" Kaitlin paused. "…dusty old shop."

A wistful smile touched Arthur's lips, considering Kaitlin's offer. He thought of the possibility of freedom, though it felt like a distant dream. He had been owned by eight different people before this. At the end of their lives, all of them chose the simplest path. His hope of ever leaving had long since evaporated. "What are you suggesting? You'll allow me to depart and risk being trapped for the next few hundred years?"

The weight of his past owners' broken promises pressed down on him. It was hard to trust anyone. He watched Kaitlin, his expression a mixture of hope and scepticism. The soft glow of moonlight illuminated her face, and he saw the sincerity in her eyes. But could he trust her?

Kaitlin's hand moved to her heart, as if hoping to convey the depth of her emotions—her honesty. She was being genuine, Arthur realised, and her promise of setting him free pulled at his heartstrings.

But he couldn't forget the pain of being trapped for so long. "I've heard those promises before, Kaitlin. I can't let myself believe you unless you truly mean it."

Slowly, Kaitlin nodded, and her eyes shimmered with sincerity. She reached out to touch Arthur's form, as if trying to bridge the divide between them. "I understand, my sweet Arthur," she whispered. "But please, give me a chance to make things right. Go back to your void, do not speak the truth of what happened to my Derek, and wait until the time comes. I promise you; I will set you free."

And with a heavy heart, Arthur retreated to the void, not knowing what the future held. Alone with his thoughts, he wondered if he would ever experience true freedom again.

Quill Darlington

In the dimly lit backroom with candles flickering, Quill sorted through the contract before turning to Erin. He delved into the customer's history, discovering that the man had frequented many merchant shops in exchange for owning ghosts. Quill's heart sank as he realised he hadn't thoroughly read the note attached to the contract. It was from his friend Jason, who'd run a Ghost Merchant shop until he broke the rules. Quill sighed, reading the note, seeing his friend's handwriting again like he was still here. It described the customer as having a truly 'dark heart'. Despite this, Quill had already invited Erin to watch. Knowing that she needed to face the harsh realities of dealing with such customers, he continued with her training.

"How much longer?" Erin asked, tapping her foot on the

floor.

"Will you stop that? The customer might hear and get spooked." Quill said.

"Who is he anyway? What kind of person comes to purchase the soul of someone to control?"

Quill raised an eyebrow. "There are many reasons. These shops date back as far as death itself. You should show it the respect it deserves."

"Is this where the saying 'make a deal with the devil' comes from?" asked Erin, checking her nails.

"The devil is but one name. We answer only to The Boss. That is all you need to know." A knock thudded at the door. Quill turned to Erin and whispered, "Now be quiet and observe. That is your training for today."

Erin mock-saluted, then zipped her mouth shut.

"Come in," said Quill, standing beside the door. "Dustin, is it?"

He recalled the name from his visit to Jason's shop. Dustin nodded. He was a tall, balding man with long, fine white hair drooping on either side; his enormous belly strained against his shirt as he waddled into the backroom after Quill.

"I understand this isn't your first meeting with the ghost merchants," said Quill. "Please, take a seat."

"Mind if I smoke?" asked Dustin, though he was already lighting a cigar.

"Not at all. You're our guest, Mr Davis."

Dustin interrupted Quill by plucking a folded paper from his pocket and resting it on the table. "Sir Davis to you," Dustin coughed. "I have written confirmation that..." Dustin's eyes skimmed the contract. "Let's see, what was his name... Ah, yes. Joel Philips gives me permission to purchase a soul under his name."

Quill examined the paper, where the ink was a dark, wet crimson. Blood. "Must be a good friend."

"Money makes people do anything. You know what I'm after, I assume. Should be written in my file? Chop-chop." Dustin exhaled smoke into the air.

"I'll go fetch her."

Quill dashed from the room, frantically searching along the shelves. His hand hovered before the bottle. He hated himself for doing this, for going along with the rules put before him. Quill thought of Jason, the warning he wrote, the fate he found. The Boss would find out if Quill sent a customer away. He had no choice. He had to show Erin there was no other way.

Quill landed on Madeline. The only soul he had in stock under the age of fifteenth.

Erin appeared beside him. "He's a bit of a pig, isn't he? Too scared to offer himself up, so he pays some poor kid to do it for him. What soul are you giving him?" Erin peered over Quill's hand and snatched the bottle. "Her? But she's a *child*. What does some old man like him want with a young child?"

Erin screwed up her face, taking a few steps back, gripping the bottle hard. Her eyes bore into Quill's, pleading with him to reconsider, to find another answer. Quill took back the bottle, keeping one eye on the door as he whispered, "Erin, please. It's not our place to ask such questions. If this is what he wants, and he's making an offering, then we have no choice."

"But she's a child. Don't you care?"

Quill froze mid-stride, lines furrowing in his forehead. His eyes betrayed the anguish raging beneath his composure. He despised himself for abiding by this man's whims, but he had no choice. He couldn't say no; the rules had to be followed. Jason's fate was proof of that. "She's a ghost, Erin. He can't touch her or force her to do anything."

"You said he's been to these shops before. How many does he have?" Erin hissed.

"Eight," Quill replied, averting his gaze to the floor.

Erin shook her head, her expression a mix of disbelief and determination. She outstretched her hand, grazing her fingers against the bottle. Her eyes bore into Quill's, pleading for an alternative. "Replace her. Put me in there instead. I can hit back if needed. Let me scare him off."

"I can't change this. If you're going to work here, you must know the rules can't be bent or changed, even if you don't believe in what you're doing. No harm can come to her." Quill moved to open the door, but Erin stopped him.

"No harm? Maybe not physically, but what about up here?" Erin tapped the side of her head. "Souls can still feel things you know. We can still be scared or frightened. She's just a young girl."

Quill shook his head, turning away from Erin.

"I won't be part of this. If you're going ahead, then I'll stay on this side of the door." Erin crossed her arms.

Quill bit his lower lip, an anxious habit betraying his inner turmoil. He moved past Erin and took a seat opposite Dustin. Sweat drenched Quill's palms, his unease palpable. He pushed the bottle towards him. "Madeline is a young girl. She's very pleasant, if a bit shy."

"Great. We're done here then," said Dustin, standing and tossing the bottle into his bag. He strode from the room, leaving Quill alone with his guilt-fuelled prayers. At least Madeline would be free when Joel Philips passes. Despite Quill's attempts to make himself feel better, Erin's words scarred him. *'Don't you care?'*

How could he stand by, letting another child down?

Erin Layton

1993

Erin's eyes fixated on the calendar's date, its numbers etched into her memory. A year had passed since the day of her death, a turning point that had separated her from the familiar world she once inhabited. She pondered how often she had encountered ghosts and spirits in her brief existence, and how many individuals were aware of The Ghost Merchant shops. How many had purchased souls for their own benefit? To date, Erin had only seen self-centeredness in soul buying.

Erin set off to work. She meticulously dusted the bottles and rearranged them on the shelves, the ethereal glow from each container casting eerie shadows. Erin marvelled at the variety in their glow, each one a testament to a different soul trapped within. Some appeared still, with slow-moving colours gently swirling around the bottle, while others seemed grainy, resembling a sandstorm blowing through a desert. Erin closed her eyes and concentrated on the bottle in front of her. Sensing an angry storm brewing in her mind, she could faintly hear the voices of the souls within. She envisioned the sand running through her skin, then squeezed her eyes shut and regulated her breathing. The image of her grave came to mind, the day she died, Jacob, and the graveyard she was buried in. She could smell the damp autumn air, the feeling of wet grass between her toes. The cold stone of her gravestone. She reached her fingers out, etching along her name in golden letters. The world flickered around her.

"What's happening here?" Erin heard Quill's voice and opened her eyes. She was back in the shop.

"I was just inspecting the bottles, making sure they were properly cleaned."

"You were fading. Are you feeling okay?" Quill leaned forward towards Erin.

She looked at her body, patted her stomach. "I'm okay, a bit wobbly, now you mention it."

Quill bit his lip. "Big day today, for you. One year." Erin nodded. "Why don't you have the afternoon off? Read a book or something upstairs." Quill picked up the dust cloth. "I can give this place a clean. Keep my body active."

Erin wondered to her room, the only place that was hers in the world, and closed the door. She could still smell the lingering scent of the trees. She fell into her bed, closed her eyes again and imagined the graveyard once more. It felt so real, like she was in touching distance. She thought of the trees again, their empty branches swaying in the wind, the tiny church that sat in the centre. Her mind swirled around, all her memories and feelings blending into one. She felt an icy wind. Her head nodded up and down, her body was light, floating through the walls. Her hands were damp and when she opened her eyes, her vision was a blur of colours.

When everything cleared, Erin found herself in the cemetery where her funeral had been held. She couldn't believe she was back in the same place again.

Erin felt the gentle warmth of the sun on her cheeks. She looked around the empty space and wondered how she got here. Without Quill, she shouldn't have been able to leave the shop, let alone appear this far away by herself.

She wondered towards her grave, hoping people she loved, who missed her, would surround it. Her arrival quickly dashed her hopes. A bunch of flowers laid there, pink, white and red. A note was attached. *'Thinking of you always, Jacob.'* Erin smiled, letting out a laugh. She wished she saw him, only to know that he was doing okay. Another note was placed beside it. A strange symbol printed along the top, three circles entwined. She remembered it from her grandmother's necklace when she was a little girl. Her heart raced, wondering if the note could be from her mother, if she'd come back, visited Erin's grave. But there were no words written on it. Just a piece of old card.

She laid back in the grass for a moment, the silence her only witness as the sky turned to a violent orange above, heard footsteps from behind, rushed ones. She got up, turned around. Was it Jacob, or her mother, coming to see her? Her eyes landed on Quill, who was walking towards her, his glasses on the end of his nose. She held her breath, worried about what punishment he will give her for leaving the shop.

"Erin, you are here." He shouted, out of breath. "How on earth did you do that? I was so worried."

Erin smiled and breathed out. He was worried about her, not angry. "I'm not sure. I just appeared here, somehow."

Quill narrowed his eyes. "Just appeared?" He tapped his chin. "Curious."

Erin walked towards him, sitting down in the grass, pulling her knees to her chest. "I keep doing this, don't I? Surprising you."

Quill chuckled. "You are fascinating, Erin. I'll admit that. I've never seen a ghost like you." He brushed his hair back from his face. "It's why I didn't want to put you up for sale when you arrived, you know. I needed you in the shop to keep an eye on you."

Erin narrowed her eyes. "I can look after myself."

Quill nodded. "I don't doubt that. Maybe I'm just being selfish. It has been many years since I had the opportunity to teach anyone."

Erin wondered if Quill was a teacher in a past life, or if he'd had a past apprentice as a ghost merchant. "Any ideas on how I arrived at my grave without your help? There wasn't even a welcoming party for me. Guess after a year, people move on."

Quill's pause stretched into a contemplative silence, his eyes distant as he finally spoke, "Maybe your soul was calling you here. There is a place I visit, you know, every ten years as a reminder, a tiny bit of hope that things will be better. Maybe the pull you had to come here to see the people you remember was stronger than either of us could have known."

Erin considered his words for a moment before responding. "But instead, all it's shown me is that they don't care."

Quill looked down, seeming somewhat guilty. "I'm sure that isn't true. There are flowers."

Erin looked at the flowers Jacob left. She knew he did care, deep down. Maybe he just didn't want to hang around a graveyard on his day off. She gave Quill a small smile. "Shall we head back to the shop now? The sun was nice at first, but it's getting cold."

Quill got to his feet, using Erin's gravestone as support. "Wait, you could feel the sun on your skin?" he asked, surprised.

Erin arched an eyebrow. "Isn't that normal for someone visible like me and you?"

"No, it's not," Quill replied. "It seems your soul is more connected to the living world than I initially thought."

Erin leaned in. "Any idea why that might be?"

Quill shook his head. "Not yet. But I will find out. There are still secrets you are hiding, and there will be answers I can find."

Erin's surroundings shifted abruptly, the shop materialising around her as Quill's snapping fingers worked their magic, leaving her momentarily disoriented. Quill walked off, up the creaky staircase, his demeanour torn between being a stern figure and a kind grandfather. Erin pondered his words as she followed him with her gaze. There was something peculiar about her, something that even she couldn't comprehend. For the first time, Erin felt special. It was ironic that this feeling could only come to her in the afterlife.

Arthur Leech

Something had altered in the fabric of Arthur's existence.

Kaitlin had returned him to the void; she promised his soul's release if he remained silent about her husband's murder. Yet since their last encounter, she had not summoned him again. Kaitlin was still alive—she had to be—otherwise, Arthur would have returned to Quill's shop to await a new owner. He had long since abandoned any hope of being released to the next phase of the afterlife, whatever that might be.

Drifting through the void, another rumble in the empty expanse threw Arthur off-balance. He rotated mid-air, disoriented, as a brilliant light materialised around him. This was the moment he had waited for, when he would discover his ultimate fate and learn what awaited him on the other side.

The world spun around him as he gazed at the yellow lights overhead. Shaking his head, Arthur tried to clear his vision; he still wore his blue pinstriped suit, and when he glanced at his hands, he was translucent—a spirit, still. An incessant beeping forced him to glance up at an old woman lying in a hospital bed, her face obscured by a breathing mask. It took a moment for him to recognise Kaitlin, who had aged considerably since he last saw her. Her eyes had hallowed, with dark circles formed beneath, while her skin was thin, yellowed and mottled with bruises. With a bony finger, she beckoned Arthur closer. They were alone, yet the worried murmurs of Kaitlin's family sounded outside. On the table behind him lay his bottle.

Leaning closer, Arthur watched as Kaitlin removed her breathing mask, examining him through tired eyes. "You're as beautiful as ever," she whispered, running a hand along his cheek. It passed right through. "I'm so sorry about what I did to you, Arthur." Her voice was hoarse, and she coughed, a deep rattle emanating from her chest.

"It's all right. I'm here now. Did you call me back?" he asked, flicking his gaze to the bottle on the nearby table.

"My time is almost up. I just needed to settle things between us—between me and my husband."

Arthur smiled, brushing a stray strand of hair from her face. "What did you need me for?" he asked, searching her face for what to expect.

"Do you remember that night when we danced?" Kaitlin's voice trailed off as she appeared to stifle her laughter. "You showed me what a proper gentleman was like in the good old days. I even told my grandchildren about it. How a wonderful man from the 1920s took my hand and danced with me in the dead of night."

Arthur smiled. "You sure kept me on my toes, Ms Chapman-Webb. It was an honour."

Kaitlin's expression turned pensive. "Such a darling, even after how I've treated you. Locking you away like a forbidden secret." She turned her head towards the door. "They all think I've gone senile. Talking to myself, speaking of the past, about haunted ghosts."

"You don't look well, Kaitlin. I'm afraid our dancing days might be behind us," Arthur whispered.

Kaitlin coughed again before melting back into the pillow. "I need the book finished. I've kept it in the back of my mind, but now I'm at the end. I want to know." Kaitlin spoke barely above a whisper.

Kaitlin's stepson walked in. It was Neil, Cindy's partner. Arthur glimpsed him as he turned towards the door. "Are you all right in here?" he asked.

"I'm fine. Please, just give me a few more minutes alone," she replied, waving him away. He rolled his eyes before leaving. "Caught his Cindy taking things, you know, from the house, Derek's home office. Selling 'official' items of Derek's to super fans."

Arthur chuckled to himself. That explained her unusual trip to his desk in the late hours all that time ago.

Kaitlin placed her hand towards Arthur's. "Please tell me what happened to him. To Derek."

"Are you certain?" asked Arthur. Kaitlin nodded and then closed her eyes. "Have your family treated you well since I left?"

"Yes, I've had a wonderful time here. My life has been great. Fulfilling."

Arthur wrestled with his dilemma. Should he offer solace

through a comforting lie, or uphold his principles to reveal the unvarnished truth? His internal struggle mirrored the growing shadows in all four corners of the room. It was becoming clear how close death was. "Your family played no role in your husband's death. That I can assure you."

"I see. There were times when I had doubts. Nevertheless, having a loving family by my side was more important than the truth. At least I know their love was genuine."

Arthur leaned closer to her frail figure in the hospital bed, observing the shaking rise and fall of her breaths. "You promised to release me if I kept quiet. If I never told you."

Kaitlin smiled reassuringly at Arthur. "Please tell me the truth, and I'll keep my promise."

"Derek was murdered." Arthur said bluntly. "He was investigating a male celebrity, and though his bosses cautioned him to stop, he persisted. He compiled an entire report. Had it readied to release before he died."

Kaitlin opened her eyes fully, then, gaping at Arthur. "He was a foolish man."

"They made it appear like an accident, disgracing him in death as a warning to others, I think. To keep anyone else from exposing him, too. They threatened your son, destroyed Derek's work, and covered up the whole incident."

"Who was it? Do you know?"

"Yes, I was unfortunate to spend some time in his company when I was at the office. He replaced Derek's time slot on TV."

Kaitlin nodded, closing her eyes once more. "That vile man. He sent me flowers when Derek died; he invited me to watch the first live show. He even put Derek's photo in his dressing room." She coughed again. "Thank you, Arthur. That's all I needed to know."

"Before I depart, I want to express my gratitude for everything you have done for me," said Arthur, smiling. "I've had no one as special in my life as you have made me feel. My friend Billy is someone I've always yearned to reconnect with. I hope to see him again once I'm no longer bound here. What you're doing for me, it surpasses anything anyone has ever done."

Arthur fidgeted with his fingers, then leaned over to place a ghost of a kiss on Kaitlin's temple.

"You're a beautiful young man, Arthur. If given the chance, you would have made a woman very happy," remarked Kaitlin, closing her eyes. Arthur sat beside her, keeping her company until her breathing slowed, countless time passed, and in her last moments, hushed voices and the tearful faces of loved ones filled Kaitlin's room. Arthur remained steadfast beside her, a silent sentinel as his hand clasped beside hers, a poignant testament to the bond they had forged.

The world around Arthur faded to black, and he lost all control of his body. His bottle clattered in the distance, and nothingness enveloped him once again. He searched, gasping for escape, but light shattered the darkness, and he found himself back in the shop with Quill standing before him.

Arthur's mind raced. "What's happened? Why am I here, Quill?" he whirled, searching for escape—the door to the beyond. But he was frozen in his tracks, unable to move any further.

"Arthur, please calm down. What's the matter?" asked Quill, puzzled.

"Kaitlin. Is she here? She promised to give herself up to free me. It should be her here, not me," said Arthur, his voice trembling.

Quill searched through The Great Book and withdrew the contract. "I'm sorry, Arthur," he whispered, showing him the contract. "Kaitlin has passed away. She moved on."

Arthur heard the words, but couldn't understand what they meant. He'd allowed himself to be fooled again, to listen to her words, allowed his heart to accept that someone could love him. That someone could find it in themselves to let him be free. But here he was, back where he always ended up.

Arthur crumbled, a gut-wrenching cry ripping from his body as his anguish echoed through the confines of the shop. The betrayal was like nothing he'd experienced before. "But she promised! She promised!" Kaitlin, who he thought cared for him, had broken her word. She had lied to his face with such ease.

Quill embraced Arthur, holding him tightly to comfort him. This wasn't usual practice for Quill, but in this moment, Arthur appreciated Quill giving him the ability to feel and touch for the embrace. "I'm sorry, Arthur. I'll do my best for you next time, I promise," Quill said, but Arthur couldn't bear to hear another lie.

Arthur knew the truth then. His entire existence had been a ceaseless yearning for the warmth of another, but now, he knew, that was a dream that would never be.

Alma Edwards

Every morning, Alma watched from the kitchen window as Rupert diligently tended to the back garden, his hands nurturing the flowers and vegetables with care. Alma had shown him how to hang the peas, using the same technique her mother had taught her. Alma wondered about her mother's whereabouts; she had been absent for quite some time, and it was unlike her to leave Alma alone with a stranger like Rupert. As Alma rubbed her wrists, she realised that nothing in this unfamiliar home belonged to her. She grew tired of constantly seeing pictures of a woman she didn't recognise. She reached out to take the photo frame from the sideboard. Her fingers passed right through it.

Looking out the window again, Alma saw Rupert digging with a shovel. He wiped the sweat from his forehead. Alma couldn't shake the suspicion that Rupert held some sinister secret about her mother's disappearance. Without thinking, she charged towards him, screaming. Rupert whirled with a look of shock on his face, but Alma didn't stop. She swung her arms to hit him, but passed right through, crashing into the crops. "What are you doing?" Rupert yelled.

Alma frantically scanned the pile of dirt Rupert had been digging, searching for any sign of her missing mother. "What have you done with her? I know you've taken her from me!" she screamed. She glanced around, desperate for someone to help her. "Help! Somebody help me!" But no one came.

Rupert glanced around, then back towards the house. "We're not doing this again. Come on, let's go inside and talk," he said, resting his arm on Alma's shoulders. She felt the slightest touch of his fingers, and her breathing calmed. Maybe he wasn't here to hurt her?

Rupert carefully placed a vinyl record on the turntable as its warm crackling filled the room. Alma's eyes softened as the familiar feeling of music transported her to happier days with her husband and child.

"Alma, it's me. Rupert. Remember me?" he asked, locking eyes with her. "Look out the window, to the front garden. Remember the primroses we planted for your husband?"

Alma followed Rupert's finger to the garden, where pink, purple, and red flowers fluttered in the wind. "Yes, I remember. The roses in the vase are for Mary," she said.

Rupert smiled, slumping into his chair. "That's right. I knew you'd remember." Alma noticed that Rupert had trailed mud from the garden into the house.

She got up from her seat and headed to the kitchen. "Do you mind passing me the broom? I need to tidy up for the guests."

The elderly gentleman trailed behind her into the kitchen. "Of course not, but we don't have any guests. This is our home, remember?"

Alma turned to the stranger; confusion etched across her face. She couldn't recall inviting anyone over, yet the man before her seemed faintly familiar. "What do you mean? Who are you?"

The man sighed, "It's me. Rupert. Your husband passed away a while ago, and we've been living together since Quill paired us up."

Alma's eyes widened, and her heart raced. She had no recollection of her husband's passing or the man before her now. Fear gnawed at Alma, and she instinctively retreated, her eyes darting around the room for a makeshift weapon. "Stay away from me!" she yelled. Rupert tried to calm her, but she swung at him, knocking a knife from the side to the floor. As it fell, Alma closed her eyes, expecting the worst. When she opened them, the knife had impaled the floorboard between them.

"This has gone too far," Rupert said.

Alma saw the fear in his eyes and recognised the photo of Mary on the wall behind him. Rupert's favourite song played in the background. It all made sense now. She remembered. "I'm sorry, Rupert. I forgot again. Please don't send me back to the void! Just one more chance." Alma's legs gave way beneath her, and she crumbled to her knees.

Rupert's head wobbled as he grappled with the tough decision. "I've given you too many chances. It's time to go." With a snap of his fingers, Alma's world dissolved into blinding white.

* * *

Alma's eyes followed the dance of leaves as they swirled past the shop window. Rupert had granted her a break from the void. She turned to find a young woman with brown hair standing behind the counter. The woman was rather average-looking, with a round face suitable for a housewife. "Who are you, and where is Quill?" Rupert inquired.

"He left me in charge for the day." The girl extended her hand to Rupert. "My name is Erin. How may I assist you?"

A beam of sunlight glinted off a mirror on the shelf, catching Alma's eye. She jumped up to examine it, recalling a similar one her mother had once had in her bedroom.

"I'd like to make an exchange," Rupert leaned in to whisper, assuming Alma couldn't hear. "I've been trying to manage, but today she flung a knife off the table. It nearly went through my foot! You can find my history in the book." Alma watched from the mirror as Erin's fingers rustled through a stack of papers, her brows furrowed in concentration.

"That's strange. I thought exchanges weren't permitted under the rules. I'm pretty sure I recently read that," Erin commented.

"Well, Quill has made exceptions for me before, and I need one again... *please*," Rupert drummed his fingers on the counter.

"What seems to be the issue, exactly? She appears perfectly fine to me," Erin said, then she turned to Alma. "Mrs Edwards! Are you content with Rupert?"

Alma averted her eyes from the mirror, feeling guilty for eavesdropping. She smiled at them both. "Absolutely! Rupert provides a simple but lovely life for me. We enjoy each other's company very much."

Erin raised her hands defensively, gently pushing Alma's

bottle back toward Rupert with a finger. "Well, everything seems in order."

"Are you certain Quill isn't here somewhere? It's unlike him to be absent." Rupert craned his neck to glimpse at the back hallway.

"I'm sure. What makes you think you can find anyone better than Mrs Edwards, anyway?"

"Excuse me? What do you mean by that?"

"Well, looking at the list of your previous purchases, Alma here seems like a kitten compared to the others," Erin replied.

"Yes, that's true. She is, but she's... *broken*, in a way. I don't think she compares to my wife, that's all." Rupert glanced around the shop. "Quill knows what I'm searching for. You must find him."

"Sorry, I can't help with that. Besides, if Quill knows precisely what you desire, it confirms that Alma is the right choice. No?"

As Alma watched Rupert's face redden, she couldn't help but feel a twinge of sympathy for him.

"Listen," Rupert said, raising his voice. "She isn't my Mary, and that's all there is to it. Now, I want you to find me someone else." Alma stepped back, shocked at Rupert's frustration. He crashed his hand on the counter with a resounding thud. Erin remained unfazed.

"Mary is your wife, correct? She passed away some years ago," Erin said calmly.

"Yes, but what's that got to do with anything?" Rupert snapped.

Erin took a deep breath before responding. "Well, I can tell you right away why you haven't found what you need."

"Oh? Is that so? Enlighten me."

"Don't you see? Mary was the love of your life, the other

half of you. The pair of you were a unique fit. Trying to replace that is an impossible task, sir," Erin explained patiently. "You need to change the way you look at your current ghost. She isn't Mary; she is *Alma*, and there is a reason Quill paired you both together." Erin motioned for Alma to come closer. "You have a kind, caring heart, Rupert, one that needs to show love to someone. Alma comes with her own needs, but you have formed such a strong bond." Erin pulled out an ancient book from under the counter, and the leather binding creaked with age as she turned the pages. "You said Alma could throw an item from your home onto the ground, correct?"

"I didn't mean for it to happen. It just... *fell*," Alma whispered.

Erin pointed to a passage in the book. "It says here that when an owner creates a strong bond with their ghost, they can form a connection that crosses through to the living. Both must hold a connection between the living and the spirit. You will be able to gently hold each other's hands, interact with electronic devices, and even move or use items connected to the host." Erin closed the book, and dust erupted in clouds. "Do you see now? If she could move an item in your home, that means you have both created a trusting bond with each other. You've never reported something like that in the past, have you?"

Rupert's eyes met Alma's, and a soft smile spread across his weathered face. His hand drifted towards her, and she felt warmth emanate from his fingertips. "Alright, I'll give her a bit longer," Rupert said, his voice softening. He leaned towards Erin. "You know what? I'm very impressed with your work. Quill wouldn't have been able to charm me like you did today. Come on, love. Let's get back home. There is still enough time for us to watch the sunset next to the flower beds." Rupert turned to Erin again. "Mind if I use the little boys' room before we leave? Can't go enough at my age."

Rupert left Alma alone in the shop as she watched Quill quietly descend the stairs from above. Alma had been up there before, back in the early days when it was just her and Quill. He had shared stories of his past life and the mistakes he had made in the factory. Quill smiled at Alma but spoke to Erin, "Good job there. I almost came down to intervene, but it looks like I didn't need to."

Erin winked. "I thought you never broke the rules."

Quill's laughter filled the room, his eyes sparkling with a rare sense of amusement. "I don't usually, but Rupert is an exception."

Seeing Quill with some life in him always brought a smile to Alma's face. For so long, he had wandered around the shop like an empty shell of himself, longing for something he couldn't have. But having Erin here, his own little protégé to continue his legacy, seemed to have given him a glimmer of happiness. Knowing Quill as well as she did that helped dissipate some of the darker memories she had of him.

Quill Darlington

With each changing season, Quill observed Erin's growth, both in her abilities and confidence. She had a knack for customer interactions, which persuaded Quill to begin welcoming casual visitors into the shop, a move that boosted their revenue. Quill had remedied the incessant leak in the roof that had plagued him for years, and swept the shop free of dust.

Quill's immortality plagued him, his mind heavy with nearly three centuries' worth of memories and experiences. Every person he encountered, every conversation he engaged in, etched vividly in his mind. The sheer volume of information he stored overwhelmed him, sometimes.

He was glad Erin had kept herself hidden away upstairs today as Allegra entered the shop, her long cloth dress dragging behind her on the floor. Quill greeted her with a warm smile. Allegra's apprentice, Renee, stayed outside the door, admiring her chewed nails in the dwindling sunlight. "Allegra, my dear. What do I owe the pleasure?"

Allegra placed a leather-bound notebook on the counter. "That girl you've had working here. She's the one I mentioned to you, isn't she?"

Quill stumbled back. He had hoped he'd kept Erin hidden enough for Allegra not to have noticed. "Girl?" he asked.

"That's right. Renee said she saw her working behind the counter," replied Allegra, leaning closer to Quill. "Not trying to keep her to yourself, are you?"

"Not at all. I just wanted to observe her for a while."

Allegra laughed, then glared at Renee, whose head was tilted, listening in. "You keep your nose out of this, girl!" she snapped. "I felt her presence, Quill. It's been months, and you still haven't introduced us."

Quill's eyebrows furrowed. "Months?" he muttered, his thoughts racing. Had Erin been working for that long? Time was a strange concept for him. Allegra abided by the time scale of the living, even if her years extended beyond a mortal life. "You know what it's like when you live forever. A few years can feel like a few weeks sometimes. I'm sorry, but life seems to slip past me."

Allegra raised a crooked brow, then flicked through her notebook to a clear page. "So? What have you found out? I might be able to help, you know, if you just let me in."

Quill left the counter to begin arranging the stock on the shelves, pulling items to the front. "Well, she's turned the place around. We're actually getting normal customers in and welcoming in the public."

Allegra gave a raucous cackle, filling the shop with her

infectious laughter. "Very amusing, Quill. But what about her... *odd* behaviour?"

Quill glanced at Wilson in the window, who arched his back while watching Renee from the outside. "Hard to say. It feels like she is living in the afterlife with me, but also the living world, like you, though it's impossible to be in both."

Allegra scribbled something in her notes. "Unusual, yes, but not impossible. Had she made a deal with... The Boss?" Allegra averted her gaze, focusing on the floor. "Catch them on a good day, and you never know what you get."

"No, Erin was a normal girl whose ancient relative bartered her soul. She has such a way with customers and spirits. She can speak to them—I caught her the other day speaking to Arthur, she can enter their voids, and interact with any soul she wants. That is a power even I don't possess."

"The family member that set all this up. Do you remember her name?"

"Gertrude Griffiths. She offered a grandchild seven generations along, which was Erin. Nothing odd about that. Many spirits here came from similar circumstances."

"I can ask around. You haven't told The Boss about this apprentice arrangement, have you?"

Quill glanced around the empty room, then leaned in, whispering, "No, I have not. I don't bother them if they don't call on me. They leave me to get on with what I've been dealt, and I'm happy with that."

A creak on the staircase had them both spinning as Erin appeared from the room upstairs. "Oh, sorry. Am I interrupting anything?" she asked.

"Nothing at all, dear," answered Allegra. "I'm just paying my dear friend a visit. To say I've noticed a difference between him and this shop would be an understatement." She moved towards Erin to introduce herself. "My name is Allegra. I run 'The Witch Stuff' around the corner, past the pub."

Quill stepped in between Allegra and Erin; he did not wish for Erin to be influenced by Allegra just yet. "Oh, I'll have to visit when I can have a look around the village," said Erin.

"You can walk out of the door, can you?" Allegra asked, stepping closer.

"Not yet, no, but I've covered the Halloween shift for Quill last year, and got the leak in the roof fixed, so he now owes me another favour," Erin explained, flashing a smile at Quill.

Allegra matched it. "Well, he is a man of his word. Please, pay me a visit. I can show you around. I better be off now, Quill." She swung the shop door open, glaring at Renee. "And what have you been doing whilst I've been busy with meetings, young lady? I didn't once see you reading through the recipes or ingredient lists I gave you." Allegra stormed out of the shop, with Renee struggling to keep the pace behind her.

Quill locked the shop door, then sat beside Wilson. "So... a favour?" he repeated.

"Yeah, that's right. You said that during Halloween, the world between the living and the dead is at its weakest."

"Yes, that is true, but I can grant you access to roam the village on any date I choose. We don't have to wait for Halloween."

"I want to take someone with me. A guest," said Erin.

"I see. Who did you have in mind?" Quill rose and moved behind the counter. "I must say, Erin. I can't allow you to return to your boyfriend. It simply cannot be done."

"I know. I wanted to take Arthur out around the village."

"Arthur? Arthur Leech?" asked Quill.

"Yes. We speak to each other now and then inside his void. He's fun, and he's loyal to you. He can be trusted," said Erin, clasping her hands. "I wanted to do something for him. He's been so down since he returned. It would be nice, don't you think?"

Quill didn't like where this was headed. If Erin developed a connection towards Arthur, who knows what would happen to the power lying dormant inside of her? Yet it seemed like she had created a bond with Arthur without Quill having the slightest idea. Maybe he should allow her request. At least she was being honest with him. If Quill forbade too much, she might go behind his back, where everything would get out of hand. "Okay. Just this once. You can go for a few hours. But this won't be a regular thing."

"Thank you, Quill," Erin said, hugging him. He tensed, locking his arms beside his body. Frozen, he was at a loss for words. Finally, Erin released him, flashing a wide smile. "I'm going to tell Arthur the good news now," she said excitedly before skipping towards the storeroom. Wilson stared at Quill blankly, and he felt his stomach knot. He hadn't felt this anxious in years. He glanced at the floor, hoping The Boss wouldn't learn of the many rules he was bending.

Arthur Leech

Arthur exited the shop, but not before sparing one last glance at Quill, who fixed his attention on some old parchments, oblivious to Arthur and Erin as they strode the cobbled paths. The setting sun created long shadows on the pavement, appearing like mountain bumps. Arthur had observed this street for years from inside the shop, watching the view change with every sale made over the decades. Never had he imagined he would have the opportunity to walk outside, to be treated like a living human once again. Erin paced ahead, and a warm smile played on Arthur's lips. Why had she chosen him? Out of all the souls trapped in that shop, why was he chosen to share this newfound freedom?

Erin had entered his void with a burst of energy, announcing their day out. Arthur's excitement was shocked into silence. He didn't ask questions. Though Quill had been kind to him, kinder than most men, he had never broken the rules for Arthur or even entertained the thought of allowing him to venture beyond the shop window.

He'd almost given up after what Kaitlin had done to him. He didn't know who he despised more, her, or himself, for allowing her to get into his mind.

Erin and Arthur ambled beneath the sunlight until they reached an intersection. On the corner, a rustic flower shop displayed brightly coloured roses in buckets, and behind it was the pub, situated before acres of open fields. They paused, relishing their newfound freedom. Erin had only passed a few years ago, but it had been seventy years for Arthur. The world had changed significantly since he left it, and although he tried to keep up with the changing times, being outside and freely observing the world made him feel like a ten-year-old again.

The tranquil village of Ringwood appeared like a postcard from years past. Arthur glanced at the florist's bucket of roses. One pound each. He remembered them costing a few pennies back in his day. Arthur knelt beside the rose, anticipating a scent he hadn't experienced in decades. The faint sweet aroma enveloped him.

A young woman in green overalls, with her hair tied up in a bun, popped her head around the door. "Can I help you? They're only a quid. Us ladies appreciate a rose from time to time," she said, winking.

Arthur turned to Erin, whose cheeks had flushed. "Oh. I'd love to, ma'am," said Arthur, standing and feeling his jacket pocket. "But I'm not carrying any cash with me." He glanced at Erin, then gently tugged her arm, guiding her toward the vibrant array of flowers. "Take a smell. The sweet aromas will be memory enough for our outing." Arthur winked at the shop owner, then grabbed Erin by the hand as they crossed the empty road towards the fields. Along the wooden fence was a stile, which Arthur jumped over before offering Erin a hand. She made the jump on her own.

They trod along the dirt path, the trees offering shelter from the sun. "So, what's the plan, then?" asked Arthur.

Erin studied the ground as they walked, her steps slow and deliberate. "I don't know, really. I never planned much beyond going past the shop door."

"I see. Well, we can follow this track. The sign said it loops around to the village—maybe we could even watch a film. I've always wanted to go to one of those big cinemas," Arthur suggested.

Erin scratched the back of her neck, kicking grit into the air with her feet. "Yeah, although it's kind of rustic around here. I don't think there's a cinema nearby, and Quill said we couldn't leave the Village."

Arthur couldn't recall the last time he felt so free. Being outside, in the village, having people see and speak to him changed that. At Kaitlin's estate, he enjoyed wandering through the gardens and vast land, but he always did it alone. With Erin at his side today, it felt like the days where he'd once lived—*truly* lived.

Erin tapped him on the shoulder. "What's on your mind?"

Arthur shook his head, stopping to peer across the open field. Past the trees, and the horses grazing, he could see a scattering of stone homes, thatched roofs. A life someone lived that he was jealous of. "Just thinking about days gone by, about my life before I became... this." Arthur gestured with his hands, creating a shadow with the sun. "How did you convince Quill to let us out?"

"I didn't really convince him," Erin said. "I just asked him questions about being dead, about the shop. I can do things he doesn't expect, which is why he gave me a job. I think he wants to watch me, to see what I can do, and while it's strange, it beats being sold off like a sales item..." Erin froze. "Sorry, I didn't mean you."

"It's alright," Arthur said. "I've been in this state longer than I was alive. This is all I know."

The dirt path led to a blue iron gate where a narrow stream and a stone bridge lay beyond. Arthur leaned against the wall, peering into the water. No reflection stared back. Erin leaned over, her reflection in the water, looking back at him as she put an arm around his shoulder. Arthur wasn't sure why she had a reflection and he didn't, although she seemed to be able to do lots of things he couldn't. "Do you have any family or friends you miss? A lover perhaps?"

Arthur jolted upright, his eyes widening. "*Lover?*"

"Well, you're a dashing young man in a suit. There's no way you were single," Erin said, grinning as she leaned against the stone wall.

"I never got around to it," Arthur said, not wishing to delve into his past. No matter how many years it had been, the memories still hurt.

Arthur squinted toward a shop named 'The Witch Stuff,' though its ornate lettering made it a challenge to read from a distance. White stone crafted the shop, accentuated by black-painted window frames. The storefront display of colourful stones, broomsticks, small black cauldrons, and skulls drew the pair closer. "Shall we take a look? It might be interesting," Arthur suggested.

The pungent scent of lavender perfume hit Arthur as soon as he entered the shop, and he suddenly realised his senses had drastically improved since smelling the roses. The walls displayed more of the same: rings, jewellery, glass bottles of dried herbs, and other items. A girl sat behind the counter, her dark hair plaited into two French braids. She glanced up when they entered, then refocused on her book. "Shall we buy Quill a gift? To say thank you?" asked Erin, leaning down to search the bottom shelves.

"Yeah, he'd like that. What do you buy a man who's lived forever, though?" Arthur whispered, reaching for a smooth, blood orange stone.

"Interested in the Carnelian stone, are you?" A croaky voice sounded from behind him. He turned to find a weathered woman with a wrinkled face watching him, her hair wild like a caveman's. "Don't look so scared, boy. We're white witches in here. No harm will come, as long as you buy the items you leave with." The woman chuckled, then stepped back. Arthur's instincts were to watch the woman with caution. She made him feel uneasy, but the relaxed way Erin's eyes fell upon her made him question his first impression.

"What is a Carnelian?" Arthur asked carefully. "And why should I buy it?"

Ignoring him, the old woman turned to Erin, smiling. "So, he let you out. *My, my, my.* You do have him around your finger, don't you?" The lady glanced back at Arthur, then selected one of the orange stones. "This will give the owner strength, courage, and protection from sickness. It would be a splendid gift for a leader or a father figure in your life."

"Well, we'll think about it. Won't we, Erin?"

"It would be a great gift for Quill, my dear."

"You know Quill?" asked Arthur.

"He may seem void of friends, but Quill and I go way back, my darling. Mind if I steal your date for a moment?"

Arthur shrugged. Erin wasn't his date. He wasn't here to speak for her. Erin glanced a look towards Arthur, a smile creeping onto her lips.

"No, go ahead." Arthur turned to the young girl behind the counter. "Hi, I'm Arthur," he said, though received only a mere grunt in response. Instead, he pretended to examine the rings and earrings on the counter, while straining to catch snippets of the conversation between Erin and the strange woman.

"Take this stone as a gift from me to you and keep it in a safe place that is yours. You are special, Erin. I told Quill this many months ago, but it seems he kept me from you. Keep this stone close, and it can be our bond. There is a lot you do not know about yourself, and I can help you find your true meaning. Quill means well, but he's an old man stuck behind a rule book. Us women must stick together. When the time is right, I will call upon you. Are you listening?" Arthur stole a glimpse of Erin, who nodded.

The witch strode towards the counter and clicked her fingers at the young girl. "How can you have your head in a book when such a handsome man presents himself to you?" She shook her head with a tut. "Such a beautiful face for such a haunted soul. I'm Allegra, by the way." Allegra gripped Arthur's jaw, tilting his face to meet hers. Allegra's piercing green eyes stared deeply into his. Arthur froze. He wasn't used to people being able to touch him so freely. After so many years, it felt alien. "You have quite the story to tell, don't you? Much heartbreak and even more regrets." She smiled, flashing her sparse teeth that remained. "Such sorrow for a young man."

Allegra turned, collecting a handful of herbs from the side. "Give Quill my regards. Assure him I won't tell The Boss about his *breaking of the rules* while training." With a mischievous cackle, Allegra sauntered toward the rear of the shop, her laughter echoing throughout the room.

Arthur shrugged at Erin before they walked home in silence. The bitter wind picked up and leaves covered the walkway. Arthur wanted to ask Erin about her conversation with Allegra, yet that would only lead to Erin asking him the questions he wasn't ready to answer about his own past. He couldn't expose his heart again, not after what had happened last time. So instead, he kept quiet.

Quill Darlington

Quill scowled at the calendar on the wall, relieved that Halloween was over for another year. He'd never enjoyed the spooky holiday, yet in recent years, the celebrations had become increasingly extravagant and demanding. Every decade seemed to bring a fresh wave of expectations, and Quill felt exhausted by all of it.

The bell above the shop door chimed, and Quill sat up, ready to greet the customer with the well-rehearsed line Erin had taught him: "Welcome to The Ghost Merchant, where we sell whatever your mind and heart desires."

He thought it could use some work, but he did his best to sound welcoming. After all, the shop now catered to everyday customers, not just the damned—much to Quill's annoyance.

For centuries, he'd ran the shop attempting to push away custom, but he wanted to give Erin a chance and listen to her suggestions.

Quill's heart sank as an old Indian man hobbled towards him with a walking stick; his thinning hair was slicked back, and the noticeable hump made his short stature even more pronounced on his neck.

"Are you Quill Darlington? The seller of souls?" The man asked.

Quill's eyes widened, and he rushed to the shop door, turning the sign to "closed." He didn't want any other customers to witness what was about to happen.

"I'm so sorry, sir. I wasn't aware you were here for that kind of item." Quill turned to The Great Book, confused. He was certain no one had booked in to see him. "I don't seem to have your information, sir. How did you hear about this custom?"

The man propped his walking stick on the counter, then rubbed his fingers together. "A friend of yours sent me here. Isaac, I think he said his name was."

Isaac Constantine. Quill's old friend and fellow Ghost Merchant. Quill relaxed somewhat.

"Why did he send you here? He has a perfectly wonderful shop to offer a ghost."

The man flashed a toothless smile. "Yes, he showed me some of his wares. But when I mentioned my business interest here in Ringwood, he told me of you. I like to buy local if I can."

Quill rifled through his desk, collecting the key to unlock the door to the hallway. It was already unlocked. "Come this way, Mr..."

"Meka. Asif Meka."

Mr Meka followed Quill down the hallway. Erin was inside Arthur's void again, her chatter rumbling through the room. Quill coughed, and Erin appeared with a guilty look on her face. She scuttled to the front of the shop, grabbing the broom as she passed.

"Please, take a seat, sir." Closing the door, Quill sat opposite Asif at the table. "So, what is it you're looking for?"

"I'll say what I told the man in London. I need a charming gentleman, with plenty of life in him—someone who is up for a joke and a laugh. Good with customers and can take orders."

"I see. And what are you planning on using the spirit for?"

"Do you need to know that?" asked Asif, clasping his hands together.

"It will help me find a match for you, sir," Quill replied, trying to keep his professionalism.

Asif was all business, despite his supposed desire for a lively, sociable ghost. Quill suspected he was not really interested in connecting with a spirit at all.

Quill worried about Erin's sudden closeness to Arthur. He knew first-hand, forming an attachment with a ghost was never a good idea. In fact, it was precisely why he had parted ways with Alma. He wanted to prove he wasn't overly attached to any of his companions.

"I'm buying the pub across the road. The Tavern. It's been closed for a while now. I got it for a cheap price," said Asif.

Quill arched an eyebrow. "Regarding the ghost you seek, you realise they won't be able to serve in your pub, correct?"

Asif erupted into hearty laughter. "Oh, I'm aware of that. I've no intention of having him pour drinks behind the bar. No, no. I want him scaring the customers."

Quill scratched the side of his head.

"Sorry, you've lost me. *Scaring* the customers?"

"Yes! I've heard the history of that place. It's said the old landlady haunts it. Used to be a goldmine for the tourists looking for a scare and a touch of the afterlife."

"And you want to buy a ghost to haunt the place for you?"

"Correct. It's going to be the next big thing, you know. I can host a party of eight or ten people and get the spirit to rattle a few things around the room. I'll be laughing all the way to the bank."

Quill shook his head. "Well, I don't get to say this often, Mr Meka, but this is a first, even for me," he said. "But who am I to judge? All I'm here to do is get the contracts set up. Now, did Isaac take you through what you need to sacrifice in order to take on a spirit?"

Asif nodded eagerly. "Yes, he did, and I've already figured it out. I want to set my boy up with a foolproof business. The next five generations of Meka's will run this pub, with the ghost on hand. That will be the legacy I leave behind."

If Asif was serious, whoever Quill took on this task would be gone for many years. He felt his heart sink, as a name came to mind. Quill tapped the pen on the table and considered Asif's proposal. "You want the ghost to stay with your family for five generations? That will require an enormous commitment."

"I understand that. Whatever life I have left, I'm happy to sacrifice it. Just give me enough time to set things up for my boy. That is all I ask."

"I'm afraid you don't get to choose. If you sign today, your years will be deducted, but I cannot tell you how many you have left. Do you still wish to proceed?" Quill asked, handing the pen to Asif.

Without a second thought, Asif snatched the pen and scribbled his name at the bottom of the contract. "When do I get to meet him, then?"

"I shall give you the bottle on the way out. You can introduce yourself at your leisure. Now please, follow me."

Quill heaved a sigh, pushing himself up from the table. His eyes flickered towards Erin, who walked towards him. Asif passed her on his way out, and Quill picked up Arthur's bottle from the shelf. "Erin. Would you be able to pass this over to Mr Meka? He is waiting in the shop for you," he said, his tone clipped.

Erin's eyes went to the bottle; she gasped, recognising Arthur's void immediately. "You've sold him?" she asked, her voice cracking. Quill nodded, and disbelief painted Erin's features. "But why him? Why not someone else? Anyone else?"

"I'm sorry, Erin. I know you grew close to Arthur, but he was the best match," Quill replied.

"Best match? Really?" Erin snapped.

"Listen, getting attached to spirits never ends well. This is another lesson for you to learn from. If you are ever going to become a ghost merchant, you need to learn them. Even the hard ones."

Quill's throat tightened at the pain etched in Erin's eyes. Though he detested upsetting her, he knew that abruptly tearing off the bandage was the only means to prevent her from forming undue attachments to the spirits. "But I like him. I don't want him to leave," Erin protested, her grip tightening on the bottle.

"Eventually they all do, dear. The sooner you realise that, the better." Quill placed a comforting hand on her shoulder. "Believe me. I learned that the hard way."

"Should I not get attached to you, then? Are you going to leave me?" Erin challenged, studying his expression. Quill blinked, turning his face away from Erin's. Looking anywhere that didn't land in her direction.

"Not for some time yet. Now, go on. Bring Mr Meka the bottle and let him get on his way," Quill said, trying to steer the conversation away from his own feelings.

"Can I say goodbye to Arthur first?" asked Erin, clutching tightly to the bottle.

Quill's heart ached at what he had done. Was he cruel for being tough on Erin? If she was ever going to become a successful ghost merchant, she couldn't allow herself to be weak. His own softness had been his downfall in the past, and he couldn't let it happen again—not to anyone else, not to Erin. As she hurried away, Quill faced the window. He'd been punishing himself for two hundred years now; as he looked at his reflection, it was clear he still had some time left before he could face any forgiveness.

Erin Layton

1994

Erin's eyes remained locked on the raindrops dribbling down the windowpane, a sight that usually brought her comfort. Yet she couldn't escape this undeniable sense of being an outsider within her own room. While Quill had done his best to make the place feel like home, it still felt foreign to her.

The sight of the red and yellow duvet Quill had chosen left a bitter taste in her mouth. It reminded Erin of her childhood, of a time when things were simpler, when she was under her father's care. But that world felt like a lifetime ago, though she longed for it, nonetheless.

On her bedside table, a silver picture frame stood alone,

with no photograph behind the glass. It reminded her of Jacob, who had once gifted her a similar frame on their fourth date, with the promise of filling it with a memory of them both. Erin bit her lip, hoping to banish thoughts of Jacob from her mind. It was unlikely he thought of her, given how much time had passed and how much their lives had changed.

As she trailed her fingers over the blood orange stone—the gift from Allegra—Erin wondered about the truth of her situation. Quill had always been kind to her, but his recent actions in taking Arthur away had her questioning his true motives. Was he someone she could trust, or was he hiding something sinister?

What about Allegra? Could they trust Allegra, or was she leading Erin down a dangerous path?

Erin crossed to the window and peered out over the overgrown courtyard below—another project Quill had neglected over the years, for nature to reclaim. Yet despite his shortcomings, Erin felt an odd sense of protectiveness towards him. He did his best in a rapidly changing world, even if she didn't always agree with his methods of doing so.

Erin couldn't help but miss Arthur, who had been gone for what felt like an eternity. She yearned for his infectious laughter and the rare moments he brought joy to her small world. Erin had bonded with him; he was like a younger brother to her—or older, depending on how you gauge time in the afterlife. Either way, an empty void now remained in Erin's life. One that was hard to fill.

The last customer had left, leaving Erin alone with Wilson by her side. Absentmindedly, she petted Wilson, waiting for the moment to flip the sign to 'closed.' A tap rattled on the window, and Erin gasped, flitting her attention to where Allegra peeked, looking through the glass. Before Erin could speak, Allegra pushed open the door.

"Mind if I come in? I see Quill is out." Allegra didn't wait for a reply before closing the door behind her and entering, her heels clicking against the wooden floorboards.

Erin nodded and Wilson leapt from his seat to greet Allegra.

"He's letting you run the place on your own and sending you outside on dates. He really has taken a shine to you, hasn't he?" teased Allegra.

Avoiding the question, Erin tried to sound nonchalant. "How do you know he's out?"

Allegra let out a cackle. "My apprentice is keeping him busy chatting."

"What, the silent girl who works in your shop? Keeping *him* chatting?"

"I'm an excellent teacher. Well, not that good, so I'll have to be quick." Allegra glanced around furtively. "Do you still have that stone I gifted you? The one from the shop?"

Erin withdrew the stone from her pocket, holding it between her thumb and finger. Allegra's eyes widened as she reached to take it. "Good. Now, make sure you keep it on you tonight. Hold it in the palm of your left hand."

Erin snatched it back from Allegra, turning the stone over. "Why? Have you put a curse on me or something?"

"Quite the opposite, dear. I want to help you discover where your curse came from." Allegra's eyes met Erin's. "If you want answers, the only way to find them is to search your past. Hold on to the stone tonight, dear. If you want to come, I shall call you. If not, then you will never gain the answers you seek."

Erin narrowed her eyes. "How do you know I'm cursed, anyway? Is that why I can do all these strange things? Is that why Quill keeps such a close eye on me?"

Allegra ran a finger through her tangled hair. "Our darling Quill spoke to me about you when you arrived here, us witches know more than you think. The link you hold between both worlds, that is what caught my attention, but I need some clarity before I can be sure of the answers. That is what tonight is about."

Erin hesitated. "What if Quill notices I'm gone? He isn't exactly a fan of sleep and relaxing."

Allegra closed the palm of Erin's hand, pushing it towards her chest. "Magic is a powerful tool, my dear. He will think you are in your bed resting. No other thoughts will cross his mind. After hundreds of years of only looking after yourself, thoughts about others are often put aside."

"Well, I'll think about it. Having answers, even if it won't change anything, must be better than not knowing at all."

Allegra turned to leave. "I look forward to working with you, dear. The night will be electric with emotion, but the gift I see in you cannot go unnurtured forever."

Erin leaned against the counter as the last remnants of daylight faded outside. Silence descended upon the shop, interrupted only by the distant hum of passing cars and Wilson's soft breathing by her feet. Her thoughts and emotions churned together in her mind, like a tempestuous sea caught in a storm.

She couldn't escape the sense of unease as she thought of the night ahead. She never imagined she would sneak out in the night, especially not to Allegra's store. Yet the promise of answers was too alluring to ignore. Erin had always felt like an outsider, like she didn't quite belong in the world. And now, with the possibility of learning the truth about how she ended up here, that feeling grew ever stronger.

The stone pulsed in Erin's palm, like an unspoken bond had forged between them, as though some kind of power or magic awaited to be unlocked. Closing her eyes, Erin took a deep breath to calm her nerves. It was a tremendous risk following Allegra's plan, but the potential rewards were too great to ignore.

What would Quill think if he knew of her plans? Ever since her apprenticeship started, Quill watched over her like a protective father, yet she couldn't shake the feeling he was keeping something from her. Something important.

Erin Layton

When the clock struck three, a sudden burst of light overcame Erin until the darkness swallowed it whole. Erin's eyes adjusted to the warm glow of a nearby streetlamp framing a shop window. Candle flames surrounded her, casting warped shadows across the walls.

Before her, Allegra loomed, and her apprentice Renee quietly peeked over the counter, concealed by the shadows. Three women sat cross-legged on the floor, each with wild, grey-speckled hair poking out from under their hoods. Their flowing garments of linen added to the otherworldly atmosphere of the shop.

Erin's heart raced as her eyes darted around. Allegra offered her hand to Erin, a calm gesture amidst the tension. Erin took a sharp breath, the weight of the moment settling on her shoulders. She had come to Allegra's shop to search for answers, but now she felt like she had stepped into something far beyond her comprehension.

She stepped forward into the circle of women, and Allegra's words did little to calm the pounding in her chest. "We must be quick. Quill cannot know I have taken you." A knot tightened in Erin's stomach as Allegra directed her to sit in the centre of the room on a single pillow. Tiptoeing over the jars and mysteriously filled bottles scattered across the floor, she felt the eyes of the seated women.

"Who are they?" asked Erin, trying to discern their features.

"My sisters—*our* sisters," Allegra answered, scattering a handful of dirt on the floor. "We are all part of one coven. A web of connections. From mother earth to our hearts. We are all special, Erin, including you."

Erin had stumbled into a world she barely understood.

"I'm not special," she protested. "A distant family member sold my soul off to the ghost merchant, nothing more."

Allegra's eyes narrowed, and Erin felt a sudden jolt of fear. "Oh, but you are, dear. You can speak to the spirits. You retain free will and control of your own thoughts, even in the bleakest of times. You can cut through into the void, travel to places a spirit shouldn't."

A cold sweat broke across Erin's skin. How did Allegra know so much about what she could do?

"We need to do a test," said Allegra, "to find out where your heart lives, to see if my hunch is true."

Test? What kind of test? Erin asked herself. She stared around the room until she settled on Renee, who stared back at her, unblinking.

"What do I have to do?" Erin whispered.

Allegra leaned in, smiling. "Think of your mother and her home. The smells, the sounds, the feelings—all of it."

"I... I only knew my mother when I was young. We never had much of a bond. She left when I was a child. I have hardly any memories of her."

"Her mother, then. Your grandmother. Where did she live? Did you know her?" Allegra pressed, her voice commanding the attention of the room. The witches sat around, murmurs coming from under their hoods. Erin didn't know what they were saying, didn't understand why they were here. But she felt a power from their bond. As they held hands, each one connected.

"Yes, I spent some of my childhood with her. We visited most weekends with my mother before she left. My Grandmother lived in the same house her entire life, which was handed down to her by her mother."

"Perfect. It all makes sense." Allegra licked her lips. "Think of that place, Erin."

Erin's mind surrendered to a haze of nostalgic memories, where the colours and textures of her grandmother's house materialised. The creaky wooden floors and the peeling wallpaper, the ticking clock on the wall, and the old family photographs, forever captured in time. Erin heard the rustling leaves outside and the gentle hum of bees in the summer. She tasted the homemade apple pie her grandmother used to bake with the cinnamon sprinkled on top.

A piercing sound jolted Erin back to reality as Allegra's voice echoed through the room. "Erin, focus. Can you hear me?" The room blurred as Erin opened her eyes, trying to regain focus, sensing the eyes of the other witches locked onto her every movement. "Erin, can you hear me?" Allegra repeated.

"Yes," Erin said, suddenly disoriented. "I can hear you."

Allegra rested a hand on Erin's shoulder. "Good. Now, tell me what you saw."

Erin exhaled, the memories of her grandmother's house fresh in her mind. "I saw a puzzle on the table, and flames dancing in the fireplace. I heard laughter coming from the kitchen, and the smell of cinnamon and apples."

Allegra's eyes widened, glinting with excitement. "Yes, that's it! That's where your heart comes from. Your grandmother's house. That's where the magic lies. The answers." A chill trickled down Erin's spine. The concept of magic had never crossed her mind until now, but Allegra made it feel real. The other witches in the room began quietly chanting, their faces alight with wonder.

Erin's heart pounded as she stepped back into her grandmother's old, dark living room; a sliver of moonlight shone through cracks in the curtains.

"You did it, love. Well done," whispered Allegra, gripping Erin's arm.

Erin glanced around the room, and a shiver traced a cold path down her neck. The room, the same one she had visited as a child, had been left to decay, hidden by dust and cobwebs. "Does anyone still live here? Am I really here?" she muttered.

"This could be real, dear, or merely a fragment of your mind. Is there an attic? A basement?" Allegra asked, her finger tracing along the dusty bookshelf.

Erin nodded, scanning the room. "There's an attic. The stairs to it are on the second floor."

Allegra grabbed a book from the shelf and followed Erin up the creaky stairs until they paused at a solid oak door with a brass handle. Erin remembered sitting on these floorboards, legs crossed, as a young girl wanting to go past the door. "Grandma always told us not to go in here. It might be locked."

"My sweet child. We are witches. A little locked door won't stop us. Go on, open it," urged Allegra, her voice low but firm.

Erin hesitated, her hand trembling as she reached for the handle.

With a deep breath, she forced the door open. The hinges squeaked, and she winced, hoping not to have alerted anyone to their presence. They stepped inside, Erin's heart racing at the thought of what they might find.

"What are we looking for?" Erin asked, trying to keep her voice steady as she bumped into a pile of boxes.

Cobwebs spread across the wooden beams and dust piled onto every surface. No one had been up here in years. But something felt off. Erin couldn't put her finger on it.

"Over here," Allegra said, gesturing Erin over to where she frantically arranged a collection of old family photos and papers on the floor.

"What is all this for, Allegra?"

Allegra didn't answer. She was too busy rifling through the pages of an old picture book, her fingers trembling as she flipped through the images. Finally, she found what she was looking for, then thrust the book towards Erin.

"Do you recognise her?" she demanded, pointing to a woman in a black-and-white photo. Her hair was much darker than Erin had ever seen it, but those eyes could not belong to any other, the bump in her nose the same one Erin remembered looking up at. She nodded. It was her grandmother.

"Ah-ha! Look here!" Allegra pulled out another photo, even older than the first, and tapped the crumpled piece of paper. "You know what that is, right?" she asked. Erin looked at the mark, the lines overlapping, the shapes it created, the same one she saw by her grave, the blank card left for her. "The sign of a witch—of a coven. This woman must be your great grandmother."

Erin studied the symbol painted along the back of the paper. "I've seen that before. My grandmother had a necklace that she kept in her jewellery box. I haven't thought of it for years, but she let me play with it when I visited. I'm sure the pendant had the same image on it as this."

"Everything adds up. It's a coven."

Erin thought about Allegra's shop, where she remembered a similar symbol on the walls and in books positioned on display. Even the shop's front logo had the symbol.

When she was a child, Erin's mother would scold her for holding the necklace. Why would she argue with her own mother over such a trivial thing? Her past was making sense now.

Allegra grabbed Erin's hand. "Come on. Let's get back to the shop."

As they left the attic, the bedroom door stood ajar, and as Erin glanced into the bedroom, a wave of emotion washed over her. Her mother, the woman who had abandoned her all those years ago, lay there, still as the night, in slumber. She appeared much older than Erin remembered; her once vibrant blonde hair was now a dull, lifeless grey resembling wire. Erin yearned to enter the room, to shake her mother awake and demand answers to the questions that had haunted her for years. But Allegra's grip on her arm tightened, tugging her away from the open door.

"I want to go in. I want to see her and ask her why!" snapped Erin.

Allegra's expression softened, though her grip remained firm. "I'm sure no one is here. It's a trick of the mind. Anyway, you're dead. Digging up old wounds won't help anybody. Come on."

Erin lingered a moment longer, her eyes fixed on her sleeping mother. Allegra was right, yet the pain of abandonment still cut deep. If only her mother would wake up to see what her daughter had become, she might understand the damage her departure had caused.

"Come on," Allegra urged again, tugging Erin towards the stairs. They re-entered the lounge, stopping in the spot where they had arrived. Her surroundings flickered and shifted and blurred. In the blink of an eye, she was back.

As the pair stood in the shop's centre, the witches from before were now gathered towards the back wall. Renee stayed in place, her eyes locked on something behind Erin. She turned to find Quill, arms crossed and cheeks flushed with fury. Allegra stepped in front of Erin.

"Now, Quill. Before you get mad, it was all my idea," said Allegra.

Quill pushed Allegra aside, his eyes focused solely on Erin. "I trusted you. Come on, let's get you home." Turning to Allegra, Erin heard him whisper, "We'll talk about this later."

Erin's heart sank like a leaden weight in her chest as she walked alongside Quill. The night air bore a frigid stillness, and the shallow puddles on the cobblestone path rippled with the unease of truths never told. As they turned the corner towards the alleyway, Erin's steps faltered. She had messed up, and Quill's disappointment pressed upon her.

"I'm sorry." Erin's voice cracked as Quill stopped in front

of the shop door, turning to face her with a dark and unreadable expression.

"Do you know what position you have put me in? This place isn't some game. It's serious, and there are consequences for breaking the rules. How many warning do you need before taking that seriously?"

Erin blinked. He was right. She had been reckless, had heard mentions of The Boss from Arthur, from Quill himself. "I won't disobey you again."

Quill opened the door and leaned against the counter. His gaze was distant as he ignored Wilson, who meowed at his feet. "It isn't just me you have disobeyed, Erin. There are people above me who make the rules." Quill paused. "The Boss will act if they find out. If I don't report this behaviour, there's no telling what will happen."

"Then don't tell them. Keep it between us, a mistake I made. That's all it is."

Quill shook his head. "It isn't that easy. It was bad enough when you went to grab Jacob at your funeral." Quill sighed. "Another Ghost Merchant, Jason, was his name. A fine man, much braver than I. He went against The Boss. You know what happened to him?" Erin shook her head. "He's no longer here. Soul gone, into nothing but dust and darkness. A forgotten memory. That is what fate awaits you if The Boss finds out."

Erin looked at the floor. Anger swelled in her, emotions mixed around in her head. A moment ago she was on the brink of finding out about her past, and now she stood here with Quill, unsure if she had a future. "One more chance? I promise."

Quill let a smile appear on his lips with a sigh. "One more chance," he said. "But you must know. I don't enjoy playing by these rules, not all the time. But the risk is too great now. Don't make me regret this."

Erin nodded, repeating *one more chance* in her mind.

Arthur Leech

It had been months since the Meka family had purchased Arthur and locked him away. Asif attempted to introduce him to his family, who all gasped at their old man, unable to fathom the purchase of a ghost. Asif's brother and uncle had pulled him aside, questioning his mental stability, while Asif's wife sat in stunned silence.

Arthur's new role involved performing cheap tricks for the family's guests. He would nudge a bell on a table or whisper to Asif the cards held by different players during poker. In only a few weeks, he had helped Asif to earn thousands, and also prove his existence to the doubting family, yet this was only the beginning of Arthur's work.

Once the pub opened and the bar filled with drunken guests, Arthur considered the real reason Asif Meka had purchased him. To entertain the damned with cheap thrills. At first, Arthur found amusement in blowing cold air down an old man's neck or frightening a group of young girls on a hen do. Their laughter and screams at every creak or shadow excited him; he loved contributing to their joy, but it soon felt meaningless.

Asif forced Arthur to sit around while desperate people cried out for their loved ones, hoping to contact them from beyond the grave. He would move the Ouija board an inch, spelling out what the customers wanted to hear. It was heartbreaking for Arthur, who knew the sad truth. Their family members had moved on to the next part of their journey. All the while, Asif Meka filled his pockets.

Now and then, Arthur would steal a glance out the window, hoping to glimpse the Ghost Merchant shop. A dark and narrow alley hid it from view. He yearned to see Quill or Erin—even once. His only friends in this strange afterlife. Sadly, Asif ensured he was bound to roam the pub, and the pub only.

Asif's hushed voice pulled Arthur's mind back to the present day. "How are things going, sir?" asked Arthur.

"Well," Asif said, grinning. "The future is bright, Mr Leech. My family will prosper in my sacrifice. I owe a lot of that success to you. You must know how thrilled I am with your work, and I much appreciate your commitment to the role."

Arthur tried to hide his scepticism. "I feel there is a *but* coming..."

"I worry our customers are becoming too exposed to the bumps that occur in the night," continued Asif. "Your little tricks of scaring the customers worked once, but they are becoming aware of what is to come."

"So, what do you want me to do about it? I'm just a spirit,

Mr Meka. I'm limited in what I can do." Arthur replied, waving his arm through Asif's body.

"We need to up the stakes! Thrill the paying guests and spread the word of the haunted pub of Ringwood. The customers will flock to experience it!" Asif declared, standing up. He spun dramatically, his arms outstretched as his walking stick dangled from his grip.

Arthur rubbed at his temples. He felt like a performing monkey trapped in the circus. "Will I be expected to follow a script?"

"Quite the opposite. I want you to dazzle the guests. Change your surprises at every booking. Scare the regulars: throw a table, break a vase! Shatter a light bulb!"

"Are you going to give me magic powers? Or shall I pop downstairs and ask the devil myself, Mr Meka? I think you are overestimating my ability to scare the public."

"Don't put yourself down, Mr Leech. I believe you can achieve it… with the perfect setup, of course."

"Help from your own hands?" Arthur raised a brow.

"Yes, yes! That's it. I can set up a few things here and there. All you need to do is let them off at the right moment, and we will have a proper show," Asif said, scribbling something down on an envelope.

"And how soon will I be taking on my new role?" Arthur asked, bracing himself for the answer.

"We have a booking tomorrow night. I will set it up ready for them! Go on, Mr Leech. Get practising," Asif said. He left Arthur to grapple with his new role while facing the solemn truth of how little people had changed over time. The same old tricks and schemes alive and well in the world, like they had been back when he was alive. Was this really all there was to the afterlife?

***

As the guests settled into their seats, a sense of dread built inside of Arthur as the pressure mounted. Heart pounding, he tried to maintain his composure.

Candlelight flickered, casting shadows on the walls, and glinting in the silverware and fine china that lined the table. However, the atmosphere was far from elegant. A palpable tension gripped the air, as though the room itself held its breath in anticipation.

The guests seemed oblivious to the lurking danger. They chatted away, sipping on their wine, and enjoying their meal. But Arthur knew what was to come.

Agnus, the birthday girl, was a plump woman with rosy cheeks and grey permed hair, who reminded Arthur of Queen Elizabeth. Agnus' grandchildren had booked this meal as a surprise for her seventy-fifth birthday.

When Asif signalled him to begin, giving three quick winks of his left eye. Arthur leaned towards Agnus, blowing gently on her neck. She clapped her hand against her skin and shuddered. The other guests laughed, but this was only the beginning. The real scare was yet to come.

Asif stood, scanning the room. "Tonight's menu is pre-prepared for Agnus's special day. Will you all join me in giving a round of applause for the birthday girl?" As the guests clapped, Asif dimmed the lights. "Not only is tonight a special night for our guest, but for the pub as well. For you see, tonight is the one hundredth anniversary of Phyllis Padberg's death."

Agnus's eyes surveyed her family, a smile gracing her lips. "Who's that when she's at home?" she asked, with a curious country lilt.

"Phyllis was the landlady of this very pub," explained

Asif, his eyes glinting with mischief. "This room we're in now was the old storeroom. The very place she *died*." Asif winked at Arthur, signalling what Arthur should do. Arthur knocked the vase on the bookshelf, yet not enough for it to fall. Asif glared at him again before stepping behind Agnus. "She stood at this very spot when two hands wrapped around her neck." Arthur tried again, and with the second attempt, the vase fell to the floor, shattering into thousands of fragments. The entire room erupted with screams. The two grandchildren jumped from their seats, then promptly sat back down, feigning composure.

As the evening continued, the guests enjoyed their food: British roast beef and vegetables. One of Arthur's favourite meals when he was alive. When dessert was served, it was time for Arthur to pull off the last piece in Asif's plan. The big scare of the night.

Asif gestured Arthur into the kitchen, pointing at a bowl of ice cream. "This is it, Arthur. The big finale."

"What needs to be done, Mr Meka?" he asked, glancing at the chef and his helper, who worked on the other side of the kitchen. Too stressed and overworked to notice Asif talking to himself.

"Once the ice cream is served to Agnus, that's your sign to let rip."

"In what way?" Arthur asked, his curiosity piqued.

Asif's arms flew up into the air. "I want chairs falling over, the alarm clock on the shelf to go off. Do whatever you need."

When the waiters arrived with the deserts, Asif stood beside the door with a grin on his face. Turning to the shelf, Arthur prodded the alarm clock. The ticking grew louder as it neared the shelf's edge, and with a sudden jolt, the clock fell. An alarm echoed through the room and startled Agnus, who dropped her spoon. The ringing continued and deafening screams merged with the chaos. The lights flickered, plunging the room into darkness in acute bursts.

Asif played his role perfectly.

A chair abruptly shot into the air, propelled by a mysterious mechanism. It landed on the table with a thud, followed by more screams as two guests rushed to Agnus, who had fallen to the floor. Her grandchildren stifled their laughter, their amusement replaced by panic.

The light flickered on again. It was Agnus's daughter calling out for help. Arthur leaned over to find Agnus gripping her chest, her wrinkled face contorting as her breathing quickened. In the doorway, Asif's huge smile faltered to one of shock.

"Help! We need help in here. We need a doctor!" Asif shouted as chaos erupted in the pub.

Arthur stood vigil beside Agnus, his presence unwavering as the room gradually cleared of onlookers. He knew what fate awaited her now, and all he could do was sit with the lady as she drew her last breath. Eventually, her eyes faded to nothing as her soul left her body, and he couldn't help but wonder if he'd done enough to soothe her in her final moments.

Quill Darlington

The grating wail of metal rang in Quill's ears as he disembarked from the train. He turned, greeted by a chaotic sea of commuters who surged in all directions. At this time of morning, most commuters wore suits as they hurried to work. Quill dusted off his cap and settled it back onto his head with a brisk motion. He had been visiting London for centuries, and despite the new plastic signage, the station's beautiful design had remained unchanged. As Quill took a deep breath and glanced at the clock, he realised he was already running twenty minutes late for his meeting. The train schedules certainly hadn't improved over the decades.

Barging past the crowds, Quill jogged up the concrete steps towards the exit. Traffic jammed the streets, and deafening horns blared; yet, as he turned to follow the block through Whitechapel toward Brick Lane, the busy streets gradually thinned, until he heard the faint sound of music and chatter from nearby markets and cafes. Despite his urgency, Quill followed the same walk he had taken for the past two hundred years, having etched every corner and alleyway to memory like the back of his hand.

As he approached the small square garden, a shell of a building stood before him. A tear rolled down his cheek. The site carried a heavy burden of memories, a mix of joy and sorrow etched into every corner. As he wiped away the tear, he felt a friendly hand on his shoulder. Quill turned to find Isaac Constantine standing beside him, dressed in a brown cotton coat that covered most of his body. Beneath the coat was a deep red waistcoat.

Isaac's appearance remained untouched by time, his familiar smile radiating the same warmth it always did.

His embrace was firm, a testament to their years of friendship. The weight of history pressed down on Quill as he fixed his gaze on the weathered factory, its remnants whispering tales of days long forgotten. With each visit, more of the walls had crumbled away.

"Strange, isn't it? Not having Jason this time. He's usually the first to arrive," Quill said.

"Yeah. I miss him too."

Quill sighed. "Well, that just leaves us two, then."

Slowly, they paced towards what once was the entrance but was now a broken arch entangled with vines. "I had one of your recommendations arrive a few months back. Thanks for that one."

Isaac chuckled. "The man who wanted to buy a ghost to create a haunted house? Thought you'd appreciate that."

"He didn't last long. Some poor dear died of fright, and

they shut the place down. I still don't know what became of the spirit I sent there. Suppose I won't for some time."

"You still care, then... about the work?" Isaac's tone softened.

"Someone has to," Quill replied. "If not for us, then those souls would have no hope."

Inside the factory walls was a workbench poking through overgrown weeds. Isaac took a seat, peering out across the factory floor. "I never thought Jason cared all that much, not after the first few years, but it didn't stop him from running a successful merchant shop. Maybe we are the foolish ones. Maybe we cared too much."

"Perhaps." Quill nodded. "He didn't move on by choice, though. He must have had some guilt remaining in the back of his mind somewhere."

"Not that he'd admit it." Isaac paused and peered skyward. Where their office used to be, where Quill would watch the workers. They all acted like they were above it all. "This place still haunts me, Quill. How much longer will it take to forget what happened here? Why are *we* the ones left behind?"

A leaden weight of memories pressed upon Quill's chest as he gazed into the vast expanse of the open sky. He couldn't shake the feeling of shame—a constant reminder of the past. He turned to Isaac, hoping to find some solace in their conversation.

"At least he trained up a new merchant before he left. I'm surprised Oli didn't come here to meet us to at least keep the tradition going," Quill whispered.

Isaac's eyes shifted downwards. "Oli worked for Jason for years, didn't he? I think Jason was ready to move on long ago."

Quill nodded. "Have you got yourself an apprentice?"

Isaac glanced back at Quill, his gaze softening before he diverted his focus to the ground once again. "Yes. Not long after we last met, I found myself one."

Quill glanced up at the sky once more. "I see. Jason's influence?" he asked, his voice tinged with curiosity. He didn't want to mention Erin yet.

"Partly, but can you blame me? We can't do this forever. Once we find a replacement, we can move on at any point. Maybe we've paid our dues, mate. Maybe it's time to let go."

Quill's thoughts returned to Erin. "A special spirit arrived to me a few years ago. At first, I was against it. But she was so different. I couldn't sell her, not until I was sure what she was." Quill's throat tightened.

Isaac glanced at Quill in surprise. "I never thought you'd allow it. I know how you frowned upon the others for doing the same," he said.

"Only Mike. He barely did ten years' work before he left. He never truly cared, not really. I still feel our punishment is far from over. Not that any of it matters anymore." Quill looked along the factory walls, remembering the workers and the sounds that plagued this place.

Isaac raised an eyebrow. "Oh?"

"I caught her disobeying the rules. I didn't want to risk The Boss finding out after what happened with Jason. I couldn't bear the thought of her soul being taken, but knowing I've kept this secret haunts me."

Quill's gaze drifted to the old machines that would once rumble on both sides of the factory, where the children and young women toiled in the heat.

"A rule breaker isn't always bad, Quill. We wanted to be like that once, remember?"

"And look what happened when we did nothing. That mistake has followed us ever since." Quill sighed. "I can only imagine what would have happened if we spoke out." Quill tapped his pocket, where the note of names he'd carried all these years remained. "Haunted me each day, as sure as the sun rising and the moon filling the sky," Quill replied sorrowfully. He stopped in his tracks, gazing at the arched windows on the left side of the building. He counted them, knowing exactly where he stood. "This was where little George worked. Do you remember him? The orphan whose parents died here, where he ended up working years later to meet the same fate." His voice cracked, and tears welled in his eyes as an unbidden surge of emotion pressed down upon him. "You never know what breaking rules can lead to, Isaac. I'd hate to risk Erin. I couldn't go through that again."

Isaac curled his arm around Quill's shoulder, offering some comfort, but the pain of regret still lingered in Quill's heart. "They were lucky to have you looking over them. You cared about the kids, showed them the only love they'd ever known. The spirits are lucky to have you, too. I know you care about them just as much, even if that's breaking the rules."

Quill's eyes grew misty as he turned to his friend. "Do you think I should forget about it? Let her continue her training like nothing happened?"

Isaac nodded with conviction. "If she's as special as you say, then yes."

"But I don't want to use her for my own gain."

Isaac's grip tightened as he turned to face Quill. "You've punished yourself for long enough! It's been hundreds of years. That's a greater punishment than any judge could have given. It's time to let go, to let those ghosts rest, and to forgive yourself."

Quill surveyed the surrounding ruins, a reminder of the terrible past they shared—the reason they had all promised to meet here every ten years, to never forget what they had been a part of. "Will you be here for the next meeting, Isaac?" Quill asked, his voice small. He already knew the answer.

Isaac shook his head vigorously, tears cascading down his cheeks as he wiped his nose on his sleeve. "No, I'm ready. I've had enough of the sleepless nights, the death... the sadness. This will be our last meeting, and I want you to do one thing. Find forgiveness in yourself. You will be the last one standing, the last link to all of this." Isaac waved a hand towards the building. "You owe it to yourself and to the kids. End it, do your job, train this person up and allow yourself to move on."

Isaac pulled Quill in for their final embrace, one that lasted longer than any before. Quill stood, frozen, as the last link to his past walked away, never to return.

The weight of that horrible day was now solely on Quill's shoulders.

Arthur Leech

Asif Meka had suffered a significant loss. With the passing of Agnus, the Tavern soon lost its reputation, and the pub struggled to regain its former glory. When Arthur last saw Asif—many weeks ago now—he appeared thin and weak, and the looming presence of death clung to his slim frame. Asif was a man who had given up, failed, and knew that his payment was due.

Arthur stood as a silent witness as the pub's thriving hub of activity became a desolate, abandoned relic, with its empty tables and dusty bar stools. The regulars no longer came, and the special events once igniting the pub with energy and fervour were now a distant memory.

While Asif tried his best to keep the family pub afloat, the public lost faith in him and The Tavern closed its doors.

Arthur, who now wondered the pub floor, spent most of his time studying the drinks on the dusty shelves, finding solace in the faint smell of fruit cider lingering in the air. Even in the darkness, with the windows boarded up, Arthur saw the potential hidden within The Tavern's walls.

Arthur's lifelong aspiration had been to step into the role of a landlord, to possess his own bar and cultivate a lively community within its welcoming confines. A place that accepted everyone. The dream had never faded, even after death. Reliving the days of his past life, his work in the clubs, one of the few times he ever felt happy, was behind a bar. In total control.

As Arthur was studying the bottles behind the bar, he heard the front door creak open. He hurriedly made his way towards the stairs to see who had arrived, hoping it was Asif. Instead, he saw Asif's eldest son, Dev. Arthur imagined Asif must have once looked like Dev. He stepped into the dimly lit pub - the sharp attire, impeccable posture, and the mane of thick, dark hair that spoke of a shared heritage. Whenever Dev visited with his father, Arthur felt awkward and out of place, like he was intruding on a family gathering.

"Arthur? Are you here?" Dev called out, unsure.

Arthur emerged from the stairs, greeting Dev with a smile. He didn't smile back.

He let out a laugh. "God, you really are real. I've never actually seen you before."

Arthur propped his elbows on the bar. *How could Dev see him when Asif was his owner?* Arthur thought. "I guess Asif won't be joining us?"

He put his hand on his forehead. "No, father will not be joining us," Dev replied.

Arthur's heart sank. While Asif's health had been

deteriorating, he hadn't expected such news so soon. "I'm sorry, Dev. Are you all coping okay? It's always so hard when a loved one is sick."

"Father died three days ago, Arthur," Dev wiped his finger across the dusty bar, where it gathered in his nail. "I'd almost forgotten about this place until I had to go through all the paperwork. I forgot about you as well. Not sure I ever believed in Dad's wild stories, but here you are, like the contract said."

Arthur froze. Asif was dead, yet Arthur was still here. How was that possible? "How am I still trapped here? I should have left when Asif died."

"Father, in all his wisdom, wanted the family to be set for years to come," Dev explained. "He had you marked down for five generations. It's no wonder he kicked the bucket so fast."

Arthur's heart plummeted. This family had bound him for years, possibly decades. Frantically looking around the bar, Arthur wondered if he would be stuck here, alone, for all that time. "What are you doing with this place?" he asked Dev.

"Wow, Father really did make an impact on you. All business, till the end," Dev groaned. "I want to sell it. It has no use to the family, and honestly, neither do you."

Dev's words pierced through Arthur's spirit as the sting of long-forgotten wounds resurfaced. Despite his charming demeanour, Dev's tone was cruel and callous. "So, do you plan to keep me in the void until the five generations are up?"

"Void? You mean that little bottle? We have no idea where that is. Father put it somewhere, I'm sure, but we can't seem to find it. Can't you just... I don't know, haunt this place or something?" Dev shrugged.

Arthur sighed, fearing generations spent alone in the

darkness. Endless days and nights. He needed to think of a plan, and then suddenly, an idea came to him. Arthur snapped his fingers. "I know! You should do this place up and get it running again. You can use me to run it! I know everything that needs to be done. I've spent countless hours watching it run before. I know it like my own home."

Dev stared blankly at him, pushing his hair back from his face. "You? A ghost running a pub?" He laughed, stepping back into the middle of the room.

Arthur was unfazed. "What if I speak to Quill and have him make me visible? That way, I can work here for you and keep your future safe like Mr. Meka wanted."

Dev stopped in his tracks, his keys tightly gripped between his fingers. "You really want to run this place?" Arthur nodded. "And I wouldn't have to see that Quill guy, or help you or anything?"

"Exactly. I can get it all sorted for you. It will be easy money once it reopens. I can live here and run the place at no cost to you." Arthur leaned forward. "A businessman like yourself wouldn't turn down an offer like that, would you?"

Dev tapped his foot, mirroring the same mannerisms of his father. "I'll think about it. I will come back in a month, and if you've sorted it, I won't sell."

"Thank you Dev. I won't let you down."

Dev rolled his eyes, heading to the front door. "Making deals with a ghost wasn't on my bucket list, you know. But you have one of those faces I can't say no to. I'll be back in a few weeks. Don't let me down, Arthur."

Dev slammed closed the door, and as his footsteps faded, a sense of relief washed over Arthur.

Yet one major obstacle was in his way—the unchangeable fact he was a ghost. He couldn't walk into a bar and start serving drinks. To do that, he'd have to make himself visible, tangible to the physical world once more.

On his outing with Erin, the witch had spoken to Arthur as if he was a normal person. So had the florist. Quill was the only one who could make him visible again.

Arthur rushed up the stairs to the window, peering out at Quill's shop across the street. He needed to come up with a plan, to lure Quill inside and convince him to help.

Quill Darlington

Quill's hands trembled as he delicately set the glass into the frame, his fingers brushing gently against the edges of the painting. He had poured his entire soul into it, hoping to emulate Isaac's kind spirit. Quill had etched every detail of his friend's face onto paper—from the sparkle in his eyes to the subtle creases around his mouth when he smiled. As Quill's eyes lingered on the completed painting, a swell of emotions rose within his chest and tears blurred his vision.

Quill looked at his fingernails. Dried paint remained on them. Another friend he had to say goodbye to, another who'd found forgiveness, who had trained someone up to replace them.

With meticulous care, he adjusted the paper, smoothing out any creases or folds that might detract from the image of his dear friend. As he secured the back of the frame, he took a deep breath and turned it around to face him.

Isaac had been a loyal companion, a shoulder to cry on, and a source of comfort when Quill had needed it most. And for that, he was eternally grateful.

Quill placed the frame beside the others on the shelf. All three of them. His former colleagues and friends, who had all become ghost merchants. Memories of the factory's horrors and the unspeakable atrocities they had witnessed together cast a shadow over Quill's thoughts. He blinked and saw whirring iron and welded metal. Broken bones and broken children filled his mind.

Wiping the frame clean, Quill returned to the shop's main room, where Wilson lapped at his water bowl. The frozen air outside seeped in through the cracks; condensation smeared the windows.

The fear of The Boss's wrath loomed, but as the days turned into weeks and the weeks turned into months, he heard nothing. No fines or summons, no angry reprimands. The shop went along as usual, with the souls adding up in the books and no sign of trouble on the horizon.

He and Erin had got away with it this time. But Quill knew it was only a matter of time before their luck ran out. He didn't want to live like this forever, constantly looking over his shoulder and waiting for the other shoe to drop.

The wind whipped through the village as Quill braved the outside world. It was the perfect weather for a solitary walk; he decided—and he was unlikely to run into anyone he didn't wish to. With each passing generation, Quill found it increasingly difficult to remain anonymous as family lines remained in the village. After all, how could an old fool like him still be running a shop in the same spot after so long?

The villagers must have their suspicions.

As he strolled past The Tavern, a loud crash sounded from inside. Although locked tight since closing, Quill couldn't resist a closer look.

Through the boarded windows, nothing but darkness emerged from The Tavern. An unsettling tension hung in the air, and suddenly, the banging halted. It was as if something watched him from the shadows. Quill knew he shouldn't linger, but something pulled him to step inside.

Cobwebs hung from the ceiling like macabre ornaments. The stale stench of beer and mould greeted Quill as he took a step forward, the floorboards creaking beneath his weight. His eyes landed on a broken chair lying on its side.

"Hello?" Quill called, yet the only response was that of the howling wind. Quill adjusted to the dim light, then spotted a stack of old newspapers. Shaking his head, he wondered why anyone would leave such a place untouched for so long.

As Quill turned to leave, something caught his eye. A small glimmer of light reflecting off something in the corner. He headed towards it, and only then did he notice the figure standing in the shadows.

In the darkness, Quill strained to discern the figure's identity, but he could only distinguish a silhouette motionless in the shadows. He called out again, "Who's there?"

"Quill? Is that really you?" echoed the voice of the silhouette. Quill recognised it instantly. "It is you!" Arthur jumped over the bar and rushed towards Quill. "Did you hear me from outside?"

"That was you?" Quill asked, surprised.

"Yes. I've been trying to get your attention for weeks. I didn't realise how little time you spent out of the shop before.

I was running out of things to push off the side."

Quill lowered Arthur's arms and tried to calm him. "Why are you still here? Shouldn't you be with your new owner now?"

"I should be," Arthur explained. "Asif's son came to visit, but he wants to sell the building and leave me here."

Quill felt a wave of guilt. He'd placed Arthur in this situation, knowing full well what the outcome would be, only to teach Erin a lesson, but all that's happened since was her teaching him.

"I see," Quill said. "It seems Asif was the only family member who was keen on this arrangement. I thought that might be the case."

"You did? Why didn't you advise him not to offer so much for my ownership?" asked Arthur, crossing his arms.

Quill shuffled his feet. "Well, it's not the job of the ghost merchant to put off a sale. We must accept what we are offered."

"I see, another one of your *rules*." Arthur said, moving back behind the bar with heavy footsteps.

"Oh, Arthur. What happened to the cheerful man from a moment ago?"

"Well, it's the same story, isn't it? I'm left stuck in a place waiting for the inevitable. Back in the void, ready for another owner to offer another broken promise," replied Arthur, his spirits clearly dampened.

"A member of this family might let you leave when the time comes. There is always hope, Arthur," said Quill, trying —and failing—to lift his spirits.

"Not anymore. I've been burnt enough to know I'm stuck here."

Quill stroked his chin. "What would make you feel better?

There must be something I could do?"

Arthur glanced up at the offer, his mouth agape. "Well, ah, never mind. You'll never go for it," he said, slumping once more.

"No, go on. I'm listening." Quill encouraged.

"Really?" In between the gap of Arthur's folded arms, Quill watched his eyes widen. He bolted upright. "Well, I was talking to Mr Meka's son, and I suggested running this place for him for the duration of my contract."

Quill narrowed his eyes. While he was used to Arthur's elaborate view on life, this was extreme. "So, you want to run a pub? Play the role of landlord for a few decades?"

"That's right. It's good to have dreams, isn't it? To not give up hope. Why shouldn't I do it?" said Arthur with a hint of defiance.

"There is the slight problem of you being dead, of course."

Arthur crossed through the bar to stand beside Quill. "That's where you come in. Do it to me again. That day you let me out with Erin."

"What about it?" Quill's brows furrowed. "That only allowed you to roam the village; it didn't bring you back to life."

"I don't need to be *alive*, just visible to guests and visitors. Like you and Erin are. Do that to me again," explained Arthur, his eyes alight with hope.

Quill pushed his glasses back up the bridge of his nose. "I'm confused. When I let you out with Erin, it was only her who was visible to others, not yourself."

"No, no, it wasn't. I waved at people. I spoke to the flower girl and the old witch in the shop."

Quill stepped away from the bar. "You did? Fascinating."

"It is?" Arthur bridged the gap between them.

"Let me work on this. What you are asking of me isn't... *standard* practice. It would mean bending the rules. I'd need to use other means for it to go unnoticed. Maybe I need to make a visit to Allegra."

"That's the witch I met," Arthur said.

"Leave it with me. Allegra has some explaining to do," Quill said.

Quill Darlington

For years, Quill had accepted his role as a ghost merchant without question, but now, he couldn't help but wonder about the wrongness of it all.

Erin had once said that she and the other souls felt like prisoners, slaves who had never asked for this fate. Quill had been dictating the afterlife for so many souls without their consent, and the realisation made him uneasy.

"Erin, I want you to run the shop for me today. I'll be here to watch over, but you will take the lead."

Quill had slowly been giving Erin more responsibility. Even with her rule breaking, she still needed to learn.

Erin looked up from her magazine. "Oh? Who's booked in?"

"Well, no one. But you never know who might walk

through the door."

Erin rolled her eyes, flipping impatiently through the pages of the magazine. "An empty reward," she muttered under her breath.

Quill froze, affronted. He had hoped giving Erin some responsibility would make her happy, but clearly, it wasn't enough.

"I'm also giving you the ability to walk free," added Quill. "Around the village and into shops. Wherever you want, actually."

Erin's face glowed. "Really? Wait, what's stopping me from getting up and going then?"

Quill chuckled nervously, realising that there was in fact nothing stopping her from doing just that. "Your responsibility for the job, of course. This is a once-in-a-two-hundred-year offer, Erin. Please don't leave me regretting my trust in you."

Erin shoved her chair away from the desk and strode toward Quill, her hand reaching for Wilson's fur. "Don't worry. I know that the life I left behind is no longer there for me anymore. My future is here, if you'll have me."

Quill breathed a sigh of relief, but before he could turn away, Erin spoke up again.

"Quill, did you not want to ask me about what happened? About where Allegra took me? Or has she already filled you in on the details?"

Quill paused, unsure of what to say. "No, Allegra is very loyal to me and to you. Your business is none of mine." Erin's mouth fell open. "When you're ready, and if you want to talk, then I will listen. I've spent too long thinking about the past, trying to control the narrative. But no more."

Erin smiled. While Quill still had a lot of things to figure out about Erin, he was thankful to have her by his side.

The doorbell rang, and in walked Dustin Davis. He was wearing a grey sweatsuit, his fingers laden with gold rings. A clueless young man trailed behind him, likely hoping to find an easy way to fame or money. Quill turned his attention to Erin.

Dustin stopped in the middle of the shop, ignoring Erin behind the counter by immediately facing Quill. "Mr Davis. Is it really that time already?" Quill asked.

"Seems to come around earlier each time, doesn't it? Can we go to the back room?" Dustin snapped his fingers, and his friend quickly closed the shop door. "And it's Sir Davis. Remember?"

Quill's eyes flashed to Erin to gauge her reaction. It would be an excellent test to show Erin's seriousness for the job. "My colleague would be more than happy to help. Erin, please take Sir Davis to the back room? I will follow you shortly to check everything has gone well." Dustin narrowed his eyes at Quill, who flashed a smile. The young man who accompanied Dustin followed them both into the back and as Erin closed the door, Quill heard the heaviness of her footsteps increase. Listening from the other side, Quill crouched.

"So, Dustin, what can I do for you? I see no appointment marked." Erin's words appeared forced, as if spoken through gritted teeth.

"Not everyone needs to make an appointment, darling. I'm a loyal customer here, so you will treat me with some respect."

Quill clenched his fists, but he couldn't interrupt the meeting. Instead, he apparated through the door. Erin's face flushed red.

"My apologies, sir. Please tell me what you are seeking with us today," Erin said, feigning politeness.

Dustin remained standing with his arms folded. Turning to the young man, he nudged him forward. "Get a contract ready and get him to sign it. I need another soul."

Erin's eyes burned. "Are you happy to offer your soul after death?" she asked the young man, who, with a look from Dustin, nodded. "I'm going to need you to speak." Erin pressed. "I need your name, for starters."

The man scratched his head, and Dustin shoved him again. "Mike. Mike Richardson."

The name took Quill by surprise. After saying goodbye to Isaac and Jason. Mike left so long ago, the first to move on of the group, but his absence didn't make hearing his name any easier.

Erin tapped the pen between her fingers. "And you're happy to exchange your soul for the soul of another?"

"Go on lad, just sign it and then you get the cheque," Dustin interjected.

"Yes, I'm happy with that," said Mike. "What's it matter, anyway?"

"Death is eternal, which means it lasts a lot longer than life. You are literally sacrificing years of your life for this exchange. It's not something simple to throw away. You know it's serious, right? It's *real*." Erin replied, her eyes fixed on Dustin.

"Excuse me, woman. Watch your tone!" snapped Dustin. "Quill, get in here and sort your staff out!"

Quill sensed Erin's anger brewing, like a gathering storm preparing to unleash. He had to act quickly before she did something she would regret.

"Sir Davis, can I help?" Quill asked, entering the room.

"Get this contract sorted, won't you? And find me a soul—the usual type—then let me out of this godforsaken place!"

"Erin, please. Gather the jar on the middle shelf. It's in section D. Third from the back."

Erin slammed the pen down, shoving her chair away. Storming past Quill, she whispered, "You aren't giving him another child's soul, are you?"

"What did she say?" asked Dustin, turning towards them both. "Go on! Get to work, girl."

Erin slammed the door, leaving Quill alone with Dustin and Mike.

"The usual type will be difficult to find, Sir Davis. Perhaps you could be more specific?" pressed Quill.

Dustin watched Quill, narrowing his eyes. "I don't have time for your games. Just get me what I need and let me leave."

The boy tapped Dustin on the shoulder. "Can I go now?"

Quill smiled and moved Mike towards the table. "Sign here, lad. That will be all I need from you."

Erin returned with a bottle in hand as Quill co-signed the contract. Dustin snatched the bottle from her, then left the room, with Mike trailing behind like a lost dog.

Erin's eyes bore into Quill's, her hands pressed firmly on her hips. "Say it. Go on. Tell me you don't think this is wrong."

Quill sighed, slumping his shoulders. "We've been through this before. We can't pass judgement. If he has payment, then he gets what he asks for."

Erin groaned as she tossed her hands up in the air. "You know what? I can't *wait* for the day you are gone and I'm in charge! It's no wonder you can't sleep at night, knowing the pain you've caused these children. Isn't it enough that they lost their lives so young? To then send them to live with *that* monster? It's a fate worse than death."

With that, Erin spun on her heel, her steps clicking against the floorboards like the final notes of an unfinished symphony. While Quill tried to shield himself from the reality of what he had imposed on those innocent children, the weight of his actions was a burden that never left. But it wasn't up to him to make the rules. This commitment was simple. Sell a soul for a soul. The contracts had loopholes and conditions, but when it came down to it, that's all The Boss cared about—a soul for a soul.

He tried to not think of what happens if The Boss sends you away, the place Jason had gone to under The Boss's watch. The dark is all Quill knew. He wanted to save Alma from that fate, wouldn't wish it on anyone. He needed to stick by the rules as much as he could. The unknown scared him the most. Quill's judgement day would come, but not until it was time to leave. And that's the only judgement he waits for.

Quill inhaled the crisp air as he stepped out of the stuffy shop, grateful for the reprieve from Erin's sour mood. Crossing the cobblestone streets, the silence of the woods enveloped him, despite the crunching of leaves underfoot. He strolled along the forest path, allowing his mind to wander and his senses to absorb the natural beauty around him. The trees towered overhead, forming a canopy for the sunlight to filter through.

He remembered the time Allegra spent in the woods, the times she had forced him to go foraging with her, and countless hours exploring the forest in the past. Quill hoped to find her today, to distract himself from the heaviness of his work.

Winding through the woods, Quill followed the path with ease, breathing in the scent of damp earth, while relishing the rare sense of peace only nature could offer.

When he eventually came upon the crystal-clear waters of the stream, Quill took a turn off the path and ventured deeper into the woods. The occasional chirping of birds accompanied his travels as he followed the trail, his eyes scanning the ground for signs of Allegra.

When he emerged from the thicket of trees, he spotted Allegra crouching in a clearing of bluebells. Her brown linen hooded cape covered her head, and a small knife glinted in her hand. An abundance of greenery surrounded her: roots, flowers, and nettles.

Quill quietly approached, not wanting to startle her. "Do you need any help?"

The hint of a smile played on Allegra's lips as she glanced up at him.

Standing, Allegra strode to an ancient oak and trailed her fingers along the rough bark. "What changed, Quill? I thought Erin, and I were in your bad books."

"A friend had a few words in my ear. I'm not here to be anyone's enemy, although I fear I've already upset the balance."

Allegra frowned, sensing the tension in Quill's voice. "Easily done when you have such a lively spirit. You always wanted to know what it was like to be a father. Now you do."

Quill gave a rueful laugh. "What? Always thinking you're doing right when, in fact, you're only messing things up? Sounds about right."

Allegra gripped the knife, carving into the bark and slicing it from the tree. She collected it in a small leather bag that

The Ghost Merchant

hung around her wrist. "I assume you have tracked me down for a reason. Finally ready to ask about that night?"

Quill smiled and collected a piece of bark that fell to the ground. "Do I need to know?"

"No, not if you don't want to." Allegra said, her voice slightly guarded.

Quill hesitated before changing the subject. "There was another thing I wanted to ask, actually. About The Tavern pub."

"Oh, I'd love to go out for a meal. I thought you'd never ask." Allegra beamed.

Quill suppressed a chuckle. He raised a brow at Allegra instead, knew she was teasing, and he had to admit sometimes it was welcome. He held great respect for Allegra, even envy with how she looked at life in such an easy and simple way. Quill wondered if he would do well to introduce some of that thinking into his own.

"I need a favour."

Allegra raised an eyebrow back. "The run-down pub that's haunted? My, my, my. What on earth could you want there? This has nothing to do with that charming young man I met when Erin visited my store?"

Allegra turned from Quill, following the stream back towards the path. Water sprayed onto the pair, and Quill relished the sudden coolness. "So, you could see him? He mentioned that."

"Quite odd, isn't it?"

"He wants me to make him visible. To run the pub for his owner. Can you help?" asked Quill, his face unmoving.

Allegra halted in her tracks with a cackle. Bending down, she plunged her arm into the ice-cold water to yank out some moss. "Not asking me to break the rules, are you? It seems young Erin has influenced us all."

Quill stepped forward, ignoring the hammering of his heart.

"Can you help or not? Arthur is a good man. He deserves the chance at happiness."

Allegra wiped her wet hand on Quill's top. "I can help, yes, but I will need the assistance of another witch to do so."

"It will be an excellent lesson for your apprentice Renee, then." Quill teased with a slight smile.

"Hmm, no. I don't think so. She can watch, but I have another in mind. Leave it with me, Quill. Your handsome young boy will have his wish. And I will graciously accept my thank-you meal, sometime in the next decade." Allegra said, a mischievous glint in her eye.

Erin Layton

Erin roamed the quiet village streets to escape the torment of her thoughts, taking advantage of the newfound freedom Quill had permitted. The rules of the afterlife were not fair by any means, but it wasn't Quill's fault, not really. He didn't make the rules, only tried to follow them.

As winter descended upon the village, Erin recalled her final months with Jacob in New York. She shivered, though the cold no longer affected her. Instead, her body trembled from the bittersweet memories clinging to her like frost. In New York, on Erin's last day, he'd offered her his coat—a simple gesture, one she appreciated more now than before. Erin had grown attached to the simple life of the village, with its absence of traffic and crowds of people. She passed the same horses each day, leaning across the fence with handfuls of grass in their mouths, and waving at the locals.

Erin meandered through the quaint village streets, blending seamlessly into the simple life of the community. If anyone asked, she was Quill's niece, having moved from London for a quiet life. Although no one truly cared about Erin's backstory, the lies made her feel *alive,* and that is what counts. Peering inside the post office, Erin thought about sending a postcard to her grandmother's house. Would anyone reply? What about her mother? Was she really there the night Erin visited with Allegra? Perhaps the truth was better left unknown.

A crooked finger brushed against Erin's shoulder, and she jumped, whirling to find Allegra, who smelled of lavender and essential oils. A sly smile tugged at the witch's lips as she said, "Don't startle, dear. Quill has granted me permission to have this little chat with you."

Erin glanced around, as if expecting to find Quill watching. Wondering if this was a test of his.

"I have a job, and I need your help," Allegra continued, turning to walk along the pavement. "Follow me."

Erin quickened her pace to match Allegra's. "What kind of job?"

"Oh, I think you will approve," Allegra said, a sly tilt to her smile. "That handsome young fella you introduced me to needs your help."

"Handsome fella? You mean Arthur? Where is he?" Erin asked.

"He's been here the entire time, my love," Allegra said, stretching out her arm. Erin followed her gaze to The Tavern Pub, a mere few steps away from the Ghost Merchant. All this time, Arthur had been right here, and Quill had never said a word.

The Ghost Merchant

Inside the derelict pub, dust and dampness thickened the air, accompanied by the stench of stale beer. Sun rays slivered through the gaps in the boarded windows, casting light in sparse places. Every corner held shadows. Erin crept forward; her footsteps echoed, accompanied by her pounding heart. Allegra's apprentice, Renee, flanked them. The three women moved in unison, their eyes scanning the room for any sign of movement.

As Erin and Arthur locked eyes, a rush of relief surged through her. Her friend was back. Despite being here for all this time, there was something different about him—something sad. "Arthur, I can't believe you were here this entire time!"

"Did Quill send you? I'm so glad you've come. He said he would find a way to bring me back, to make me like you." Arthur's gaze shifted behind Erin, realising she had company. "The witches are here. Where's Quill?"

"Don't worry, my handsome lad. I assured Quill I'd get the job done," said Allegra, beginning to place candles on the floor, forming the shape of a star. "Come here, boy. Stand in the middle."

Without looking at her, she tossed Renee a box of matches. "You get lighting these up, dear. Erin, you come and stand beside me. There will be plenty of time to catch up later."

Whenever the candles flickered, the room sprang to life. Shadows danced along the walls and an electric tension crackled through the air. Allegra spun, her long-ragged cape whirling with her as she circled Arthur, scattering herbs across the floor.

"We get one go at this boy. Are you sure you want to continue?" Allegra asked, her voice dark and foreboding. Her eyes pierced into Arthur's soul.

Arthur glanced back at Allegra, wide-eyed. "What happens if you fail?"

"Then you go to wherever it is lost souls go. No one has ever returned from there, so I can't tell you if it's any good or not."

Erin turned towards Arthur, her heart pounding. "There must be a safer way to do this."

"It's okay, Erin. I'm willing to take the risk. I mean, a witch as old as Allegra must know what she's doing."

Allegra raised an eyebrow. "You're lucky I don't send you there myself after that comment. Lucky for you, my handsome man, Erin will be the one taking the risk—not me."

Erin whirled to face Allegra, gripped by fear. She was in way over her head. "What *exactly* are we doing?"

"We're bringing Arthur back! Dear Quill instructed me to get it done, whatever the cost. All you must do, Erin, is stare death in the face, resist, and power through until I'm finished. Then our darling friend will be just like you. Visible to the public, and able to keep his charming looks forever more."

Erin tried to centre her breathing as the unknown filled her with a sense of dread. She couldn't let Arthur down. Taking an unsteady step forward, Erin took her place beside Allegra, who interrupted the tense silence with mysterious incantations as the power surged around them.

This was it. There was no turning back. Erin steeled herself for whatever lay ahead. The fate of Arthur's soul hung in the balance, and it was up to her to save him.

Allegra moved closer to Arthur, chanting with her eyes closed. The smoke thickened until Arthur was no longer visible, yet the shapes of Allegra and Renee either side flashed and distorted within the candlelight. Fear and doubt crept into Erin's mind. Was she ready for this? Could she really bring Arthur back?

Allegra opened her eyes and faced Erin. "Are you ready, child?"

Erin nodded.

"Find the darkness. Let it take you to Arthur. Find him; grab hold of his soul and Erin," Allegra clung tightly to her hand, "don't let go."

Erin closed her eyes and cleared her mind. She felt the darkness—an abyss that threatened to swallow her whole, but she forced herself to focus, to keep moving towards Arthur.

Erin's body jolted, and suddenly, she was falling. She landed hard on the ground, the breath knocked out of her, and when she opened her eyes, she was no longer in the pub.

She stood in the middle of a desolate wasteland, where the sky was a sickly shade of green and the air pungent with the stench of decay. Faint whispers and moans came from all around, and Erin felt a wave of terror wash over her, yet she had to keep moving. Keep focused.

In the distance, a figure huddled on the ground. It was Arthur, his face twisting and contorting in pain. Erin ran towards him as the ground shook beneath her feet. She couldn't make it. A wall of fire rose before her, blocking the path ahead.

She forced down the scream building in her throat. There had to be another way. She searched for a clue or sign—anything that showed her what to do next. And then she saw it. A faint glimmer of light far off in the distance. It was small, but it was there. And she knew to follow it.

Allegra's desperate screams roared over the crackling fire, her words trembling with fear. "Libertas, Mortis, Lumen!"

Tendrils of smoke curled around Erin, obscuring her vision and suffocating her senses. It felt as if the very air had turned against her, and she gasped for breath. Allegra screamed again, her words echoing through the sky.

"Libertas! Mortis! Lumen!" Erin's heart raced and a deafening bang echoed behind her. "Erin, close your eyes!" Allegra yelled. "Find the darkness and let it take you to Arthur!" Erin obeyed, squeezing her eyes shut to block out the surrounding chaos. But as she stepped forward, a figure loomed before her, larger than life. The ground shook beneath her feet as the dark giant approached with its thunderous steps. Sharp jolts of pain ripped through Erin's mind. She stumbled forward, determined to reach the darkness. Streams of black trailed behind her, joining the shadows dancing along the ground.

In the abyss, the giant's eyes blazed like fiery beacons, casting a crimson glow that pierced through the oppressive darkness, revealing the desolation that stretched endlessly in all directions. "Each soul is mine to keep," its voice boomed through the emptiness. Erin shuddered; her breath caught in her throat. Yet she held her ground, fixing her eyes on the giant as it spoke again. "The soul should be mine. But you can have it, sister of the night. *If* you can escape with it in hand."

Erin could hardly think, her mind clouded with fear and confusion. Why did it call her sister of the night?

By her feet was Arthur's body. He laid in the dust, bruises scattered across his face, and blood staining his clothes. His legs and arms twisted in ways they shouldn't. Kneeling, Erin pulled him up and threw an arm over her shoulder, clinging to his frame.

"Erin, that's it! Come back!" Allegra's voice echoed in the distance. "Come back to us with him!"

Erin searched frantically for a way out of the darkness. The giant was gone; its red eyes had vanished without a trace. Erin spun, desperately searching for a way back to her friends. "You can do it. Follow my voice," Allegra's pleas grew stronger. "Follow your sisterhood, Erin, and return to us!"

Erin staggered, the brunt of Arthur's soul dragging her down, as if an invisible force had tethered to her. She refused to let go. She was bringing him back to the world, tearing him away from the clutches of the giant. As she drew closer to Allegra's voice, her steps grew heavy, her feet struggling to lift from the ground. She clenched her jaw, pushing forward through the pain. She refused to falter, and determination blazed in her eyes as she reached the end.

Allegra fell to the floor, her hair matted like a bird's nest; even Renee looked like she'd ran a marathon. Arthur stood with shaking feet and brushed off his suit. He was whole. Colour had returned to his cheeks and his dark hair was as thick as ever.

"You did it. I'm really here!" Arthur screamed, patting his chest. He jumped onto the bar and collected an empty bottle while Erin turned to Allegra, pulling her into her arms. "Is she alright?" Arthur asked, turning to Renee. Renee shrugged and opened the door, allowing the light in. She blew out the candles.

Erin held up Allegra's head. "Allegra?" Erin shook her body. "Allegra, wake up! It's Erin and Arthur. We made it back." Erin turned to Arthur, whose recently coloured cheeks had faded.

"She needs to rest," Renee said, folding up the cloth. "Help pick her up. Throw her arms over your shoulder and help me get her back to the shop." Renee collected the candles and wiped away the trail of herbs with her shoe while Erin and

Arthur struggled to get Allegra upright. They each put an arm over Allegra's shoulder, lifting her off the ground. Renee grabbed her feet, and together, they walked through the street to where the witch shop was a few feet away. They had to move quick.

"Thank you, all of you." Arthur whispered before facing Erin, his expression sobering. "There's something I needed to say to you."

The shop bell rang out when they shoved the door open, placing Allegra gently onto the ground. "Really? Right now?" said Erin.

"I saw a man leave the shop recently. A celebrity."

"Dustin Davis? Trust me, Arthur, you want nothing to do with him. I can fill you in on any world events you've missed, but let's make sure Allegra's alright, eh?"

"I know who he is," Arthur replied, peering sheepishly at Renee, who appeared lost in thought. "He's the celebrity that killed my old owner's husband. He was behind his murder. There's a huge cover-up to protect him."

Erin narrowed her eyes. "I told Quill he was wrong'un. He's buying the ghosts of children, you know."

"We need to do something. He can't get away with this. Kaitlin's husband deserves justice."

"Well, if he won't be punished in life, then maybe it's up to us to sort him out in death. I'll see what I can do. But with Quill around, I'm not sure I'll have much luck."

Arthur's eyes glinted with determination. "We'll find a way. We'll make sure he pays for what he's done."

Erin Layton

With the arrival of the new year on the horizon, Erin's longing for Allegra deepened, like an ache in her chest that refused to fade. Renee had informed them that Allegra was recuperating well and receiving care from a local witch in their coven.

Amid her burgeoning responsibilities within the shop, Quill had grown Erin's workload, not just on the human side of owning a store, but also on the afterlife side of things, too. When he received the news about Arthur, he blushed, as though an embarrassed parent had discovered their child had misbehaved.

Erin suspected that Quill giving her more duties was his way of making amends for what he had done wrong, yet also to test her loyalty. Being a ghost merchant wasn't all that different from any other retail job she had worked in the past. It was all about meeting targets, but the targets set by 'The Boss' were straightforward. Quill had told her it was simple: a soul for a soul.

But Erin thought there must be more to it than that.

Quill sat at his desk, hunched over a parchment, scribbling furiously with his ink pen. He perched his glasses beside him, ready to wear them at any moment. Erin sat across from him, twirling a loose strand of hair around her finger.

She placed The Great Book on the desk, then trailed her fingers along its spine. The book was a strange thing; it almost felt alive.

With no appointments due for another week, Erin browsed its many pages, studying the entries of other Ghost Merchant shops around the world, curious about their owners and clientele. Ghost Merchant shops spread far and wide, from bustling cities to remote towns. Erin wondered about the souls who had passed through their doors. Were they like her? Trapped in a limbo between life and death? Or were there other kinds of ghosts, ones who chose to remain in the afterlife?

Perhaps she had landed on her feet with Quill as her mentor. She imagined other owners to be cruel, locking her away or selling her to the first buyer. Or perhaps they would have sold her, and a kind owner would have eventually sacrificed their soul to set her free. But there was no use torturing herself with such questions; she was here, and here she would stay.

An emptiness overcame Erin as she looked around the room. She, too, was now part of this place—a piece of someone else's past. But she wanted to be here to help, to offer solace and comfort to those who needed it.

The sheer number of contracts on display overwhelmed her as she rifled through the shelves out back. Neatly organised folders, each containing the name of someone who had sold their soul and their owner, filled the shelves. The room was quiet, the only sounds being that of Erin's tapping feet as she read through them all.

She scanned through the names, and her eyes fell upon a folder with the name of a young child. A four-year-old girl who had been here for over twenty years. Erin felt a pang of sympathy for the poor child. She had not even lived, not really, and now she was trapped in an endless void. What about the child's family? Did they know what had happened to her? It was a tragedy.

Then, her eyes fell upon another name. Dustin Davis. Erin's blood boiled at the thought of him. Yanking out his folder, she flipped through the contracts. He had purchased over forty ghosts from different shops all over the world, and each soul was that of a child. Erin felt sick to her stomach at the thought of all the innocent lives he had made miserable.

Her mind drifted to the young man Dustin had brought along recently, who had signed his life away for a few cheques and the high life. He truly was a monster—a sinner. He should pay. Erin had to do something.

Acting on impulse, Erin's trembling hand reached for the pen. She defied her own doubts and struck out the man's name, boldly replacing it with Dustin's in swift, determined strokes. She repeated this process for all of his active contracts, freeing each soul upon Dustin's death. Her hands trembled with a mixture of fear and anger. If they caught her, the consequences could be dire, but the thought of freeing those innocent souls gave her the courage to continue.

Erin took out Dustin's latest contract and scrawled a note at the bottom.

Upon the death of Sir Dustin Davis, his soul shall be returned to The Ghost Merchants of Ringwood, England. Any souls under Dustin Davis ownership shall be released.'

It was a risk, but Dustin had to be stopped, which meant taking matters into her own hands. It was her small way of making a difference in the world.

Erin carefully set the pen aside, her hands wet and clammy. A weight lifted from her chest as she slowly exhaled, having taken a perilous step toward her own path of justice, crossing a line that could never be uncrossed. She could never go back, but at least she had done something to stop the evil that Dustin represented. As she left the room, Erin felt a sense of purpose, a feeling she had not felt in a long time.

Quill Darlington

Quill inhaled deeply, savouring the brisk, frost covered air enveloping the village. A tranquil stillness clung to all corners of Ringwood, offering a respite from his busy mind. The usual hustle and bustle had faded, replaced by a sense of calm that was almost palpable. It was a time of year he looked forward to as the visitors left and the streets emptied.

Dressed in a thick, mustard-coloured scarf and red cotton gloves, Quill journeyed down the empty street. Though the winter chill never affected him, Quill maintained a facade of shivering, his breath forming faint clouds in the air. He couldn't afford to let down his guard, always mindful of watchful eyes.

Approaching The Tavern, Quill peered, looking into the window where Arthur stood with a welcoming smile lighting up his features. He gestured animatedly to the progress of the builders outside.

Quill had heard rumours that Allegra was back at the shop, having finally returned after a long absence away. He needed to speak with her, to discover what she had done to bring Arthur back, and get some much needed answers.

Quill approached the Wiccan shop, where Renee struggled to erect a window display, her slight frame barely able to handle the weight of the large wooden board. Quill watched as she clumsily attempted to secure the display with pins clasped tightly between her lips and sweat forming on her brow. Despite her efforts, the display seemed to get the better of her.

As he entered the shop, a small bell above the door announced his arrival. Renee turned to face him. Removing the pin from her mouth, the fairy lights draped above Renee's head twinkled as they fell. Quill couldn't help but smile. "Is Allegra better now?" he asked.

Renee scrunched up her face, considering her response. "She's in the courtyard, doing nothing while I struggle." She said. Quill thanked her and made his way to the back of the shop.

Navigating the narrow kitchen, the pungent aromas of dried herbs and flowers enveloped Quill like a fragrant cloud and made his senses tingle. Dried frogs were hanging from strings with pegs clipped to their feet, their desiccated bodies swaying gently in the breeze. Buckets were below them to catch anything that fell, and jars of herbs, stones, and jewels lined the shelves. The corner held a high pile of assorted fabrics, cotton, and linen, each carefully labelled and organised.

Quill spotted Allegra outside, sitting on a stone bench

before a fountain, where two robins splashed in the water. He sat down beside her. She seemed tired, despite her long break away. Her hair was pulled back in a loose braid, and dark circles lingered under her eyes. Despite this, she smiled warmly at him.

"How are you, friend?" Quill asked.

Allegra slowly turned to him, offering another weak smile. "I'm well. Better for being back home. I visited my sisters, and well... it wasn't as peaceful as I'd hoped."

"Family or...?"

"No, my sisters from the coven. There is never any rest to be had when visiting a sisterhood, it seems. It's part of the reason I've had Renee work to the bone since I came back," Allegra replied, turning to the two robins with an open palm full of seeds. The birds hopped over to peck at the food. "Turns out I'd been letting her get away with far too much," Allegra continued, wiping her hands clean. "It's difficult, isn't it? Leading the younger generation into this world."

Quill took off his glasses and meticulously wiped the lenses clean with a cloth. "It's not something I've prided myself on. I put it off for all this time for a reason."

Allegra looked at him, eyebrows raised. "And what reason is that, Quill?"

Quill hesitated, unsure if he wanted to reveal his true thoughts. There was a weight of responsibility that came with overseeing so many people. Each day, he had to consider the impact of his decisions on their lives, and although there were higher-ups to call the shots, Quill felt a sense of duty to carry out their orders, even when he disagreed with them. How different would his life be if he had chosen a different path?

Allegra reached out and gently grasped Quill's hand. "You

have a chance now to do right by Erin."

Quill released a weary sigh, slumping his shoulders. "You have been more of a mentor to her than me. She looks up to you, Allegra. All I am is the boring shop owner with a book of rules."

"But she stayed. Even when she had the chance to leave. This place is a pull for her. She will flourish here under your watch."

Quill reclined on the stone bench, his brow furrowed as he fixed his gaze on the statue before them. The intricate stone work detailed the witch exactly as Quill remembered her. From her sharp face to the billowing fabrics she used to wear. "What is it about her, though? You took her away that night, did you not? You never disclosed what that was about."

Despite the exhaustion of Allegra's expression, her eyes still shone with vitality. "I took her to a family home to find an item. To check my hunch."

"And that hunch was?"

"I wanted to know more about Gertrude Griffiths, the woman who sold Erin's soul to you over a hundred years ago. The reason Erin is here today," Allegra explained. Quill nodded. "Erin's powers for free will, for bending the rules... It all added up."

Allegra glanced at the statue. "That statue there in the centre is the former head witch of this coven, Lydia Abbius. She had members arrive from all over to help chip away at the stone until it was a perfect likeness of her. Knowing her days were numbered, she wanted the statue finished before she died. She always wanted to be looking down on what she created."

Quill nodded again, recalling the woman from centuries

ago. "Ah yes, Lydia Abbius. She wasn't my biggest fan, I'll give you that. Knew how to keep a strict house, and never once smiled."

"She was a harsh teacher, but I won't say a bad word about her. I am here today with a strong coven that will withstand years, thanks to her guidance." Allegra grasped Quill's hand. "It's a powerful thing to know when your time is up, Quill. Us witches can sometimes get lost so easily in the extra years we have, but Lydia knew when the game was up; she knew when to let go."

"But what does that have to do with Erin?"

Allegra's expression grew solemn. "When Erin arrived, the feeling I had felt all too familiar. I searched through the coven memberships, went years back. Turns out the day Gertrude arrived to sell the soul of her seventh-generation grandchild, she also visited this shop, too. She made a deal with Lydia."

"A deal? Lydia wasn't one to make deals," Quill said, glancing up again at the statue.

"Correct, unless you are from another coven, that is."

Quill's mind raced. Did Erin come from a bloodline of powerful witches?

"What deal did Gertrude make with Lydia? I don't understand. Erin is still under my control. She is dead, a spirit trapped within the rules."

Allegra's piercing eyes burned into his. "She has her mind, Quill. She repels the natural order of the afterlife. She's untainted by death, and she questioned things from the very beginning, did she not?"

"She did. She even got a foot outside of the shop door within minutes."

"Gertrude must have asked Lydia for Erin to keep her sharp witch's mind. We cannot be controlled, not by anyone.

If the coven is blooming and the sisterhood stands, then all our minds will be clear and free. Erin being dead obviously muddled things slightly, but as we know from dear Arthur, these walls can be broken when pushed."

"Was that night with Arthur a test? To see if Erin had the power of a witch?" Quill knew Allegra wasn't strong enough to do what she did to Arthur alone, and looking at Renee struggling in the window, it was clear Allegra's extra help came from elsewhere.

"Yes, it was to see if Erin truly had the blood flowing through her."

"Do you think I should release her? Let her find her coven?" asked Quill, his eyes drawn back to Lydia's statue once again.

Allegra stood, unsteady on her feet. She gripped the water fountain for support. "Here's a wild idea, darling. Why don't you ask her?" Allegra said, twisting her fingers into a fist. "They are your rules. Only you can choose to break them."

Allegra shuffled off then, back inside her shop. The dull sun shone above Quill, leaving him alone in the courtyard. Should Erin be free? When a soul arrives here, it stays for good, until The Boss takes it or exchanges it for another. It could be years until anyone discovered Erin being missing, as long as Quill kept running the shop, of course. He could hide it. Allow Erin to be free, but Quill would damn himself if he ever leaves the ghost merchants, or if The Boss was to discover what he'd done.

His time wasn't over. He had penance to pay. As long as he had that, he could train Erin up fully before allowing her to decide her future.

Arthur Leech

Arthur's fingers moved methodically across the gleaming surface of the Brosimum redwood bar. Each stroke of the polish revealed the rich, natural grain of wood beneath the newly installed lights. Arthur grinned. Dev Meka, the owner of The Tavern, had entrusted Arthur with the budget to bring the pub and restaurant up to scratch, and the work was nearing completion. He had selected the perfect fabrics for the seating, designed the menu, and even ordered a jukebox that was due to arrive in a few weeks.

As he peered around the bar, Arthur couldn't suppress his smile. This was the first time in his life—and afterlife—that he felt like he had truly made something of himself. Pride swelled within him at the result of his tireless efforts.

Feeling content with his accomplishments, Arthur glanced

at the clock. He needed to meet Erin. Walking outside was once a rare treat for Arthur, but now it was a part of his everyday life. He couldn't wait to spend time with Erin in the beautiful surroundings of the village.

As he made his way down the cobblestone path, Arthur kicked the fallen leaves, enjoying the satisfying crunch beneath his feet. Spotting Erin sitting on the fence up ahead, he waved to get her attention. She dropped to the ground, caking her bright yellow boots in the mud. Arthur chuckled as he approached. "What you got in there?" he asked, gesturing towards her bulging shoulder bag. "Is that a present for me?"

Erin gave a subtle, inviting nod towards the winding forest path. "Not here," she whispered. "Let's go into the forest, near the stream. Did you see anyone on your way over?"

"No, not a soul. Literally," Arthur replied, jabbing Erin playfully. Upon noticing Erin's lack of enthusiasm, he added, "Oh, this meeting is a serious meeting then, I take it?"

They remained quiet until they reached the stream, swollen from the rain that had fallen over the past week. Arthur knelt and threw a stick into the river, watching it disappear with the current. "So, what's up? This all feels very official. Quill really has got you trained up, hasn't he?"

Erin's lips curved upwards and her eyes lit up. "I didn't want anyone to bump into us, that's all. I made sure to leave Quill busy in the shop." She glanced around before crouching beside him, clutching tightly to her bag. "This is between us. *No one* else can know."

As curiosity got the better of him, Arthur leaned forward to glimpse whatever Erin had stashed in her bag. Yet the contents remained a mystery. "Okay. I promise. What is it?"

Erin paused, eyes locked on Arthur's. He wondered what was hidden. What could Erin have that needed to be kept such a secret? Could it be something dangerous enough to risk his new life?

"Remember that man, Dustin Davis?" Erin whispered.

"How could I forget?"

"Well..." Erin glanced over her shoulder again. "Quill left me to look over the contracts. I came across his. Quill's pen was right there, and..." She opened her bag and held out a glass bottle, where inside was a soul—dark like an oil-clogged sea. "I altered a few things. I freed the souls of the children and replaced the offering with his own soul."

Arthur's eyes widened as he pointed at the bottle. "You mean that's Dustin in there?"

"Keep it down," Erin said, shoving the bottle back into her bag. "I didn't think he'd die so soon. When the bottle arrived this morning, I nearly died all over again."

"And Quill knows nothing about this?" asked Arthur.

Erin shook her head. "Not a clue. His death hasn't even made the news yet. He's been so busy with the shop, I don't think he'd notice even when it does. Dustin wasn't exactly a nice guy, was he? Maybe Quill won't even care."

Arthur's thoughts drifted to Kaitlin. The thought of Dustin's secrets finally coming to light was a glimmer of hope in an otherwise bleak situation. Perhaps now he was no longer alive. The media—and those who had protected him—would have no reason to maintain his reputation.

A rustling came from the bushes, and behind Erin, Renee appeared, with twigs in her hair, and linen bags slung over each shoulder. She stared blankly at Arthur and Erin, then offered a small smile. A mouse darted from beneath her into the foliage. "Doing some work for Allegra. Don't mind me."

She brushed herself off and followed the mouse deeper into the forest.

Arthur flashed a smile at Erin. "For how strange this village is, she has to be one of the weirdest things here."

"I hope she didn't see Dustin's bottle. Maybe I should put it away," Erin said, nervously glancing at it.

"What are you going to do with him?"

"Nothing. He can be kept forever in the void." Erin replied bitterly.

"The void is too good for him. He should be punished, not living in a land of half sleep," said Arthur, narrowing his eyes.

"Did you forget what I can do? I can visit the void whenever I like. He won't be having a relaxing afterlife. Don't you worry about that!" A sly smile crept across Erin's features.

"What if Quill finds him? There will be a missing soul in the books if you keep him hidden."

Erin's eyes widened. "You seem to know a lot about the goings-on of a ghost merchant."

Arthur glanced away. Defensively. "I do not. It's just me and Quill had a deal once. That's all."

Erin scrambled to face Arthur. "Oh, really? What deal is that? Unlike him to be making deals. He's always so... *uptight* with me."

"He got to know me. My soul was passed around more than most. When I'd arrive back in the shop, he'd fill me in with the details of what's been going on in the world. Sometimes he'd talk about himself or work—mainly work, now I think about it," Arthur said, a touch of sadness in his voice.

"All he talks about is the shop and how important it is to

stay professional. Little does he know what we can really do in there, if you're brave enough to bend the rules," Erin said, tapping her bag with a mischievous glint in her eye. "How did you end up here, anyway? You've never said."

Arthur's mind immediately flashed back to that fateful day, and his heart pounded with the memory. Pain shot through his body, as if it were happening all over again. He took a deep breath to steady himself.

"Me? Well, it's boring really," Arthur said, feigning composure.

"Come on, you know all the gory details of my story. Tell me." Erin pushed.

Arthur squirmed. He didn't want to relive that moment, but he knew he should. Maybe it would help? "It's difficult for me to speak about," he admitted.

"You sound like Quill. All secrets when it comes to your own death, but happy enough to know all the gossip about everyone else's," Erin teased, though a note of concern traced her words. "Come on, you must trust me by now. I'll send you back to being a ghost. I can get Allegra over right now," Erin teased, and though she was trying to lighten the mood, it wasn't working.

Arthur breathed in, the cold air catching in his chest. He rubbed his arm, fighting back the tears threatening to spill.

"Arthur. Oh, I'm so sorry," Erin said, wrapping her arms around him. "I was only kidding. You don't have to tell me." She glanced around, pulling the bottle from her bag. "Come on, cheer up. Here, give Dustin a shake. Wake him up. It will make you feel better!"

"Sorry. I don't know where that came from." Arthur wiped away a stray tear. "It's not something I've spoken about before. I guess bottling it up all this time didn't really help," said Arthur with a shaky laugh. He wiped away another tear, his emotions getting the better of him. "I can tell you, if you'll listen," he said finally, his voice raw with emotion.

Erin placed Dustin in her bag and nodded, turning to face Arthur straight on. The sound of rushing water and distant birds helped calm him as he inhaled an icy breath, preparing to tell his story. He was ready to relive his last moments and release the pain that had haunted him for so long, at last.

Arthur Leech

1923

As midnight approached, the city of London's dark and quiet streets became a vibrant affair. Church bells rang out, the echoes of which reverberated through even the narrow alleys, setting the stage for an exciting night ahead. Rich brandy and intoxicating perfume scented the night-time, and amidst the flickering streetlights, Billy and Arthur weaved their way through the maze of underground bars. The soulful melodies of jazz seeped into the streets, entering their very souls as they moved from one dimly lit venue to another. The city was electric, its energy pulsed through their veins as they eagerly sought the next adventure awaiting them.

As they rounded the corner, the warm, inviting glow of an exclusive wine bar caught their eye and beckoned them inside. With a devilish grin, Billy turned to Arthur and asked, "Another tonic and brandy, my friend?" With a quick nod, they made their way inside.

Billy's weariness from a week of toil was clear in his slumped posture. Arthur, however, held a determined spark in his eyes. He was eager to turn this night into an unforgettable adventure to lift his friend's spirits. After working gruelling hours at the bakery, followed by an exhausting night shift at the bar, they had earned this evening of revelry and release.

As they wove their way through, they bypassed couples on the dance floor, their vibrant dresses creating a whirl of colours and patterns that merged with each movement. The band on stage was a blur of motion and energy, the rhythm of their music pulsing through the crowd.

Cocktails lined the edge of the bar, and Arthur and Billy found themselves perched at the end on stools, the air swimming with the scent of alcohol. Billy slumped on his stool, his head in his hands, while Arthur watched the couples on the dance floor.

The men confidently swept their partners off their feet, and a sliver of envy pricked at Arthur's heart. Their joyous twirls and laughter seemed just out of his reach. He had danced with countless women before—thanks to his mother's strict teachings in his youth—but he never felt as carefree and joyous as the men on the dance floor did with their partners. Despite his efforts to enjoy himself and connect with women, he always ended up at home alone, leaving Billy to wander off with yet another new flame.

But tonight, Arthur was determined to push those thoughts aside. He simply wanted to enjoy the moment.

A tap on Arthur's shoulder brought him back to the present. A tall red-haired girl grinned at him, then glanced at Billy, who was still slumped over. "Does he belong to you?" she asked, squeezing between them both. The scent of her jasmine perfume brought Billy back to life, and his head appeared out from between his mountainous arms.

"Hello handsome," she said, rubbing his back. He straightened then, beaming.

"Can I get you a drink?" asked Billy. "Arthur, get the lady a French 75 and another brandy for us."

Arthur nodded and raised his hand to the barman. Last night Arthur was in the same shoes: working behind a busy bar, thinking about home. He suddenly felt awkward standing beside Billy, whose focus was entirely on this new lady.

As they waited for their drinks, Arthur glanced around the club. The dim lights created an intimate atmosphere, with the jazz band in the corner adding a lively feel to the room. Couples swayed to the music, lost in each other's eyes. Arthur took a deep breath, savouring the moment.

"So, what's your name?" Arthur asked, tapping his fingers along the bar.

She turned to him with a flick of her curled red hair. "Dorothy, but my friends call me Dot."

Billy whimpered, dropping his head back into his arms as the drinks arrived. Arthur passed the cocktail to Dot and smiled. "Sorry about him, he's had a... *rough* day. His lady split with him, and her nickname was Dotty."

Billy coughed in a poor effort to hide his sobs. Arthur scratched at his neck, then smiled at Dot. "Maybe you should give him some space? Enjoy the French 75." Dot strode away, disappearing into the dance floor.

"What are we going to do with you?" Arthur said, slinging his arm around Billy's shoulder. He slid the small brandy glass towards him. "Come on, sit up. Get this down you and crack a smile."

Billy turned to Arthur, his eyes glimmered more than ever with his recent tears. Arthur hated to see his friend sad. No girls ever noticed how big and fragile Billy's heart could be. "Can we go, Arthur? Can we get away from here? All I can think about is Dotty." He whimpered again, followed by a hiccup.

Arthur nodded, and they weaved through the crowded dance floor once again toward the door. The jazz music slowly faded as they stepped outside, greeted by the cool air. The city lights illuminated the cobbled streets. Arthur put his arm around Billy's shoulder and guided him away from the club.

"Come on. Let's find a quiet place where we can sit and talk. I'm here for you, buddy." Arthur squeezed Billy's shoulder, and together, they walked in silence.

Arthur and Billy had reached a point of intoxication where their legs could no longer keep them upright. They stumbled along the pavement, giggling as the sounds of the city faded behind them. As they approached the iron bars of Regent Park, Billy tugged on Arthur's sleeve, insisting they take a shortcut through the Park.

Arthur hesitated. There had been recent reports of muggings and beatings in the park at night. Trying to reason with Billy, he suggested they head home the long way, but Billy was already clinging to the iron bars at the entrance.

"Come on, Arthur! We can get back home quicker this way," Billy exclaimed, his eyes filled with a wild determination.

With much reluctance, Arthur followed his determined friend through the brick archway, the dark expanse of the park unfolding before them. The path was eerily quiet, the sounds of the city replaced by the rustling of leaves and the distant hooting of midnight birds. The park's darkness enveloped them, leaving only slivers of moonlight to guide their way.

Arthur's heart pounded in his chest, his senses on high alert. He tried to keep up with Billy's drunken skips, yet stumbled over tree roots and rocks in the path. Every sound made him jump as he imagined the danger lurking in the shadows.

As they continued deeper into the park, Arthur regretted their decision. But they couldn't turn back. Billy's determination had led them this far, and he was too drunk to listen to reason. The only thing Arthur could do was stick by his friend's side.

The darkness seemed to close in around them. The sound of leaves crunching underfoot amplified, and Arthur's heart raced.

Billy turned to Arthur, his ocean-blue eyes shimmering with affection, like stars reflecting in a tranquil sea. The sweet, alcoholic scent of brandy tinged his breath. "I love you," said Billy, and Arthur's heart skipped. "You are the only one who's ever there for me."

Arthur smiled, wrapping his arm around Billy's shoulder. A sense of warmth spread through his body. "I love you too, Billy," he said, and he meant it. Arthur had always been there for Billy, through thick and thin.

Billy continued skipping, but this time dragging Arthur with him. "You can't be cold. Come on, jump up and down," he said, stopping in the middle of the path.

Arthur rolled his eyes, yet his lips curled, betraying him. He joined in with Billy, feeling a little silly but also happy to be spending this time with him alone.

Billy swung his arm around Arthur's neck, and they continued walking, a comfortable silence between them. Arthur couldn't help but think about what Billy had said earlier. *'I love you.'* Though it had been said in a drunken haze, it made Arthur's heart flutter. He had always wondered what his feelings for Billy meant, though he knew he should never act on them.

Throughout all the wild nights they had spent together, chasing girls, and revelling in the moment, a tinge of loneliness always overcame Arthur when he returned home alone. It was a feeling he couldn't quite shake. But as he walked alongside his drunken friend, relishing the warmth of his embrace, he couldn't help but wonder if Billy felt the same way. They had an indescribable bond, a friendship that Arthur had never experienced. He missed Billy every time they were apart, but had assumed he was the only one who felt that way.

They were almost out of the park, but Arthur had to ask. The words were on the tip of his tongue and he couldn't hold them back. It was the perfect time; the sky was dark and filled with stars, and they were both tipsy. Now or never.

"Bill. Did you mean it? What you said just then?" Arthur's voice was low, almost a whisper.

Billy stopped hopping on one leg and turned to face his friend. "Come on, we're nearly home. Did I mean what?"

"When you said you loved me," Arthur clarified, ignoring the jump of his heart.

Billy stepped closer to Arthur, a smile creeping across his face. He slapped Arthur on the back twice, a gesture that was supposed to be reassuring. "Of course I do. Now come on, we should get a move on."

A sigh of disappointment escaped Arthur's lips, and he drew to an abrupt halt. Shoulders slumped, Arthur glanced up at the starry sky. Billy did love him, but not in the way Arthur wanted him to. It was crushing, but at least he knew the truth.

As Arthur hurried to catch up with Billy, he noticed four men looming by the gates. The street on this side of town was deserted. "Billy!" Arthur shouted. Billy turned around but stumbled over his feet, accidentally knocking into one man by the exit. Billy burst into laughter, though no one else did.

Arthur rushed over to the group, hoping to retrieve Billy and leave. "I apologise for him. He's had a bit too much tonight," Arthur explained, pulling Billy up to his feet. The three other men crowded around them, blocking their path.

"Everything's alright here, boys. We're just heading home," said Billy, patting his trousers to dust them off. As he turned to the gate, three men cornered Billy, who stumbled back into Arthur.

The men blocking the exit stepped aside, allowing Billy to walk between the two others. "You two going home together?" One of them asked. Billy laughed and went to deny it, his words silenced by a punch to the gut. Arthur was about to intervene, but a man from behind kicked him to the ground. The men towered over Arthur, while Billy groaned in the background.

"You two fags or what?" asked the man, landing a kick on Arthur's face. That word stung through him. He hated hearing it, never thinking it would describe him. Hugging his head, Arthur begged with them to stop, insisting they were just friends. Billy rose to his feet and punched one man, but the other three quickly piled on top of him, kicking and punching him in a relentless pursuit.

Arthur scrambled to his feet. He yelled for them to stop and screamed for help, but no one came to their aid. He grabbed one of the men and pulled him away, knocking him spinning into the others. Arthur helped Billy to his feet.

"Come on, let's get out of here," Arthur said, jumping over the two men on the ground and pulling Billy with him. They rushed towards the gate with its iron bars and red brick archway.

"They thought we were a couple?" Billy said, brushing off his top.

Arthur's heart raced, its thunderous beats echoing in his ears as he sprinted down the deserted street. His eyes darted, scanning the surroundings for any sign of help. He glanced back to see the four men behind, their footsteps echoing on the pavement. But when he noticed Billy hobbling behind him, he knew they were doomed.

"Billy, please! They're right behind us!"

"I can't keep up, mate. My foot's twisted," gasped Billy, wincing with each step.

Arthur stopped in his tracks. He couldn't leave Billy behind, not like this. "I won't leave you," he said. Arthur grabbed Billy's shoulder and locked eyes with his. "I know you didn't mean it when you said you loved me, but I did. I meant it."

Billy's eyes clouded with confusion. "What does that mean? What are you trying to say?" Billy stepped back, brushing Arthur's arms off from his shoulders.

Before Arthur could reply, the group of men caught up with them. The main one sneered at Billy. "He's the fairy, is he?"

The men closed in around him. Arthur couldn't bear to see the expression on Billy's face as the strangers drew close. With one last look at his friend, Arthur turned away, unable to stomach the fear and pain in Billy's eyes. The first punch landed on his side, knocking the wind out of him. Arthur gasped for air, trying to catch his breath, but another blow hit him square in the head. The pain was intense, almost blinding. Falling to the ground, the hard concrete scraped his cheek. He lay there, helpless and vulnerable, as the four men rained blows upon him, kicking and stamping with vicious force. Dirt filled his mouth, and blood poured from his nose and lips. He could hear his own screams mixing with their laughter and their taunts. Through his blurred vision, he saw Billy's feet, rooted to the spot against the brick wall, watching on. Above, the stars twinkled, as if oblivious to the horror taking place below. Arthur's body convulsed with pain; he was close to his end. Closing his eyes for the last time, he felt Billy's hand on his. He couldn't answer Billy's question; couldn't tell him he was okay because he wasn't. He was leaving this world, leaving behind his friend and everything he had ever known, and when the pain finally subsided, a profound emptiness replaced it. That lasted forever more.

Erin Layton

Erin wanted to speak, to tell Arthur how much his story had moved her, yet words seemed inadequate in that moment. Instead, she simply held his hand, relishing the warmth of his skin against hers, while the sky shifted from a soft pastel canvas to a riotous blend of violet and pink. Erin's emotions mirrored the turbulent horizon, and though she yearned to release her anger, she found solace in Arthur's presence.

As the sun dipped, a cloak of darkness descended, cocooning Erin and Arthur in its embrace. They lingered there, reluctant to return to the harsh realities of the world. But eventually, Erin knew they would have to face the day. For now, though, she was content to remain there with him, watching the stars in the endless expanse.

As the weight of Arthur's story settled in Erin's mind, it was as if she could sense his heaviness, one that came with carrying around a secret for eternity. She peered up at the horizon, trying to understand the emotions Arthur must have grappled with all those years ago. "What was it you loved about him? About Billy?" she finally asked, breaking their silence.

Erin's question hung in the air. Arthur's body stiffened at the mere mention of the word *'love.'* Afraid she had sounded judgemental, Erin spoke up to reassure him. "The moment I knew I loved Jacob was moments before I died, but I don't think I ever told you that." Her throat tightened as she voiced the words out loud, the memory fresh in her mind.

Arthur tilted his head to look at her, confusion etched in his expression. "How did you know?" he asked.

Erin shifted onto her front, propping her chin in her hands. "A feeling, I suppose. We were on holiday; jet lag was over. We'd had a great night before and we had been shopping that morning." She felt the cold air creep in. "We were having fun, and I looked at him, and suddenly, things felt different. Any doubts I had vanished, and I said to myself then: I love this man, and I'll spend the rest of my life with him."

Arthur appeared to relax somewhat, mirroring Erin's pose as he turned onto his front.

The night sky twinkled with countless stars, while the forest had come alive with the sounds of nocturnal creatures, their voices and movements a symphony of life in the darkness.

"That's rough," Arthur finally said.

Erin's chest tightened, but she didn't want to dwell on her own story. She wanted to allow Arthur the space to share his. "Not too dissimilar to your story, I guess."

Arthur turned to face Erin, and she felt the intensity of his gaze. "Billy was a friend, though. We were never anything more than that," he said, his voice low.

Erin nodded, though she couldn't help but wonder about the rest of the story. "Do you know what he ended up doing with his life? After you died? I know the rules say you shouldn't delve into your past, but..." she trailed off, suddenly feeling guilty for asking.

"Quill actually assigned me to Billy's son; he was one of my owners," Arthur said, much to Erin's surprise. "His son arranged it all; he said his father was ill, and he'd always talked of his friend Arthur, who died. It was a coincidence really that he came to Quill's shop. But I was there."

Erin sat up; her curiosity piqued. "So, there *is* more to the story, then? What happened?" she asked, leaning in closer to hear Arthur's response.

"He rejected me," said Arthur. "When we arrived at his home, Billy was dying. I was there when he left the world. I don't think he even believed a ghost could be there beside him." He paused, his eyes filling with tears. "His son banished me back to the void, blaming me for taking away his last moments with his father, and a few weeks later, after Billy died, I was back in the shop again. I never found out what happened to his son."

A lump formed in her throat as she listened to Arthur's story. It wasn't fair; she thought. Arthur deserved to be loved as much as anyone else. She rose from the ground, brushing the dirt off her clothes. Erin couldn't remain passive; she could no longer watch her friend suffer. She offered her hand to Arthur, urging him to stand.

"I know this isn't the same," she said, giving Arthur's hand a reassuring squeeze. "But I think Billy was a fool. It's never too late, you know. To find someone."

Arthur watched her with doubt-filled eyes. "You really think so?"

Erin nodded, a smile spreading across her face. "I know so. You're a wonderful person, Arthur. Anyone would be lucky to have you in their life." Erin clung to her bag, checking to make sure Dustin's bottle was still safely inside. "I should get back. I need to hide this somewhere before Quill finds it and starts asking questions."

"Give him to me," Arthur said, holding out his hand. "I'll store him in the cellar at The Tavern. He deserves a cold, dark room, and he'll be safe there—away from Quill's prying eyes."

Erin gratefully handed over the bottle, shaking it violently as she did. "I hope he's suffering," she muttered.

As Erin returned to the shop, a sense of accomplishment washed over as she reflected on how she had aided Arthur in sharing his past. She cherished the trust they had built, knowing her secret was now shielded by their newfound connection—a sense she had been missing since death.

Alma Edwards

The bungalow, once filled with vibrant energy, had succumbed to an air of sombreness. The laughter and joy that had once echoed within its walls had now faded. Gone were the days when Rupert and Alma would spend their time gardening, cooking, and listening to the radio, joking and laughing together. Instead, Rupert's days were now consumed with sleep, punctuated only by nurses who attended to his needs throughout the day, changing his bedding and washing him.

When the carers left, Rupert let out a low groan, his once bright eyes now dull and sunken. Alma rushed to his side. She knew he was in pain, and she couldn't help but feel helpless as she stood beside him.

"Are you well?" she asked, though she already knew the

answer.

Rupert managed a small smile, his eyes betraying the true extent of his suffering. "Always will be," he whispered as Alma squeezed his hand as best she could. "I'm glad my Mary didn't see me like this. It broke my heart seeing her in pain. No one should have to go through that."

The corners of the room seemed to fall away into darkness, shadows creeping into her vision. "You will be with her soon," Alma whispered. She knew her time was nearing, too. "When you see her again, talk about me. Tell her I helped keep you going."

"Alma... Don't talk like that."

"Please, don't speak, but promise me you will remember me in death, when I am all but a memory. Please speak of me. Talk to Mary about the flowers we planted for her, for my family. At least then, I won't be totally forgotten."

Rupert's hand tightened around hers. He was struggling to let go, just like Alma was.

She felt his love and his pain; it was all-consuming. She tried to hold on, to cling to him, but she knew it was time.

As Rupert's heartbeat slowed and his breathing shallowed, Alma felt a wave of sadness wash over her. She had been with Rupert for so long, through all the trials and tribulations, and now she was leaving him. She wanted to stay, to comfort him, but she knew it was not possible.

Tears cascaded down Alma's cheeks as she drew near to Rupert's ear, her voice quivering with emotion. "Thank you," she whispered, her words carrying the weight of a thousand memories.

As the darkness closed in, Alma thought of her husband and her children one final time. The moments they had shared during her brief life with them, the laughter and the tears, the joys, and the sorrows. Alma knew where she was going. There wouldn't be anyone waiting for her, but at least Rupert would soon be reunited with his wife once again. And that was enough of a spark to make Alma happy.

Closing her eyes, a sense of peace washed over her, and with one last whisper of 'Thank you,' she let go and drifted away into the darkness.

The voices started again. She could hear his laugh. *Jean's* laugh. Alma was afraid to open her eyes, scared of what she might find before her. Alma's heart raced as she gazed upon her beloved husband, Jean. It had been so long since she had seen him, and the flood of memories returning to her mind made her feel as if she was reliving their life together. The touch of his hand on her shoulder sent shivers down her spine.

Was this really him? Or was it another cruel trick of the voices that had haunted her? Was she about to be torn away from her reunion, to be banished to the darkness forever? But as she peered at him more closely, she knew it was real. The way Jean stood, the sound of his laughter, the smell of his hair, the touch of his skin—everything was just as she remembered.

Tears streamed down her face as she held Jean's hand, pulling him closer to her, desperate to feel his embrace once again. As Jean's hand made contact, Alma's heart swelled. The warmth of his touch ignited a torrent of feelings, washing over her like a gentle wave.

But as she reviled in the joy of their reunion, a commotion sounded behind her. The sounds of her sons' laughter rang out, and she turned to find them playing together. They were just boys again, carefree and full of life.

She stood there, taking in the sight of her reunited family.

Her heart soared. Her family, all together in one place. Even if this had been a cruel trick before her soul was banished, she could leave content.

Peering back at Jean, she took in every detail of his face, just in case she'd never be able to see it again.

"Is this real?" she asked.

"We have been waiting for you, my love." Jean wrapped his arms around Alma, lifting her off the ground and kissing her all over. Alma grinned as her two boys ran towards her, suddenly transforming into tall, handsome men, just like their father. She swiped at the tears. "You... you are both so grown up," she said, tightly embracing her boys.

Suddenly, a cough interrupted the reunion. Alma spun to find Quill pushing up his glasses. "Quill? What's happened? Are you here to send me away?" she asked, her heart sinking at the thought of leaving her family again. "You said my soul was running out of time. That my life with Rupert was my last chance. If I failed, then I'm glad to know he was able to move on. At least one of us got a happy ending."

A warm smile graced Quill's face as he exchanged a meaningful nod with Jean. "It's time. Are you ready?"

"I don't want to go, not now. What will happen to me?" Alma's voice quivered at the prospect of leaving her family again. "I'm sacred."

Quill draped his arm around her neck. "Alma, you are free to go. Be with your family and let go of the past."

"But, what about Rupert? My contract? I was about to be taken by the darkness. I felt it. I saw the moving shadows in the room. What happened?"

"Your contract is up; it's all signed over. Now, go. Be with your loved ones."

Alma felt puzzled. "But how?" she asked, desperate for

answers.

"Rupert exchanged his soul for your freedom. Just in time, it seems. I knew he was the right customer for you, Alma. Now, go. Be free. And thank you again for always being there for me." Quill then faded, leaving Alma to process the news.

Jean's eyes locked onto Alma's as he gently clasped her hand. In that gaze, a world of unspoken affection passed between them. "Are you ready, my love?" he asked. "We've been waiting such an awful long time for this."

With a tender, lingering kiss on Jean's cheek, Alma conveyed her love and gratitude wordlessly. "Yes, I want to make sure I give the respect Rupert deserves, though, for everything he's done." She called her sons over. "I want you to listen, boys. I want to say sorry for when I went away, that I forgive everything that happened before I died. But you need to know I was well cared for. That there was a man looking after mummy while I was gone." She wrapped an arm around their shoulders. "He was a gentleman; he was kind-hearted. He showed me so much care and love. Wherever we go, I want us to grow some roses—red ones. One for her and one for him. So they are never forgotten."

She promised to remember Rupert, the gentle man who gave her everything. She remembered the life she lived, and the painful end. The reason she ended up in the ghost merchants in the first place, and she allowed a smile onto her face again. She held her husband's hand, and with each step they took toward the light, a profound sense of peace and closure washed over her like a comforting embrace.

Erin Layton

Erin discerned the echoes of Quill's footsteps reverberating from upstairs—a rhythmic thud, punctuated by brief pauses. He had been retracing the same path for hours since Alma had moved on. She'd never seen him so upset, so confined to his thoughts. Erin's gaze shifted to the bottle on the shelf. Within Rupert's void was a calm, shimmering rose-gold that swirled gently. Erin picked up the bottle and placed it at the centre of the table in the back room. Pulling the cork, Erin stepped back as Rupert materialised before her. Stretching, the elderly man surveyed the room before his gaze settled on Erin.

"Rupert, it's nice to see you again," Erin said, smiling.

Rupert's eyes lit up as he opened his arms to embrace Erin. "So, this is what the afterlife feels like," he mused, moving his arms through the air. "No pain in the joints. That's something, I guess."

Erin pressed her lips together, but the corners of her mouth twitched. She was in awe of Rupert's sacrifice. His selflessness was undeniable. Working at the Ghost Merchant had exposed Erin to the darkest facets of humanity, which had almost eroded her faith completely. Rupert had revived it.

"Did Alma move on, okay? I signed everything I needed to with Quill," Rupert inquired.

Erin nodded. "Yes, she reunited with her husband and boys and then departed. I think Quill's taking it hard, though." Erin's eyes drifted upward, where Quill's footsteps still echoed.

"Good, I'm glad she's happy," said Rupert, glancing around the room with his hands clasped behind his back. "So, what exactly did you want, then?"

Erin chuckled, feeling foolish for summoning Rupert. Her initial plan to sing his praises and express her happiness for his selfless act now seemed somewhat awkward.

"I wanted to know why you did it, I guess. Though I haven't been here long, no one has given up their freedom when the time came—except you, that is," Erin admitted, watching Rupert's face for any sign of regret. He must have had some? That tiny spark of wonder, of longing to see his wife again, knowing that he wouldn't.

"Well, I gained a few years of happiness with Alma—years I never would have had if I stayed alone in that house." Rupert glanced at the floor. "I made a promise when I first entered this shop. I said I'd give myself up, and I did. My mind is clear. That's the most important thing."

Erin despised her job at times, where mostly, everything

felt hollow. When someone did something good, she wanted to celebrate that. Rupert had given up any chance of seeing his wife again, and Erin wanted to make sure he knew how thankful Alma was, how he had reignited a glimmer of hope in her.

"Stay right there," she said as she turned towards the shop door. Ignoring the blistering wind, Erin ran down the alleyway and stopped outside the flower shop. She glanced up at the sky, where the grey clouds and a low sun caused long shadows to stretch across the street. The door was locked and a closed sign hung in the window. Erin banged on the door once she spotted the light at the back of the shop. She waited and banged again until Karina Potts appeared, glaring at her.

"Erin, what do you want? Shop's closed."

"Sorry, Karina, but I needed to ask a favour. Do you have a spare rose I could grab?"

Karina's eyes narrowed, and she let out an exasperated sigh. Quill had told Erin stories of Amanda Potts, who used to own the flower store before; her daughter was a spitting image of her mother, apparently. Alongside her terrible attitude towards customer service. Karina unlocked the door and stepped aside for Erin. Moving towards a bucket on the wall, Karina plucked a single white rose and extended it towards her.

"One condition."

Erin smiled. "Yes?"

"You get the gutters of the shop repainted. They've been chipped and flaking since I was a little girl."

"Of course," Erin replied, reaching towards the rose.

Karina snatched it out of reach. "And the shop lettering could do with a fresh coat, too."

Erin nodded. "Of course. I'll see to it myself. Now... the rose?"

Karina passed Erin the rose and turned to the door. Rushing back to the shop, Erin stopped to listen. Quill was no longer pacing; there was nothing to greet her except silence. She didn't know if that was a good or bad sign.

She marched into the back room where Rupert was seated at the table, gently petting Wilson.

"Here." Erin proudly presented the rose to Rupert and placed it beside him. "It's not much, I know, but I remember you talking about your love for flowers and the garden, and well..."

Rupert cut Erin off, his eyes sparkling as he looked at the rose. A single tear swelled and dripped down his cheek. "Thank you. It means the world to me. My Mary's favourite."

As Erin put Rupert back into the void, she placed the rose beside the bottle. She wanted to scream out to Rupert, to tell him how proud she was, how happy he'd made her, but Erin knew Quill would frown at that behaviour. At least with this simple gesture, she was allowed to break the rules in her own little way—a small way to say thank you for Rupert's sacrifice.

Quill Darlington

Quill's hand trembled, hesitating over the vacant spot left on the shelf where Alma had once been. A melancholic smile played on his lips, and he couldn't help but smile through the tears that threatened to well in his eyes. Alma's suffering had finally ended, so why did an emptiness gnaw at Quill's soul?

As a ghost merchant, Quill had learned to detach himself from his role. While the job was often unrewarding, his friendship with Alma was the exception. However, she had moved on, like most of his cherished ones, and that was something he needed to accept. They had all moved on from this world, leaving him behind.

Quill switched off his lamp, waking Wilson as he made his way along the creaking floorboards. Erin's lights were still on in her room. The sleepless nights were the worst part about being dead. The living took for granted the relief of sleep. Quill felt the urge to knock on Erin's door and confess his upset about losing Alma. But he thought better of it. Erin had her own life, and with it, she needed space.

Quill ventured into the silent village, where the moonlight cast shadows across his path. Each step echoed in the calmness, and he found solace in the gentle caress of the cool breeze. Amid the serenity, Renee's figure emerged, a silhouette swathed in flowing garments that danced gracefully with the wind.

"What are you doing out so late?" asked Quill, eyebrows raised.

Renee turned to him, her eyes lacking the spark he had become accustomed to. "Allegra sent me out to charge some rocks, or something," she said, her voice devoid of enthusiasm.

Quill peered up at the full moon. "Ah, an apprentice like you doesn't believe in everything you are taught then?" he said, failing to disguise his amusement.

Glancing at the small pile of stones beside Renee, Quill wondered about the true purpose of the task. It seemed an odd way to teach an apprentice, but he was sure Allegra had her reasons.

"It's stupid. When I came to this coven, I expected more. I heard great things about Lydia Abbius. She trained Allegra, and I built her up to be something she hasn't turned out to be. Having a tutor like Lydia should mean greatness. Allegra seems to have massively fallen behind my expectations."

Quill laughed, remembering Lydia's high demands for her coven. "It's true. Lydia was special. Few witches like her. If she trained Allegra, then surely that should be enough for you to trust her teachings, no?"

Renee watched Quill with half-open eyes before turning back to stare at the road. "It's been years, and I've hardly grown. She favours your *apprentice* more than me."

"Jealousy doesn't sit well within a coven, Renee. Even I know that much."

Renee collected the stones into her pouch and stood. "I'm not jealous of anyone. I just want to finish my training and have my own coven. I'll lead a better house than Allegra ever could."

With that, the apprentice stomped away into the night, her cape flowing behind her as she walked. Her silhouette reminded him of Lydia then. The determination in her stride, her shoulders pulled back, the air of confidence surrounding her. Their likeness truly was uncanny.

Erin's organisation impressed Quill. She had a natural talent for the practical side of the job, and he was pleased to have her here. Erin moved from room to room, arranging the new souls and scanning the book for stock and potential matches.

Erin let out a cough in front of Quill, startling him. "I noticed the gap out back, on the shelf. I left it, but I wondered how you were getting on?"

Quill raised his eyebrow. "Alma? It's okay. You can fill it if you like. She's gone now." Quill pushed himself to his feet and walked towards the counter. He shuffled some paperwork and turned to Erin. "How are you finding things? Is there anything you'd change about the training?"

Renee's complaints swelled inside Quill's head. He'd never asked Erin how she was finding things. For all he knew, she could be just as unhappy as Renee was with Allegra.

Erin smiled. "No, it's all... perfect."

"Erin. Speak the truth," Quill prompted.

Erin tucked a strand of hair behind her ear. "Well. There is something I wanted to implement. Let me run it by you."

"Go on."

Wilson peered up at Quill and meowed. *It's always the young who think they can change an institution,* Quill thought.

Erin moved behind the counter and opened the Great Book. "With Alma leaving, it got me thinking back to her... issues. Rupert struggled with it, at least a little. He was ready to give her up when he visited here, but I was able to talk him around." Erin paused. "What I wanted to do was start conducting check-ups on the customers, to see how they're getting on with their spirits, and how the spirits are getting on with them."

Quill raised his eyebrows. "You want to ask the spirits?"

"Yes. Look at Dustin Davis, for example." Quill noticed Erin's voice crack at the mention of his name. "If we carried out checks and the spirits were unhappy, we could re-assign them."

Quill chuckled. Erin's attachment to Arthur had already led Quill to bend the rules behind The Boss' back, but hoping to treat the stock with such kindness was beyond reproach. "Do I need to remind you that once we sell a spirit, we surrender any right to them until the contract's finished?"

Erin's eyes flickered, devoid of hope; it reminded Quill of his days in the factory, where he played the heartless manager to the children, crushing their hopes and dreams one by one, all under the order of someone above him. He felt like a hypocrite, enforcing rules he himself had rebelled against. Yet here he was. Two hundred years later, still doing the same thing.

"I'm sorry, Erin," he said, shaking his head. "Maybe when you are running your own shop, you can follow your own rules, but for now, while my name is on the door, we follow what we are told."

Erin's fingers tightened around the Great Book's edges, her knuckles white. With an exasperated sigh, she slammed it closed. "But the rules here don't work! Not for everybody, only the customers," she exclaimed. "Spirits were people once, Quill. Like you were, or has it been so long that you've forgotten how it felt?"

Quill recoiled, but before he could reply, Erin stormed from the shop and slammed the door shut with a bang.

Wilson jumped out of his seat and onto the floor, rubbing his head along Quill's leg. Quill petted him on the head and sat down behind the counter. Training Erin as his apprentice was challenging, at best. He had never had to share his space before, nor listen to someone else's opinions on how to run things. The Boss made the rules, and he stuck to them to avoid any trouble.

But now he had to balance Erin's wild temperament and her willingness to better herself with her training. She was like a daughter to him, and arguments like this were normal, he reminded himself.

Perhaps it was time he allowed her to decide. She had

options, being from a bloodline of witches. Allegra had said she would leave the issue alone, and it was up to Quill to decide when or *if* he wanted to reveal the full truth to Erin.

The shop was his life, and Quill had always followed the rules to keep it running smoothly. But now, he realised, some rules needed to be broken, especially when it came to doing what was right.

The Tavern had never been more popular. Although the locals still frequented the bar, its newfound popularity drew crowds from all over. Arthur had transformed it into a place to be reckoned with. He worked the bar like it was his true calling, serving up drinks and engaging in conversation with the patrons.

Quill sat beside Erin on a bar stool, feeling somewhat out of place amidst the lively surroundings. She had purposefully positioned her back to him. Smiling, Arthur poured Quill a drink, despite knowing he wouldn't touch it. But it helped him fit in.

Arthur had grown so much since arriving at the Ghost Merchant. Quill was proud of him, just as he was of Erin. When Arthur first arrived, he was a broken shell of a boy, not yet ready for the afterlife. But by bending the rules and giving him a chance, he could grow and develop into a man. It was thanks to Erin's ideas of change that meant Arthur could find happiness here, as a landlord. To find purpose in his life.

Arthur leaned on the bar, glancing between Quill and Erin. "Come on, guys," he said. "I will not have my family fall out." He then turned to Erin. "You. Turn the stool and look at Quill," he ordered. "And you, Quill. Turn your head and look at Erin."

Quill didn't move, so Arthur grabbed their heads and forced them to look at each other. Erin smiled and then glanced away. "Okay," pressed Arthur, "Now, on the count of three, say sorry."

"But I haven't done anything..." Erin protested.

Arthur raised his hand to silence her. "One... Two... Three..." he counted, prompting the pair to say, "I'm sorry," in unison.

"I really am sorry, Erin," said Quill. "I was thinking, and... well, you have come such a long way. I wanted to offer you a chance to change the way we do things in the shop."

Erin's face lit up with curiosity. "Yeah? What is it?"

"Maybe you'd like to run the ghost merchant on your own for a while. Let me step back, step away completely. Run it as if it is your own."

Erin scrunched up her face in thought. "Run the shop on my own?"

Quill looked at Arthur, who shrugged his shoulders before moving down the bar to serve another customer. "I thought you'd be happy with the idea," Quill said. "You can see how your new ideas work."

"That's great, Quill, but I thought I'd stay working in the Ghost Merchants with you," Erin replied. "I don't want to be left alone to run that place without you there."

Quill realised he had been thinking like a lonely Ghost Merchant instead of a fresh-faced apprentice. He had assumed Erin would be of the same thinking as Renee after his brief chat with her earlier. "Erin, when you become a Ghost Merchant, you have to run your own shop. It's the natural step that comes once you finish training."

"Why can't we both stay here, though? Together?" Erin asked.

"There can only be one owner per shop," Quill explained. "If you were to stay, that would mean I'd have to go."

Erin's head drooped as Quill's words sank in. "I see," she said, turning to face him. "Since I arrived here, I've grown to the idea of becoming a Ghost Merchant, to be the best I can, and impress you. I wanted to work with you and Wilson as a team. But I never thought I'd have to run it as my own business. On my own."

Quill reached out and took her hand. "I never had children, you know," he said. "Never thought I would. I didn't think I had the time for it. But lately, I've been feeling like a parent. Watching Arthur over there, seeing him change and grow into a new person... it's a truly wonderful feeling. And watching you, Erin... you've grown so much over the past few years. I see you as the daughter I never had."

A smile crept onto her face, her cheeks blushed. Happiness danced in her eyes.

"Quill..." Erin began.

"Please, let me finish," Quill interrupted gently. "Being a parent is hard, especially when it comes to letting go. You must be ready to face the world without me, and that's the hardest part. But I know you will flourish with whatever you do, and even if I don't want to leave, knowing that I *can*, and that you'll be the best you can be, makes it clear I have done my job right."

Erin was speechless for a moment. "I never knew you felt this way. I've been nothing but a stroppy madam to you. And this whole time, you've seen me as a daughter?"

Quill smiled. "It's alright, I'm not used to speaking this openly either. But I know you'll be ready soon, and I want you to know that I'm proud of you. That's all."

As they sat in The Tavern for the rest of the evening,

nursing their drinks and chatting, they watched Arthur put on a show behind the bar and listened in on the trivial conversations of the living, enjoying each other's company.

Their time together may be short, and Quill wanted to savour every second they had left.

Erin Layton

Erin made her way across the bustling village road, passing by the flower shop where Karina was busy arranging fresh bouquets, sweet floral scents contributing to the pleasant aroma of Ringwood. Across the street, The Tavern was alive with activity.

Erin made her way towards Allegra's shop. It appeared empty, much like Quill's. A bell tinkled as she entered. Renee glanced up from her magazine, but when she saw Erin, she quickly returned to her reading.

Erin approached the counter. "Is Allegra around, Renee?"

Without looking up, Renee flicked the page of her magazine. "In the courtyard."

The sun hit her face as Erin stepped outside. She squinted, adjusting to the brightness. She immediately noticed the stone bench to her right, where Allegra sat amidst the vibrant winter blooms. Chirping birds livened up the courtyard, where towering in the centre was a gigantic statue of another woman.

Allegra's dark flowing clothes were a sharp contrast to the stone walls behind, offering an angelic quality to those who didn't know her. Allegra peered up with a welcoming smile and shuffled to one side. Erin sat beside her.

"Long time, Erin. I know I can be an elusive woman, but all I've had from you is a wave here and there from across the street. So, what brings you here today?" Allegra asked, her voice warm.

Erin took in the garden's beauty until landing on the large statue once again; it seemed to watch over them, a flash of judgement from the cold stone eyes.

"Some advice, I suppose," said Erin.

Allegra stood up, brushing off her flowing clothes. "If you are going to speak, then you will have to follow me. I can't stay out here much longer. I always have work to be doing."

Erin followed Allegra into the kitchen, hit with an overwhelming aroma of herbs and spices. Jars and glasses filled with mysterious concoctions hung on hooks across the wall, and the ceramic sink was half full of murky water. Erin gasped as Allegra dived her hands into the sink, trying to find something within.

"So, go on then. What's on your mind, girl?" Allegra asked, her attention still focused on the jars.

She'd been worried about what she had done to Dustin ever since she signed the paper. Hearing Quill the other night, seeing how much Erin meant to him, and her realising how much he meant to her. It forced her to question what she had done, and what consequences she had brought from The

Boss. If she was going to seek out advice, she knew Allegra would be the one with the answers.

"I'm worried I've brought something bad to the shop, to Quill and myself."

Allegra dried her hands. "Oh, what on earth could you have done behind his back that's worse than what we did the night we visited your grandmother's home? I'm sure whatever it is, it will be fine."

Erin bit her lip. "Have you ever seen The Boss? Are they really as powerful as Quill makes out?"

"To the dead, yes. Why? Spit it out girl. I can't help if you dance around the truth."

"I altered a contract under Quills name. Sent a soul to the shop who shouldn't be there."

Allegra paused, her eyes fixed on Erin. "Right." She drained the sink of water, brushing her wet fingertips on her dress. "How long ago? Recently?"

"A few weeks, something like that. He deserved it. I don't regret what I did, only..."

"Scared of facing the consequences of it? Yes, I understand. The rules the afterlife follows are not for everyone. But this is a serious matter. The Boss doesn't take kindly to being made a fool."

Allegra stepped towards a small table placed in the corner and sat down. "Listen. I value Quill. There are things he clearly hasn't explained to you, things I've kept quiet for him. But hearing this, I think you need to know the full story, know all the options available." Allegra said, her tone serious.

Erin knew there was more to know about herself. Allegra didn't take her away to her family home for nothing all that time ago. Her grandmother had ties to a coven. Quill had always worried about Erin's abilities from the beginning. The monster she met in the void, when trying to save Arthur, had called her sister of the night.

"Tell me. Tell me the truth. Tell me everything." Erin begged.

Allegra took Erin's hand in hers. "Your grandmother she came from a coven directly linked to magic. The blood of the witch ran through her and your mother... and you."

Erin felt a chill run down her spine. A witch. Could she truly be a witch? Erin thought back to her mother, who had left her as a young child. She wondered if her mother had known about her abilities back then, and if that was the reason she had left.

"You mean I am a witch? This isn't a maybe? Why did my family never tell me?" Erin asked.

"Maybe they were saving you from a life they didn't want for you. It isn't an easy one, but there are positives. A witch can be brought back from death, and a spirit like you—one who is so attached to the world of the living—it would be a breeze. Of course, witches should always know when their time is up. No one should outstay their welcome but you, Erin. You never even lived."

Erin's mind raced. The sensation of something missing from her past had always haunted her. But the thought of leaving everything behind, of leaving the life she had come to know and love, was almost too much to bear.

"Remember what I said, The Boss is no threat to the living. If you are truly worried about the actions you have taken, then maybe coming back to the living world is exactly what you need. Move away, forget everything you know about the ghost merchants. It's the obvious answer."

Allegra returned to the sink, careful not to spill the jar

with the frog inside.

As Allegra pulled the frog out, she spoke in hushed tones. "Now it isn't an easy trade. If The Boss finds out they've lost a spirit back to the world, then you will be punished if you ever returned to the afterlife."

Erin's nerves kicked in, and she let out a nervous laugh. Allegra spoke of eternal damnation like it was another day at the office. "What are you saying here, exactly?"

"We can bring you back; we can remove you from the spirit world, but you couldn't return, couldn't allow The Boss to know. They don't take kindly to losing out." Allegra's eyes were wide with fear, and Erin couldn't help but feel the weight of the decision she was about to make. "We did similar with Arthur. His life still has limitations, restrictions, but with you, we can take it to the next level, with the bloodline you hold."

Erin took a deep breath, her heart racing. "Let me think about your offer. I shouldn't rush this."

"Of course. It isn't an easy one to make, one you can't go back from. But it will keep you from The Boss. It will allow Quill to continue his shop. But it is up to you." Allegra placed the jar aside, the frog's eyes staring into Erin's soul.

Quill Darlington

A birthday card rested on Quill's desk for Isaac. He had started a tradition; he'd write out a card and send it each year. The act of writing and sending the card brought him a sense of comfort, as if it helped keep his friend's memory alive.

Quill placed a stamp on the envelope, then glanced out the window at the world beyond his shop. Erin had already left for the day, leaving Quill to manage the store on his own. But he didn't mind. There wasn't much outside of his shop that interested him anymore.

Quill unlocked the door, glancing at Wilson, who had already settled into his fur-cleaning routine. "Thank you for always being here," Quill whispered, giving Wilson a pat on the head.

As he unlocked the shop, he noticed Renee waiting patiently outside.

"Renee, what brings you over so early?" Quill asked. Renee pushed her way past him and closed the door behind her, a cloud of dust erupting as her long cape brushed against the floor.

Renee's sharp, beady eyes darted around the shop, scanning every corner for any hint of movement or life. "Is anyone else here?" she asked in a hushed tone.

Quill shook his head, wondering what could have prompted such a panic so early in the morning. "Does Allegra know you're here?"

Renee grinned and brushed her hands through her hair. "She thinks I'm out foraging. I need to speak to you. It's just between us." She motioned for Quill to follow her towards the back of the shop. "Can we go through here and talk? I don't want this to be overheard."

"Allegra taught you well," Quill remarked, following her into the back. The jars on the shelves rattled in response to their presence, but Quill reassured Renee they wouldn't be able to hear their conversation.

"Now, I didn't want to do this, but I'm worried about your safety, Quill. And seeing as you are held in such high regard around here, I couldn't *not* say anything," said Renee, her often moody demeanour replaced with urgency.

"You can speak freely here. It will stay between us."

"It's about your apprentice," said Renee. Quill immediately noted her refusal to voice Erin's name. "Well, you won't like to hear this, but she's been treating you like a fool. It's serious, more serious than I think you could ever imagine."

"Really? I'm not sure much surprises me anymore."

Renee shifted her weight. "She's forged a contract. Under your name. Taken a spirit when she shouldn't have, capturing them in a jar, like the ones in here."

In all his years as a Ghost Merchant, Quill had never heard of anyone doing such a thing to a spirit, nor had he imagined Erin would go behind his back like this. Quill always checked the stock regularly, especially since Erin had assumed more responsibilities. Could she have changed the books and lists right beneath his nose? "Go on. Tell me more. The stock is all up to date in the store."

"I don't know more, but she has the spirit in her bag; she showed it to Arthur. She's hidden it from you. If The Boss were to find out, there's no saying what he'd do to her." Renee wiped below her eyes, though it was difficult to tell if she was upset or merely playing a part. "I know we aren't close, but I'd hate to see The Boss punish her or you."

Quill mulled over his choices, with each one carrying its own weighty consequences. He didn't want to believe what Renee was saying, but he needed to know more, to test if she was genuine. "What would you suggest I do? Scold her? Demand she tells me where the soul is and release them? Call The Boss on her and let them decide her fate?"

Renee sighed and placed her hands on her hips. She tapped the side of her head. "I thought maybe you could return her to the void. Let her cool off in there for a few years, and hope The Boss doesn't find out. I know it isn't fair, but it would be the best solution for both of you. At least then, she could stay here, in some way." Circling her foot on the spot, Renee glanced up at him through her lashes. "You're not angry at me, are you? For telling the truth?"

Quill smiled. "Not at all. Allegra has trained you very well, Renee. Leave this information with me. I promise you it will be sorted."

Renee skipped towards the shop door. "Thank you, Mr Darlington. I feared you wouldn't believe me, but maybe deep down, I think you know Erin is trouble."

"And like I said the other night, maybe you are more like Lydia Abbius than you think," teased Quill, awaiting her reaction.

Renee abruptly halted, pivoting to offer a sly smile to Quill. "Thank you again for keeping this between us."

Quill's mind raced with this newfound information. He knew Renee viewed Erin as a rival, but regardless, Erin had crossed a line if this was true. If Renee was to be believed, Erin had not only forged a contract, she had also trapped a spirit against their will. He had to act fast. If Renee told anyone else, it could cause trouble for them both.

With trembling fingers, he flicked through every page of The Great Book, comparing Erin's recent interactions with the stock of used jars. Nothing out of the ordinary stood out. Tapping his fingers along the desk, he spotted the boxes of stock deeper in the back room. He began rummaging through the boxes and spare jars one by one until he found a box hidden at the back. A label adhered to the box. It read 'Damaged' and inside were unused jars, each one brand new without a crack to be found. But one of which was missing.

Renee was telling the truth.

But there was still the matter of who the trapped soul was. Pouring over The Great Book again, he flipped through the pages until a name caught his eye. Dustin. Erin had worked with him twice, but had refused to continue. Could he be the spirit Renee referred to? The man died not long ago, Quill remembered seeing his photo in all the newspapers. As he pondered his next move, Wilson jumped onto the counter and swung his tail from side to side.

"I know, Wilson. He was a rotten man," Quill muttered. "But rules are rules." He needed to contact The Boss and request an urgent meeting, but he needed more time. Erin still had things to learn, and Quill wanted to be the one to teach her. So, he arranged the meeting to take place in a few days' time. Punishment could wait.

Quill Darlington

Quill stood outside the worn wooden doors of The Tavern, which were bolted shut. He knocked on the door a few times, but there was no answer. Scanned the deserted street and then phased through the door. He had a busy day; he couldn't wait around.

Shadows cloaked the room; bottles scattered haphazardly across the bar, and ashtrays brimmed with cigarette butts. It was clear Arthur had left in a hurry, which was unusual for a man who never had to sleep.

Quill's voice echoed through the room as he moved behind the bar.

"Arthur, are you okay?" he shouted, but there was no response. A set of stairs led up to the flat above the pub, and Quill took them two at a time.

Once he reached the top, he saw behind the scenes of the grand pub. Arthur had left his private flat untouched. At the seams, the wallpaper peeled, and the faded, stained carpet showed its age. The small hallway before him had three doors, and he heard shuffling and panicked footsteps coming from behind the door to his left.

Quill called out once more. "Arthur!" he shouted. A mumbling came from behind the door, and then a strange man poked his head out for a quick look at Quill before disappearing again. Quill quickly adverted his eyes to the ground.

Finally, Arthur stepped out of the room, a shy smile on his face as he closed the door behind him. "Quill, what are you doing here so early? In fact, how did you get in?" he asked.

"Everything okay out there? Do you need me to get the bat to whack 'em with?" asked a voice from behind the bedroom door.

Arthur smiled, his cheeks growing red as he gestured for Quill to join him downstairs.

"I'm sorry, Arthur. Sometimes I forget that you're no longer one of my spirits to keep track of. I shouldn't have let myself in like that," said Quill sincerely.

Arthur sat on the red leather window seat in the bar. "It's okay. I wasn't in any danger. You just gave us a bit of a fright, that's all." He crossed his legs and glanced at the locked door. "I'm not sure how I'm going to explain you coming in here, though. What can I do for you? I rarely see you this early."

Quill settled beside Arthur and sighed. He thought about asking who the visitor was in Arthur's bedroom, but decided against it. What the youth get up to in private was no concern of his. "I have a full day, and there are a few things I wanted to check off my list."

"And I was at the top of that list? How wonderful," Arthur teased.

"Well, we have had quite the journey together, and few of my spirits have returned as many times as you have. For a while, I feared you'd never be able to move on from your first."

Arthur's gaze shifted to the locked door, failing to conceal the pain of his past. "You were great, Quill. I know it's difficult being a Ghost Merchant, and I appreciate how you treated me differently from the other spirits. Few can say they had it as good as me."

When Arthur first arrived at the shop, Quill thought it was an easy fix to pair him with Billy's son, but it only left him more broken and rejected.

"It's a shame it never worked out with Billy. I never thought you got over that, not truly. But I look at you now, and I can see a new man," said Quill, trying to lift his spirits.

Arthur smiled, placing his arm over Quill's shoulder. "I couldn't have done it without you. All of this I have now. It's because of you setting things into motion."

Quill hated being praised. He rarely deserved it. But knowing he made a difference with Arthur gave him thought about what to do about Erin. Arthur stood and began opening the blinds to let the orange morning light in. "Come on then, enough of this small talk. What did you need to ask me?"

Quill's pause was palpable before he gathered the courage to speak. "I wanted to check with you about Erin. Will you look after her if I need to go away? Keep her out of trouble for me?"

Arthur collected the empty bottles from the tables with a

puzzled expression. He placed them on the bar before replying, "I think Erin can look after herself."

Quill pressed on. "But if she *needed* someone, you'd step in, right?" Arthur glanced at Quill, concerned. "I know she's broken some rules, and I understand you may know that as well. But please, reassure me you will have her back."

Arthur picked up the ashtray and wiped the cigarette butts into the bin. "Jeez, I didn't know you knew about that. Erin meant well, Quill. You need to put in a good word for her with The Boss. Don't let her be punished."

"Will you look after her?"

"Of course I will." Arthur's eyes softened. "You're like our father — well, grandfather — so, of course. I'll look out for her like she was my sister."

"Good. That's all I needed to hear." Quill turned to the door then, his bottom lip quivering. He unfastened the bolt from the top. Though he wanted nothing more than to spend time with Arthur, for the first time in years, time wasn't something he had much of.

Quill stood outside 'The Witch Stuff.' He took a deep breath before stepping inside, engulfed by waves of lavender and herbs. Allegra sat behind the counter, but Renee was nowhere to be seen. He assumed Allegra had sent her off on another one of her pointless errands.

"A bit late," Allegra glanced up from her nail file, her tone sharp. "I've never been a woman who's good at being kept waiting."

"I know, but I had a few words for Arthur. I'm here now." Quill peered over Allegra's shoulder toward the back kitchen. "No Renee?"

"Sent her off to collect some cephalanthera rubra flowers.

So, we have time."

"What if she returns early with them?"

Allegra cackled. "They are the rarest flowers in the country, Quill. If she comes back at all, I'll be amazed. She can be very stubborn. You wanted to talk... about *her*, I assume?"

"Yes, she came to my shop the other day. Snuck off early under your close watch."

Allegra placed her nail file down onto the counter and blew at her hand. "I was aware."

Quill sighed at Allegra's cryptic words. "She's jealous of Erin. She wanted me to lock her away in the void for a few years. Any idea why she wants her out of the way?"

Allegra glanced at Quill, then her hand again. "Maybe."

Quill rolled his eyes and slammed his fist onto the counter. "Allegra, I'm very rarely short of time, but today I am. Please, cooperate with me here. Why would Renee wish for Erin to be kept in the void?"

Allegra snapped her fingers, and the 'Open' sign shifted to 'Closed.'

"Fine. But not a word to anyone. I can't have this reaching my coven. I can't risk it, not yet."

"What is it? Tell me."

Allegra stepped around Quill, circling him. "I've been suspicious of Renee for some time. She's shown signs of obsession with Erin. At first, it was harmless, but recently, since Erin has been permitted to explore and adventure, she's changed. She wants her to stay nearby. She won't stop going on about it."

Quill nodded as Allegra confirmed his own suspicions. "I've noticed it too. She was always odd, but most witches are. The more she's opened up, the more familiar she feels to me. I can't put my finger on why."

Allegra halted in her tracks, staring at Quill with wide eyes. She spun and waltzed into the kitchen and out into the courtyard. Quill followed to where she stopped beside the statue of Lydia, her eyes scanning from left to right, her mind racing.

Quill's heart thundered. A sense of urgency prompted Allegra's movements as a thick tension built in the air.

He opened his mouth to speak, but Allegra beat him to it, raising a finger to his lips and turning to face the statue. "Her. She was the one who made the deal with Erin's great-great-great grandmother. Correct?"

Quill nodded slowly, his mind spinning. "Lydia? Yes. Gertrude went behind my back and made a deal. We know all this."

Allegra continued her restless pacing, her eyes fixed on the statue. "Yes, but Lydia never did anything unless she gained from it as well. I always wondered why she helped Gertrude. Their covens had nothing in common, really. But it makes sense now."

"Allegra, stop moving and tell me," Quill urged, trying to keep his voice steady.

The witch cackled, pulling at her hair. "Don't you see? You said Renee felt *familiar* to you." Allegra tapped the statue with her fingers. "It's her, isn't it? Lydia found a way to come back."

Quill's mind raced as he tried to make sense of Allegra's words. "Lydia is Renee? But how? How would that work and what does it have to do with Erin?"

Allegra resumed her pacing, her movements more frantic. "Oh, she's a smart one. She always could play the long game, that one."

Quill stepped into her path. "Allegra, slow down. Explain.

What are you talking about?"

"When she made the deal with Gertrude, she must have done so based on certain conditions. Lydia knew she'd be long dead by the time Erin's soul came to you. I'll bet she put her essence into this statue. She had it made *weeks* before she died. Once Erin arrived here, she could then transfer her soul to a living body." Allegra climbed onto the bench and wrapped her arms around the neck of the statue. "Poor Renee started a few days before Erin's soul arrived. Having Erin close by is part of the deal. She must have hid it in the binding she made with Gertrude." Allegra rushed into the kitchen and returned with a worn leather book. She flicked through the pages frantically. "Ha!" She chuckled. "Look here. As long as Erin is near, her power can slowly return until she's back and fully restored. Renee was nothing but a disguise while she waited out her time."

Quill's mind reeled as he tried to process it all. "She knew Erin was of witch blood. She knew she'd be different and unlikely to be sold."

"Exactly," said Allegra, her voice rising in excitement. "Now, be a dear and get me something from the kitchen. Top cupboard in a clear bag."

Allegra's actions puzzled Quill. They needed to come up with a plan. Time was running out, and this delay would only make things worse. Quill turned and rushed into the kitchen. As he opened the cupboard, there were dozens of clear bags, each labelled. He rummaged through and found the one with Lydia's name on. As he pulled the bag into his hand, Renee banged on the shop door. "She's back, and she doesn't look happy." Quill shouted, rushing back into the courtyard.

Allegra reached out her hand. "Give that to me. Quickly. She knows the game is up." A loud crash of glass shattered the peace of the courtyard. Renee was coming.

"What do you need me to do?" Quill asked. Confrontation was never his strong suit, especially not between witches.

"Nothing, just hold her back. This shouldn't take long," Allegra said calmly. With a swift motion, she opened the content of the small plastic bag into her other hand. Renee entered the courtyard. Her eyes had blackened, and she appeared to have aged. The young Renee was gone, and Lydia stood before him, a face he hadn't seen in years. Every line and crack the same, her once tamed hair was now wild, with streaks of grey mixed in with the raven black. Quill stepped back, raising his hands. "Allegra, Lydia is here!"

Lydia's eyes remained fixed on Allegra as she lunged. Quill darted forward, his arms outstretched to halt her movements. "You don't want to do this, Lydia," he pleaded. But she swiped a hand across his chest, sending him tumbling to the ground.

Allegra smiled. "You almost did it, sister. You almost won back this coven, but you messed up at the last hurdle." Allegra taunted. She held out the contents of the bag—clippings of dark hair—and produced a flame from her fingertip, setting them alight. She dropped them to the floor. Lydia screamed and charged again towards the witch. "I'm sorry, sister, but all witches need to know when their time is up," Allegra declared.

Quill saw his chance. Jumping to his feet, he ran at Lydia, who clung to the statue's head. Quill brought them both to the ground. Lydia's nails raked across his face, sending a burning jolt through him, a sensation he hadn't experienced in centuries. He finally felt alive as the pain throbbed in his cheek. Lydia flashed her rotten teeth and gripped his face, and suddenly, he felt as if burning acid gushed through his eyes. "You feel the pain you deserve, Quill Darlington. You brought it on yourself," she hissed.

Lydia grabbed Allegra's foot again as she cackled from the top of the statue. Allegra held tightly to the statue's neck, while Lydia pulled with all her might. "Release your grip! You have lost!" Lydia screamed, spit spilling from her lips. "Let me come back!"

Allegra clung tighter as Lydia pulled until the statue gave way. Allegra and the head of the statue tumbled to the ground.

As the dust settled, Quill searched for Allegra. He heard a groan. She was curled up beside the bench, her hair clogged with dust and stone. Meanwhile, Lydia lay crushed by her own image, the head of the statue perfectly placed on top of her.

Quill pulled Allegra up and dusted himself off, trying to ignore the pain rushing through his cheek. "Sorry about that," Allegra said, shaking her head. "Some never know when to leave. Poor girl wanted back into the coven, and she gave a bloody good fight, too. I can't wait to tell the sisters about this." She cackled, standing beside Quill. "Let me fix you up."

"No. She said the pain I feel is the pain I deserve, and to be honest, it's nice to have any feeling at all," Quill replied.

Allegra watched Quill with pitiful eyes. "You need to learn to get over your past, Quill. You have suffered enough; you don't need more pain in your life." When she extended a hand to his wound, the pain disappeared at once. "What's done is done. You cannot change your past decisions. It's what you do looking forward that counts."

Allegra tumbled, collapsing beside the body of her fallen sister.

Quill rushed to her side, his arms moving faster than they

had in years to break her fall. A blend of gratitude and sorrow coloured Quill's features. He knew she was right, but it was easier said than done. The pain he had felt in that moment was something he had been avoiding for years. He thought he had buried it deep enough that it wouldn't resurface, but Lydia's attack had brought it all back. He didn't want to be defined by his past mistakes, but he also didn't know how to move on. As he stood there, lost in his thoughts, he couldn't help but wonder what the future held for him, or if he had a future at all.

Erin Layton

Erin closed her book and set it down on the bedside table. Raindrops gently tapped against the windowpane, a soothing, rhythmic melody. Rolling black clouds cloaked the horizon, obstructing her view of the usually lush fields. Erin's eyes grew heavy, and she vigorously rubbed them before glancing at the calendar on the wall. It was then that she heard a scratching noise on the other side of her bedroom door.

Erin hesitated, then peered out into the hallway. Brushing up against her ankles, Wilson slinked into the room and jumped onto the windowsill. She smiled and crouched to meet the cat's eyes. "Sorry, little fella." Her fingers gently scratched his chin. "If you want to see the world, you're going to have to go outside and get wet."

With that, Erin rose to her feet and made her way downstairs. As she walked towards the front of the shop, she realised she had locked the door and left the 'closed' sign hanging in the window. Panic set in, and she clutched the blanket tightly around her shoulders and rushed towards the counter. Quill was nowhere to be seen.

Rushing to the rear of the shop, Erin called out Quill's name. Jars rattled on the shelves and echoed through the empty store. She entered the meeting room at the back, but it was empty.

"Quill?" she called out again, her voice tinged with worry. But there was no response.

Erin turned to leave, her heart pounding in her chest. But a soft meow grabbed her attention, and she glanced up at where Wilson perched on the top of the stairs, as if beckoning her to follow him. She ran up the stairs, skipping every other step, and found Wilson waiting for her beside the living room door upstairs.

Erin hesitated, but before she could raise her hand, Wilson pushed his head against the door, forcing it open. Erin's heart skipped a beat as the hinges creaked. Grey light from the overcast sky flooded the room. The cold glow revealed a cluttered space, where books and papers covered every inch of the walls, stacked haphazardly on every available surface. Erin had always perceived Quill as a neat and organised person, but seeing his study now proved otherwise. Along the wall were a set of three paintings. Three men Erin had never seen before. She turned and slowly approached Quill, noticing the tuft of hair on the back of his armchair. Although his eyes were closed, she knew he wasn't sleeping. Something was wrong.

"Quill!" Erin shouted, jabbing his arm.

Quill shot to his feet in surprise. "How long have you been standing there?" He huffed, pushing his messy hair back into place.

Erin breathed out, relaxing her chest.

"The shop is shut. I thought you were covering this morning." Erin replied, leaning closer. "Is everything alright? You were... *sleeping*. You've never slept before. Ever."

Quill looked anywhere but at Erin. "I was arranging a few things. I had to be... *elsewhere* for a bit."

Erin raised an eyebrow, but didn't push the issue further. He obviously didn't want to elaborate. "Shall I open up then?"

"No." Quill placed a hand on Erin's shoulder. "We are closed today."

"All day?"

"Yes. We have somewhere to be. A field trip."

"I really don't feel like it today, Quill. Can we leave it till tomorrow?" Erin asked, glancing at the door. Wilson now lay in front of the exit, licking his paw. If she dared to walk out of the room, she had a feeling he wouldn't move out of her way.

"Okay, what's going on?" she asked Quill, placing her hands on her hip.

"I didn't forget the date, Erin. Come with me. I need to take you somewhere." Quill reached out his hand.

Erin knew what day it was, too. It had been on her mind all week. The rain outside intensified. Why do dates do this to you? It's just a day. No different from any other, but the memories of the past are what gives it significance. She rolled her eyes and reached for Quill's hand. The gentle warmth of the flat vanished, and wind whistled through her ears, and raindrops fell onto her hair. She opened her eyes, and she was back again, standing in the graveyard where she had been a few years ago, watching her funeral.

Erin knew exactly where to look. Her prescience led her to her burial place. It had only been a few years, hardly any time at all, but it felt significant. Walking towards her grave, Erin stopped and turned to Quill, who wiped his wet eyes behind his glasses. She gave him a gentle smile. A few people gathered at her graveside—fewer than at her funeral, but more than she anticipated.

The mourners around her grave grew clearer as they approached. "They can't see us? Right? Same rules as before?" asked Erin. Quill nodded.

"Did you want to go closer? Or are you happy here?"

Erin glanced at the people around her grave. She had come this far; she might as well keep going. "Let's get closer." Erin took a step forward, then turned to see Quill. "Come on. I need you with me."

He smiled and raised an eyebrow. "Are you sure?"

"Of course, come on." She pulled his arm, forcing him to walk alongside her. A couple stood by the grave with a small child. Erin had no idea who they were, or why they would be there on her birthday.

But then she heard his voice. It was Jacob. He wore a long rain jacket with his hood up, covering his face... but his voice she could never forget. He sobbed.

"Are you okay, Daddy?"

The child called him Daddy? He was old enough to speak, though. Erin had only been dead a few years, so she assumed he must have been a stepson, of sorts.

The woman next to him stroked his back, then crouched beside the child. "Daddy is a bit sad today. We're here to remember his friend. Give him a hug; he'd appreciate that."

The boy tottered towards Jacob. "Dad is being silly, that's

all, champ," said Jacob, kneeling beside Erin's grave.

"Why are you crying?" asked the child, staring at the gravestone. Erin almost couldn't believe what she saw. Jacob had moved on. His life had changed more than she'd ever have expected, yet he still found the time to come here, to mourn her. To keep her name alive in his life.

"This lady here was very special to daddy once upon a time, and every so often, I come here to remember her. Sometimes thinking of her makes daddy sad. But other times, when I remember all the fun we had, it makes daddy smile. Do you understand?"

The child nodded and hugged Jacob. Erin glanced away at Quill, who had now removed his glasses and dabbed his eyes with a handkerchief. "Are you okay?" he asked, putting his glasses back on. Erin nodded, wiping a tear off her own. She didn't cry because she was sad or jealous that Jacob had moved on. She cried because she was remembered. Because Jacob still held a place for her in his heart—his memory. She cried for the family he'd made, and the life he had without her. She cried because if she didn't die that day, this beautiful life of his might never have happened.

Erin watched through misty eyes as Jacob rested a colourful bouquet on her grave. The sweet gesture made her heart ache. His partner stood a few feet away, holding their child's hand while Jacob placed a gentle kiss on his fingertips before pressing them against Erin's name on the headstone.

Erin stepped towards him, reaching out to touch his hand. A wave of warmth crept through her fingers, and for a moment, it felt like they were connected once again. It was only for a fleeting moment, a final goodbye.

"I love you Erin, and I miss you every day." Jacob's voice was choked with emotion, and he swiped tears from his flushed cheeks. "If you can see me, then I hope you understand, and I hope you approve of Charlotte. I talk about you to her all the time. She laughs at the jokes I stole from you."

Erin felt a lump form in her throat, and tears streamed down her face. She nodded, unable to find her voice as Jacob pushed to his feet, his eyes still glued to her headstone. "I'll always keep a place for you in here." He tapped his chest. "And I hope you understand I had to move on."

He walked away, holding Charlotte's hand while cradling their child in his other arm. Despite a pang of sadness, she also felt relief. He was happy, and that was all that mattered.

"I approve!" she shouted at the top of her lungs, her voice cracking with emotion. Jacob didn't turn around, but Erin didn't expect him to. It was enough to say what she needed to.

Erin and Quill stayed by the grave for a while longer, watching the visitors come and go. The peaceful aura that surrounded Quill earlier had dissipated, leaving a sombre silence behind.

"Thank you, Quill," Erin said, turning to him. "For bringing me here today. I know you didn't have to, and that it would be frowned upon. But it means a lot."

"My pleasure." Quill's eyes glistened. "Erin. There is something I need to tell you," he said, his voice heavy.

Her heart sank at the seriousness of his tone. "What is it?" she asked, trying to steady her voice.

"I know about Dustin Davis. About the contract and the broken rules."

Erin's stomach dropped. "How long have you known?"

"Not long, but long enough to think things over, and to plan what to do about it," he said, his voice barely audible.

Erin turned away, gazing at the church in the distance. "I'm not sorry for what I did. I'm sorry for going behind your back, but I won't set his soul free. He doesn't deserve it."

Quill nodded. "I know. I agree. But rules were broken—serious rules—and The Boss will want punishment."

Erin had heard talk about The Boss for years. The day she pulled Arthur's soul back with Allegra, she'd come across a darkness she'd never witnessed before. Perhaps that was them. Perhaps that was The Boss. She didn't know, and after experiencing it, she didn't want to find out.

"What will happen to me? Will I be sent away?" asked Erin.

Quill's face dropped. "I have sorted it. I have spoken to them and have my instructions."

"Is that what you were doing this morning? When I found you?"

"Yes. I visited them to discuss the situation," he replied.

"I see." Erin hung her head. Too many times now Quill had gone out of his way to provide Erin with everything she wanted, but she still pushed, bent the rules, and left him no choice. "It's okay. Whatever happens. I enjoyed my time with you, Quill, and I will always remember the time we had together and the training. You did more for me than you should have."

"When we return, I won't have much time left with you. But I wanted to do this; I wanted to bring you here, to do something right for once." Quill's voice broke, and Erin's eyes stung at his words.

Erin nodded. "Make sure you keep up the stock; keep inviting customers in and decorate for Halloween. Oh, and keep an eye on Arthur for me. He may come across as Mr Confident now, but he's fragile. Oh, and Miss Potts wanted us to fix the gutters, and re-paint the shop and..."

Erin watched Quill, his eyes filling with tears as he listened to her.

"Erin." Quill bowed his head, interrupting her. "You won't be the one leaving. I am."

Erin's eyes widened, and she took several steps back. "What do you mean?"

Tears spilled onto Quill's cheeks. "I told The Boss it was me who altered the contract. I told them you were ready to take over the shop, and I accepted my fate. I was given today as grace to see you off properly, but The Boss is expecting a soul by the end of the day, and that soul will be mine, not yours."

Erin gripped Quill's arms, her tears mirroring his. "No, you can't. I won't let you."

But Quill was staring at the sky as raindrops pelted his face. He finally turned to face her.

"Erin, listen to me," Quill began. "This will be your last lesson from me. You need to know when your time is up. I've had a long life, longer than most, and it's been good. Mostly."

Pain etched into Quill's features, and Erin's heart ached for him. She couldn't imagine what it must have been like for him for all these years.

"I accepted the role of Ghost Merchant when I died. I asked The Boss to punish me until I found forgiveness. There were times where I thought I never would find it, but since you arrived, things have changed. You helped me see the world differently."

Erin furrowed her brows. "What do you mean? What changed?"

Quill drew in a deep breath, his face flushed. "And now I am going to do what I should have done all those years ago. Stand up for the ones below me, for the ones I care for. I never had a child. I never found love. But you, Erin, have become family to me, and I must protect you—save you from danger."

"No, Quill. I can't let you do this!"

"Please. Let me finish," Quill begged, his voice cracking. "So many years I spent wondering how I could ever find forgiveness. But now I know. This is how I do it. It won't change what happened in my life, but saving you—giving you a life beyond mine—it will be my way of doing it. Let me have this, for I fear it is the only chance I will get for forgiveness."

Erin didn't know what to say. She wanted to help Quill find peace, but at what cost? She couldn't bear the thought of losing him.

Quill watched her, his eyes pleading. "Erin, please. This is the only way I can make things right."

Finally, Erin relented, pulling Quill into a warm embrace. "You speak of these things you did, the unforgivable things from your past, before you go, before you walk away from me. I want to hear your story. I want to know what happened. At least give me that."

Quill Darlington

1744

In the stifling heat of the factory, Quill oversaw the children as they toiled away among the cacophony of whirring gears and clanking machines. Sweat dripped down his brow from the scorching heat radiating off the machinery. He made his rounds, keeping a watchful eye on the children. The quiet chatter of the women died down as he passed.

Other children manoeuvred beneath the machines, their fingers and elbows narrowly avoiding the deadly moving parts. Quill couldn't help but wince at every close call. Strolling by the windows offered Quill a brief respite as he gained a snapshot glimpse of the outside world—a temporary reprieve from the horrors inside the factory.

Isaac would be there, reminding Quill of how fortunate he was to no longer be working on the job the children now occupy. The managers would justify the children's labour: "It's better than leaving them on the streets!" they'd argue.

Quill couldn't dispute their logic, but something felt wrong. Unsettling.

With the factory's increasing reliance on child labour, accidents grew more frequent. Whispers of missing children rumoured the streets and the discovery of unmarked graves became an all-too-frequent topic. Quill wondered if the managers truly believed the children were better off in the factory, or if they were simply using them for their own profit.

During his break, Quill slipped away to the factory rooftop where he would rendezvous with his closest co-workers. Jason was there already—the first to take a break and the last to return. He scratched the back of his neck and bit into his sandwich. Quill greeted Jason with a nod, then leaned on the metal banister, his gaze fixed on the scene below.

Quill's voice broke the silence. "What are your thoughts on all of this?" he asked.

Jason's brow furrowed. "You're talking about the kids, aren't you?" he inquired. "I heard the bosses talking. They don't like us questioning it, Quill. I think we should keep our heads down and stay quiet."

The metal door swung open, and Isaac joined them, slinging an arm around Quill's shoulders. "Don't do it, mate. If you jump, you know I'll have to try to catch you."

Quill straightened, turning his back from the edge. "Jason says we should stop voicing our concerns about the kids. What do you think?"

"I think he's right. It could be us back down on that factory floor. They won't think twice about replacing us. We may as well have an easier life while we can," Isaac replied with a slight shake of his head.

"I agree. I mentioned it to Mike to see what he thought. He said it's more trouble than it's worth trying to change anything here. It is what it is," Jason chimed in.

Quill huffed. "Mike would jump off a cliff if a manager told him to. I don't like it. You must have heard the rumours about workers wheeling bodies out in the night."

"Those same bodies would fill the streets, Quill. Hell, it will be our lifeless corpses if we lose this job. Let's leave it. Say nothing and carry on." Jason tossed his bread crusts over the side and slammed the door as he left.

Quill raised his eyebrows at Isaac. "What do you think?"

"I don't think there is anything we can do, mate," Isaac said. With a final pat on Quill's back, he returned to work.

As the days turned into months, Quill could no longer ignore the horrors unfolding before him. He kept a mental tally of the number of children under his watch and asked some women he trusted to keep him informed about the night shift workers, recording every accident that occurred. The grim reality surpassed even his darkest imaginings. Children began arriving at the factory as early as five in the morning, toiling tirelessly until nine at night, their breaks meagre, and their meals scarce. The heat from the machines was unbearable, and the noise was deafening. As Quill wandered through the aisles of machinery, a bloodcurdling scream pierced through the factory noise. Quill rushed towards the sound. A young girl, no older than nine, waved her arms and screamed relentlessly. The machine trapped her hair and was pulling her face toward it. A young boy had rushed underneath to help. Another held onto her, trying to free her, but her head was being dragged towards the moving parts. Quill searched frantically, desperate for any tool to free the girl's trapped hair. Other children ran towards different parts of the machine, too, trying to help.

"Someone turn these damn things off!" Quill screamed, spotting movement behind the drawn blinds of the office upstairs. Someone had shut them purposefully to cut off any responsibility. Isaac arrived in haste, dropping to his knees beside the boy and girl. Another scream came from behind the machine, and Quill heard a sickening crunch. Women rushed to attend, but it was too late. The machine pulled the girl in. Blood splattered across Quill's face as her top half swung into the machine, too. Isaac tried to wrench out whoever was underneath to help, but it was too late. The boy shrieked, and when he emerged, his fingers were missing.

Jason arrived with a manager, but they were more interested in covering up the incident than helping the injured children. The managers had no regard for the safety of them. None whatsoever.

Mike arrived at the scene. It brought a glimmer of hope for a split second in Quill's mind. But hope soon vanished.

Quill glanced up, the blood still fresh on his face, and Isaac gestured towards the body of the girl. Mike's shocked expression quickly morphed into one of resignation. "How many are hurt?" he asked, a twinge of guilt lacing his voice.

Isaac huddled with the others, pointing to the machine that pulled the girl in. "Three, I think. One girl and two boys. Another lost his fingers, and I don't want to know what else happened under there," he said.

The Ghost Merchant

Jason doubled over, emptying his stomach onto the floor.

Mike gave him a stern look, then hit him on the arm. "We can't do anything," he said, his voice firm. "Let's just clear up and carry on. Push it out of your mind. If we weren't here, we would be on the streets and some other chump would fill our space. Just remember that. At least we care. Think of it that way."

Quill's fists clenched. "I can't just carry on, Mike. This isn't right. We must do something."

A manager approached, brandishing a cane. "What is going on here? All of you! Get back to work! Go along the west side and help. Quill, Isaac. Get this mess sorted out." He said, pushing the weeping children away from the massacre.

Quill's mind numbed as he cleaned up the blood of the young girl. Every week was the same; another child or young woman would find themselves at the mercy of the machines. Quill and his co-workers were the ones left to clean up the aftermath.

He had been on night shifts for two weeks, pushing wheelbarrows of bodies to the church. No one asked for the names or conditions of the dead children. When Isaac raised a question with a manager, he got struck with a cane, and his wages deducted.

They gathered every day on the top of the factory to share their stories and the names of the ones they had lost, in an empty hope of honouring the dead. With each passing month, their spirits crumbled a little bit more. The conditions deteriorated, and the prospect of being homeless became a likely possibility. Workhouse jobs were scarce, but even their security was under threat. Reports on the working conditions fell on deaf ears and would result in losing shifts.

Then, one night, all four of them worked the same night shift. Quill had written down the names of each person they had lost that night. Fifteen children and four women. Gone in one shift. By far the worst accident any of them had seen, and it had happened under their watch. How could they continue, knowing their guidance had cost those lives?

Quill had written the names and recited them to the silent night sky. "I can't do this anymore. I can't face going back into that place," sobbed Jason.

Quill turned away, staring at the view. His heart was empty, and no tears came. Clenching his jaw, he pivoted back to face the group. "Neither can I. We have watched so much death, and we have done nothing to help. Nothing."

Isaac approached Quill and took the list of names from him, grabbing a pencil from his pocket. "Mike, turn around," he said, pressing the list against his back.

Mike tried turning his head to see what was happening. "Hey, what are you doing?"

"I'm adding our names to the list. Quill, Isaac, Jason, and Mike." Isaac scribbled their names to the end of the list and handed it back to Quill. "We will be part of this. When the people rise up and fight, and they find the records of what went on here in these factory walls, our names will be with them." Isaac leaned against the metal barrier. "Are we all in agreement here? Thinking the same thing, right? This ends... now."

Quill joined Isaac's side, peering down over the sixty feet drop to the ground. His knees buckled at the thought of falling. Jason joined them while Mike stayed back. "It's okay, Mike. If you don't want to, you can stay behind. Be one of the men who changes things. But I can't stay here, not after what we have been a part of, not after what we have witnessed. I can't." Quill glanced at Isaac to his left and Jason to his right. They all had wet eyes and red cheeks. Nodding at each other, they took a breath in.

"Wait!" Mike shouted, climbing onto the barrier. "You can't leave me with this." He grabbed hold of Isaac's hand so all four men were linked together. "You got the list, Quill?" Mike asked, looking straight ahead. Quill nodded, and with that, he closed his eyes and bent his knees. He gripped tightly, holding onto the hands of Isaac and Jason, and together, they jumped.

In death, their souls bore the scars of the factory's horrors. Quill recognised he had taken the path of least resistance; he understood the weight of his unfinished duty and the deserving punishment for letting that torment persist. When he opened his eyes, he realised he was no longer in the physical world, but a dark void, surrounded by nothingness. He felt no physical pain, but the weight of his guilt and remorse was crushing.

Beside him, a presence loomed. "Do you know why you are here?" echoed a voice in his ears.

Quill nodded, his voice trembling. "Yes. I'm not ready to leave. The afterlife is not the punishment I deserve," Quill replied like he'd planned this all along, as if he knew there would be more. Of course, he didn't know that, but even in death, he felt desperate to atone for his sins.

Mike, Jason, and Isaac appeared before him. A collective understanding hung in the air. A shared purpose. One by one, they met The Boss, all agreeing to work for evermore until the day they found forgiveness, dedicating their time to the role of a Ghost Merchant.

They were scattered around the country, each bearing the

weight of their past. Quill examined his hands, now aged and weathered. He had aged forty—maybe fifty years from the man he was when alive, the stiff joints and old bones a constant reminder of the pain he'd witnessed, and turned a blind eye to.

Every decade, they convened at the factory of their demise, honouring the memory of the lost souls, remembering the ones they failed. Quill closed his eyes, bearing the crushing burden of his guilt. He knew he could never pay for what he did, but he vowed to spend the rest of his existence trying.

Erin Layton

They returned to the shop, but Quill's story lingered on Erin's thoughts. His past had devoured him, leaving Erin to grapple with the idea of Quill bearing such anguish for all eternity — an almost unbearable thought.

Despite her insecurities about taking charge of the shop, Erin now recognised the weight of responsibility for the spirits Quill held.

Quill had nurtured those spirits over the years, and she wanted to make the right choices to help others who, like her, remained trapped by their pain. It wouldn't be easy, but she was determined to fix things for him before it was too late.

She thought of Alma, the only ghost she had ever known to move on. The thought of someone finding peace from the pain of their past gave her hope that there was a way to help

Quill. She had bent the rules before—maybe, just maybe, she could do it one last time.

Wilson was sound asleep on the window seat while Quill retreated to the back room. Arthur, despite his low spirits, had proposed to host a farewell gathering at The Tavern, where Quill promised to show up before departing. Erin glanced at the clock. She had until midnight to devise a plan.

As Erin made her way to The Witch Stuff, she spotted Allegra entering The Tavern. Excitedly, Erin followed, relieved that both the people she needed were in the same place. Inside the pub, the dim lighting made it difficult to see if any customers were present. Arthur drew her focus from behind the bar, though his usual playful demeanour had dimmed. "Hey, how you holding up?" Erin asked, scanning the empty pub.

"Sad about Quill. I almost can't believe it. I've closed up for tonight; it'll just be us lot here for him. Shame Alma couldn't be here, but I suppose she's in a better place anyway," Arthur said, his hand moving to wipe an empty glass before setting it on the shelf behind him.

"I'm sure you'll give him the send-off he deserves. I saw Allegra come in here. Has she vanished?"

"She's out back, in the kitchen. Go on through. I'm sure she'll be happy to see you." Arthur leaned in closer and whispered, "I think she's feeling a little lost with the news about Quill, so go gentle."

Erin pushed open the wooden swing doors and stepped into the kitchen, greeted by the sight of grey metallic tops and sinks. Allegra's blue and red flowing top was a stark contrast to the kitchen's sterile design. She was crushing something in a small marble bowl with a pestle, grinding her teeth as she did. "Allegra?" Erin said, approaching her cautiously.

She met Allegra's eyes, which widened with delight. "Erin, dear! What a pleasure it is to see you. When I heard about Quill, well, I didn't know what to do." She took hold of Erin's arms and stared at her, wide-eyed. "What's the plan, then? You came here to fix this all, didn't you?"

"Kind of," Erin admitted. "I came to find you for the plan, though. Thought you would know a way around this. I can't see Quill taken away." Her gaze dropped to the floor. "He deserves better."

Allegra wrapped her arm around Erin's shoulder and rubbed her back. "I know, dear. That man has done so much and asked for so little."

A hint of desperation laced Erin's voice. "What can we do? Is there something we can do to help, like we did with Arthur? Get Renee over and join our powers?"

Allegra smiled, but it was a sad one. "Renee is gone. Turns out, she wasn't who I thought she was, but alas, we are still here." Allegra gripped Erin's hands tighter. "So, all is not lost. But with Quill admitting his fault to The Boss, it leaves us in a difficult situation. We can't bend the rules around this one. He wants a soul, and Quill is in line to give his at midnight."

"He wants a soul?" Erin asked, trying to see what Allegra was crushing.

Allegra dabbed her finger into the powder and rubbed it across her eyelid, staining it a bright blue. "Yes. Quill admitted fault, and The Boss demanded a soul to use for... whatever happens when a soul goes to them."

Erin rushed toward Allegra and embraced her. "You are a genius! I think I know what we can do." She turned and rushed towards the bar. "Come on, follow me."

"Erin, where are you going?" Arthur asked, jumping over the bar and following her out to the back. Erin halted beside the door to the pub garden and turned right towards the basement. Arthur and Allegra followed quickly behind as Erin searched for a light, feeling for a switch along the cold stone wall. Arthur appeared behind her, out of breath, and pulled a cord. The lights flickered, and inside the basement, countless large barrels and boxes of wine and spirits lined the store. Towards the back was a line of three small wooden shelves.

Erin's heart raced as she scoured the basement. "Is he in here?" she asked, turning to Arthur. "Is he here?"

"Erin, who? What are you looking for?" asked Arthur, confusion written on his face.

"Dustin! His spirit. The bottle I kept him in."

Allegra joined them in the basement, gasping for breath. "What on earth is going on? Nearly gave me a bloody heart attack."

Erin strode towards the back wall, where Arthur pointed at a glass bottle. "This is our answer. Allegra, you said The Boss wants a spirit, right?"

"Yes, that's right," Allegra said, brushing her hair from her face.

"And before, you told me that a spirit is a spirit in the eyes of The Boss. So, if we have one going spare, can we give them theirs instead of Quill's?" asked Erin, her voice rising with excitement.

Allegra glanced back at Erin, her mouth dangling open. "Well, I don't know. I suppose The Boss wouldn't care. It's all a numbers game, really." She clicked her fingers. "If you two don't mind bending the rules slightly, I know exactly what we can do. But we need to be quick. Quill will be over soon for the party, and we need The Boss satisfied before midnight. No sooner."

Arthur smiled, grabbing hold of Erin's hand. "Tell us what to do and we'll do it. Right, Erin?"

Erin hesitated as her mind raced with the potential repercussions of what they were about to do. Breaking the rules is what got Quill in this mess to begin with, but she couldn't let him take the blame for her mistakes. If she could safely get Quill away, then she would accept anything The Boss threw at her.

With a deep breath, Erin turned to Allegra. "What's the plan?"

Quill arrived for his goodbye, accompanied by Wilson, who slept soundly along the bar. Allegra shared stories of their years together while Erin struggled to maintain composure. Her gaze locked on the clock above the bar. As the hands of the clock inched closer to midnight, the room's tension became almost unbearable. She gripped Dustin's glass tightly in her lap, trying to focus on anything but the impending doom that loomed.

With each passing minute, fear became increasingly apparent in Quill's eyes, too. Erin's breaths came in rapid, shallow bursts, and Allegra stood suddenly, causing Quill to jump in his seat. "Right. We can't sit around and wait any longer. We have arranged something for you."

Quill's smile faltered, and he glanced at Arthur and Erin, his eyes pleading for some sort of reprieve. "No. I only have a few minutes left Allegra, can we just enjoy the quiet together?"

Allegra's narrowed eyes bored into Erin and Arthur as she approached. "Sorry Quill, but we can't be having you leave us like this." She retrieved a small silk bag from her pocket and rubbed its contents—a mix of herbs—between her fingers. "You got the soul, love?" Erin retrieved Dustin from under the jumper and placed his bottle on the table.

Quill rose, startling Wilson. "What's going on here, Allegra? Erin. Arthur. Stop this, please. I have accepted my fate."

Allegra gripped Erin's hand, her voice adopting a manic edge. "It's time, Erin. Close your eyes. The darkness is here, waiting. Speak to it, offer the soul, and don't take no for an answer. Do it now!" she screamed; her eyes widened with unsettling fervour.

Erin turned to Quill, a wry smile on her face as the darkness creeped around them. She closed her eyes and surrendered to it, the cold seeping into her bones. The clock's clanging filled the air, each chime like a hammer on her skull. Midnight. Erin stepped forward.

"Are you ready?" whispered a voice, sending shivers down her spine. Erin didn't answer. The voice already knew. She removed the cork from the jar, unleashing Dustin Davis from his prison.

He appeared before her, a faded, tired old man. "What's happening? Where am I?" Dustin shouted, glancing frantically around.

From the darkness, a long, spindly finger oozed forth, coated in a viscous, dark liquid. "Is this the soul I have come to claim?" inquired the voice.

Dustin's eyes widened. "No, don't take me. Please. Put me back inside the void, back where I'm safe!" But it was too late. A finger wrapped around Dustin, and it whisked him away, screaming. Erin winced at the sound. Although he deserved it, it still tore at her soul.

"Are you satisfied?" Erin asked, hoping it was enough.

"For now," came the reply, followed by a clap of thunder that rattled Erin's bones. Another scream echoed through the darkness, a cry for help that would never come. The air grew frosty, and Erin shivered, feeling the icy tendrils wrapping around her. A flash of golden light flooded her vision, and she crumpled. Strong arms encircled her, pulling her back to her feet.

"Erin, are you okay?" asked Quill, his voice filled with concern. She opened her eyes to see his kind face, and the gold-rimmed glasses askew on his nose. Wilson sat behind him, watching her with a curious expression.

Erin smiled weakly. It had all been worth it.

Quill Darlington

Quill extended a hand to Erin, helping her rise from the ground and leading her to a nearby chair. As he settled her into the seat, he couldn't help but notice the look on Allegra's face. The same expression she always wore when she had something up her sleeve—mischief mixed with a hint of excitement. Arthur had never been one to keep secrets hidden, and as soon as Quill had entered The Tavern, he knew something was afoot.

Quill slumped onto the sofa. He felt like he had cheated death yet again. The idea of confronting The Boss and uncovering the mysteries beyond the darkness had always filled him with dread, but now, in the early hours of the morning—a day he didn't think would have him in it—a sense of relief washed over him. "I don't agree with what just happened," he said, addressing the group. "But I thank you all. I had prepared myself for the end. Now, I feel somewhat lost."

Looking down at Wilson, Quill's heart swelled. The cat had been by his side through it all: the pain, loss, heartache. Whenever Quill returned home after losing another child under his watch, Wilson was always there, offering comfort. Kneeling at Wilson's level, Quill's voice was thick with emotion as he spoke. "Back in our old life, I struggled without you when you left. I don't know how I survived. But having you here with me now... it's been the best thing that's ever happened to me."

Rising to his feet, Quill's gaze fell on Erin, Allegra, and Arthur, who stood before him in a line. What were they planning? But as Allegra stepped forward with a genuine smile, Quill's heart skipped. It was the kindest expression he had ever seen on the witch. She ran her hand under his chin, whispering. "If you want to leave Quill, you can. Right here. Right now."

A rush of emotions flooded through him. Relief, confusion, and something else—a sense of possibility. He peered at his friends; he knew that whatever lay ahead, he wouldn't face it alone. Taking a steadying breath, Quill knew he was ready to face whatever the future had in store. He was tired. He was ready to leave.

Quill stood frozen, hesitant to take the last step towards leaving. It felt too easy to leave behind all the pain and suffering he had caused and witnessed.

"Quill, it's okay. Forgive yourself. Think of all the good you have done. Join your family, your friends. Move on, let their haunted memories go free," Erin said, stepping aside.

As Quill glanced up, a bright light glowed behind Erin,

where three figures appeared. Isaac and Mike stood there, happier and more youthful than Quill remembered. It saddened him to not see Jason, a soul locked in darkness—a fate Quill had narrowly escaped. He stepped closer, passing Arthur.

"You have made me so proud; do you know that?" Quill said, smiling as he pulled Arthur in for a warm embrace. "So very, very proud."

A gentle touch on his shoulder by a familiar, warm hand snapped him from his thoughts. It was Alma, her hair long and flowing; she looked youthful and radiant, her eyes full of life.

"Learn to forgive yourself, Quill," she said, her gentle smile soothing his nerves. "No one here blames you for what happened. They all found peace, and you can, too."

Erin stood beside him, her eyes glistening. "I'll take good care of the shop, Quill. We will never forget you; we will never stop talking about you. I promise." She bent down and collected Wilson in her hands, passing him to Quill with a pat on the head. "You take care of Quill there, Mr Wilson. Make sure you keep him company." Erin laughed and kissed Quill on the cheek. "You can go now. We will be fine without you—*because* of you."

Quill stole a final look at the family he had created with tear-filled eyes. The weight of his decision to leave behind everything and everyone he knew and loved hit him with a force he never expected. He longed to absorb every memory, every moment of laughter and love he had cultivated in Ringwood. Deep down, he knew he had done everything he could in this life, but that didn't make it any easier to say goodbye.

As he walked towards the light, he felt Alma and his

friends beside him. Their comforting touch on his shoulder gave him the strength to continue. He hugged Wilson tightly, trying to hold on to the last remaining piece of his past.

The light intensified, wrapping him in its comforting warmth. He shut his eyes as the sensation of his past life dissipated, replaced by the promise of the unknown.

As the light engulfed him completely, a sense of peace washed over him. He had left behind some good, and the people he loved would continue to thrive and grow without him. It was time to move on to the next chapter of his journey, and he was ready to leave his guilt behind, finally allowing forgiveness in.

Erin Layton

2004

Erin closed The Great Book with a satisfied smile, her pencil marking the completion of another soul assignment. She tucked the pencil behind her ear and stood from her desk, stretching out her arms to relieve the strain of sitting for countless hours.

From the window seat, Erin was pleased to see one of Allegra's proteges had already arrived to cover the shop for the regular customers. She hoped the new apprentice would learn from Allegra and become a great witch for Ringwood one day.

Stroking the cushioned window seat, Erin thought of Wilson, the white cat, and how much he loved sitting there, watching Quill work. Sadness surged within her.

Outside, Rupert was on a ladder, hanging up the fresh sign for the shop. "Rupert, be careful up there! You don't want to fall!" she called, shielding her eyes from the sun. "What do you think of the new name for the shop?"

Rupert stopped drilling, his hand still firmly clutching the tool. "He would have hated it," he said with a chuckle. "But secretly, I think he would have loved it. It's perfect."

Erin grinned at Rupert's response, pleased the name had his approval. After Quill left, Erin promised herself things would be different. She didn't want to sell souls to customers without their consent; she only signed a contract if both parties agreed.

The flower shop had come up for sale after Karina left to return to the city. Erin, Arthur, and Allegra had teamed up to buy the shop with the help of Rupert's inheritance. Erin had asked Rupert to run the flower shop for her, knowing his love for plants. After all the sadness he endured, it was the least she could do while he was under her watch.

Erin strolled toward The Tavern, which Arthur and his boyfriend had continued to run over the years. She always felt butterflies when she saw them together. Arthur had tormented himself for so long, fearing he'd never find love after Billy. But not anymore.

Erin took a deep breath, walking along the path leading to the forest. She glanced at the open fields and wondered about Quill. It was a strange feeling, knowing he was happy and at peace, yet not being able to speak with him was a hard notion to accept. Erin had faith she would see him again one day when the time was right. But for now, she had to make do with her memories.

She followed the stream that wound its way through the

forest and past the vibrant bluebells that bloomed in the spring. As she rounded the bend, Allegra was already there, standing silently beside the small grave they had made for Quill. It was a tiny spot, but a place to come and remember their dear friend.

A lump rose in Erin's throat as she approached the gravestone. Without saying a word, Erin knelt and placed Wilson's favourite pillow beside Quill's red scarf—a small offering, but a reminder of the love and friendship they all shared.

Erin and Allegra sat beside Quill's grave—a ritual they promised to do every year. Erin peered at the peaceful enclosure with the tall trees towering over them. The day they placed the gravestone here, it felt like the end of the world. Quill had always been there for them, always been in the village. His absence was still felt all these years later.

"I think about him all the time. It still doesn't feel real that he's gone," Allegra said, breaking the silence.

Erin nodded her agreement.

"Do you think he's happy?" Erin asked.

Allegra nodded. "Yeah, I reckon so. He would have been stubborn at first and made everyone's life hell. But I think he's happy now, wherever he is."

A shadow appeared then, cast over his grave. Erin turned to find Arthur standing over them. He sat down between the two and crossed his legs. "I can't be long. I've left Aaron tending the bar by himself, and you know how much he panics. But I couldn't miss Quill's special day. Ten years. Can you believe it? He's missed so much. So much change in such a short time."

The women nodded, and the three began sharing stories and laughing at their memories. Allegra retold the same stories they'd heard a million times before, but Erin and Arthur still laughed at all the right moments. Erin enjoyed speaking about him. Keeping his spirit alive felt right. Sunlight streamed through the tree branches, casting a warm golden light over Quills grave.

Erin beamed, gazing up at the freshly hung shop sign. It simply read 'Quill's,' a tribute to her beloved friend and mentor. They'd crafted the sign from local wood, sourced from the forest nearby.

Erin glimpsed a black cat lounging on the window seat inside, and she recoiled. It was the very window seat Wilson had once claimed as his own for countless years.

As she pushed open the door, the bell chimed, and the cat's head shot up, watching Erin with a mixture of curiosity and indifference before settling back to sleep. Erin sat beside the cat, stroking its back, and feeling the comforting purr emanating from deep within its chest. She gave a bittersweet laugh as a tear slid down her cheek.

Erin's gaze fell on the squeaky stairs that she still hadn't got around to fixing. Quill had always promised to fix them *'one of these days.'* Erin smiled, knowing those days would never come.

Her eyes settled on the wobbly stool behind the counter, where Quill would sit as he chatted with customers and tended to paperwork. Erin could almost picture him vividly, his wise eyes twinkling with amusement as he shared a story or some advice.

Finally, her gaze fell on the black cat again, still sleeping peacefully in the sun. Erin leaned over to tickle it under its chin, a sense of comfort washing over her. Closing her eyes, she whispered a silent 'thank you' to Quill, grateful for everything he had done for her, and for the precious gift he had left.

Erin knew Quill's memory would live on in the shop that now bore his name. She would honour him by filling it with ghosts and showing them the love and care he had always held so close to his heart. Erin knew Quill was still with her, and his guidance would always be there, too.

A Word From The Author

Thank you for reading The Ghost Merchant. I hope you enjoyed the world I created. Ringwood is a small village in Hampshire, England where I grew up as a child. The entire place always felt magical to me, and the stories of haunted pubs and witches shops were all true. It was a privilege to be able to bring that wonderful place to so many readers.

If you enjoyed the book, it would mean so much to me if you were able to post a review. Each review is paramount at getting the word out about The Ghost Merchant, and get as many eyes on this story as possible.

If you are looking for more work from me, you can find it at www.benandrewsauthor.co.uk and subscribe to my newsletter so you never miss and of my future projects.

Another Ghost Merchant Story is also available. A short novella about how Alma Edwards ended up in Quills care, set 100 years before this novel, so check that out if you are interested in expanding your knowledge of this world.

ALSO BY BEN ANDREWS

SECRETS & LIES SERIES

Secrets, Lies & Revenge
Secrets, Lies & Sacrifice
Secrets, Lies &Obsession

THE GHOST MERCHANT SERIES

Alma's Story: A Ghost Merchant Novella

STAND-ALONE NOVEL

Divided - Coming Soon

Printed in Dunstable, United Kingdom